Matthew would have liked nothing more than to take Nancy to a secluded corner of the garden and kiss her senseless.

And judging by the way the other gentlemen in the room were eyeing Nancy in her finery, he was not the only one thinking it.

He took Nancy's hand to lead her to the dance floor. His pulse quickened. He'd held many women's hands. It was a gentleman's job to lead a lady to and from the dance floor. Holding hands was often a part of dancing itself, but no other women had dazzled him like she did. Nor had touching hands made him feel hot under the collar and everywhere else. With Nancy he was on fire.

It was a sort of torture to hold her in his arms but not see her face. She followed his lead with the smallest of touches. He longed to pull her closer. To kiss her. Which was quite impossible in the middle of a dance floor. Matthew ___ himself to think of something ___ nearly plowed into the ___ a quick turn to pr___ ___ feet, placing hi___

Nancy final___ ___ saved me."

"You have a ___ ___ said, his voice low and tender. "I thou___ was waltzing with only a head of hair."

His silly jest brought a smile to her lips. The urge to kiss them heightened.

Author Note

I adore the Stringham family and I hope you enjoy this story of the second son, Lord Matthew, and Miss Nancy Black. Matthew has a way with words and Nancy, a way with knives. She's not a real lady but a criminal with a past that has come back to haunt her.

The secretary of state for war and the colonies wasn't the fictional Lord Brampton but Lord Bathurst. However, many of the events and people described in the story are real. George IV, the prince regent, did eventually become king of England in 1820. He was not a popular king because of his lifestyle and extravagance; however, he was called the First Gentleman of England because of his patronage of the arts. He left almost no mark on politics or history, except for the name of the period—Regency.

Beau Brummell was the arbiter of fashion and the leader of the dandies during the Regency period. He was also a close friend of the prince regent. After Brummell fell from royal grace, he still held social prominence. The prince regent gave Brummell the cut direct at a masquerade ball in 1813, and Brummell uttered loudly his famous rejoinder, "Alvanley, who is your fat friend?" Brummell's lifestyle and gambling eventually outran his fortune and he left England for cheaper living on the Continent.

SAMANTHA HASTINGS

—

Debutante with a Dangerous Past

Recycling programs for this product may not exist in your area.

ISBN-13: 978-1-335-59567-6

Debutante with a Dangerous Past

Harlequin Enterprises ULC
22 Adelaide St. West, 41st Floor
Toronto, Ontario M5H 4E3, Canada
www.Harlequin.com

Printed in U.S.A.

Samantha Hastings met her husband in a turkey-sandwich line. They live in Salt Lake City, Utah, where she spends most of her time reading, having tea parties and chasing her kids. She has degrees from Brigham Young University, University of North Texas and University of Reading (UK). She's the author of *The Last Word*, *The Invention of Sophie Carter*, *A Royal Christmas Quandary*, *The Girl with the Golden Eyes*, *Jane Austen Trivia*, *The Duchess Contract*, *Secret of the Sonnets* and *A Novel Disguise*. She also writes cozy murder mysteries under Samantha Larsen.

Learn more at her website: SamanthaHastings.com.

Connect with Samantha on social media.

Twitter: @HastingSamantha

Instagram: @SamanthaHastingsAuthor

Facebook: SamanthaHastingsAuthor

Books by Samantha Hastings

The Marquess and the Runaway Lady
Debutante with a Dangerous Past

Visit the Author Profile page
at Harlequin.com.

To Mylee Moon-Affleck

Chapter One

London, England, February 1813

Lord Matthew Stringham slumped into his chair and set down his portmanteau on his desk, yawning. He'd spent the better part of the day in a carriage coming back from Leeds.

Click. Thud. Thud.

Clack. Thud. Thud.

He got to his feet, recognising the sound of his grandfather's steps and not his punctual secretary, Mr Howitt. Grandfather Stubbs didn't bother to knock, but walked right into Matthew's office. 'It's about time you showed up for work.'

'Sit, Grandfather,' Matthew said, helping him into the softest wingback chair in the room. 'You knew where I was.'

His grandfather snorted, setting his cane against the chair. 'Steam locomotives, ha!'

Matthew sat back at his desk. 'They are the future,

and one day they will make me a fortune even larger than yours.'

A small smile played on his grandfather's grim mouth. 'So you say.'

'Steam locomotives will transport goods and people to every village on this island and eventually the world.'

'Well, while your head was in the clouds,' his grandfather said, 'I've been attending to our business. It would appear that the Horse Guards have heard about our superior goods. They are interested in having us provide supplies for the British army in the Peninsula.'

Matthew leaned forward in his seat. 'That's brilliant. We'll triple our investment in the shipping company.'

'At least.'

His grandfather rubbed the bottom of his long white beard. Something he always did when he was thinking.

'What's wrong, sir?'

Grandfather Stubbs was silent for a moment. 'I think it would be best if you handled all the negotiations with the lord secretary. You are of his own class after all.'

Matthew clenched his teeth. His maternal grandfather was a wealthy businessman who had his daughter marry the heir of a dukedom. But even with a daughter as a duchess, he was not included in society. The *ton* considered him a cit and a merchant. Unworthy of their presence at parties. The irony was that despite being the second son of a duke, Matthew was just as much a cit as his grandfather. He loved business and writing extremely complicated contracts to their advantage. He did the same things as his grandfather. They worked in the same office. They signed the same papers. Yet,

Matthew was acceptable in society and his grandfather was not. It irked him to no end.

'The old turnip sucker won't do business with you,' Matthew said at last.

Grandfather nodded.

'He's a fool.'

'I know.'

'And I am going to make him pay through the nose for his snobbery.'

His grandfather laughed softly. 'Oh, I know, Matthew. And it brings me a great deal of satisfaction.'

Ducking, Miss Nancy Black swore underneath her breath as a bullet whistled over her head. Someone had betrayed her. The job was supposed to be an easy smash and grab: a few English government documents to sell to a French spy. The money was good and the risk low. The British nob wasn't supposed to be home for at least another two hours. Giselle should have seen to that. Lord Whatsit should not have had a smoking pistol in his hand. She patted the papers tucked into her jacket. They were safe.

Before he could reload, Nancy charged into him and they both went crashing to the ground. She knocked his pistol from his hand before scrambling to her feet and leaving through the door. The open first-floor window— her entry point—was not an option. She couldn't scurry down to the ground floor fast enough before the toff reloaded his weapon. Grateful that most grand London houses were designed the same, she located the stairs and jumped down them by twos.

She took the last four all together, crashing directly

into the portly butler who'd been standing at the bottom. The candelabra clanked against the marble floor and Nancy felt her own bones clank inside of her. Elbowing the butler in the nose, to keep him down, she got to her feet and ran to the front entrance. Her fingers tore at the bolts as she unlocked them. She could hear the butler's yells and moans behind her as she finally opened the door.

A bullet whizzed towards her, grazing her left arm. Covering the wound with her hand, Nancy kept in her scream and ran into the street. She ducked into the first alley and zigzagged through the streets until she was out of the swell part of town. Skirting the edge of a rookery, she found a dark alcove to stop for a breath. Blood soaked her arm and her boy's clothes where the bullet had grazed her. The trail might even be enough to follow her home to her father.

Nancy sat down with a huff. With trembling fingers, she yanked up her shirt and pulled a strip of cloth from the bottom. A shift would have been better, but she never wore a dress to break in. It was too difficult to climb buildings in. She put the cloth on her upper arm, above the wound, and tied a knot with her free right hand and teeth. Gasping in pain, she leaned back against the wall of the building and let herself take a few breaths.

Someone had betrayed her.

But who?

She and her father had been a part of their current criminal gang for nearly ten years now. Since she was fourteen. Only nine of them were still alive: Alastair, Bones, Mick, Charles, Giselle, Lily, Peter, father, and herself. She would have trusted them all with her life. She had done so in the past. They'd accomplished many jobs together. She'd played beggars and ladies. Women and boys.

What was different about this job?

Was Alastair still angry about their argument in Buckinghamshire? It had been *his* fault, not hers.

Closing her eyes, she wracked her brain. Her father had planned the job. Giselle was supposed to use her feminine wiles as a professional courtesan to keep the British lord busy. Nancy had scurried up the side of the building to the window, which she easily picked open, and then took the documents conveniently located on top of the desk. Everything had gone off without a hitch, until the nob burst into his own library and shot at her.

Giselle must have not been able to distract the toff.

Shaking her head, Nancy couldn't remember Giselle ever making a mistake before now. Had she betrayed them?

If so, Nancy had to get back to the rented room she shared with her father before Giselle did. If she was willing to kill Nancy, she'd also kill her father. After stumbling to her feet, she made herself run down the lamp-lit streets until she reached the shabby building where they were living this week. Father's luck at the tables had taken a downturn these last few months and they had moved from lodging to even poorer lodging each fortnight. Nancy had hoped that this job would make them enough money to find a clean place. One without bedbugs, rats, and sewer water running through the centre of the street.

Holding her throbbing arm, Nancy went around the

back of the building in case someone was waiting for her in the front. Their room was on the first floor and there were no stairs at the back of the building. She glanced up and saw a lantern light burning in their single room. The window was open. Shivering, Nancy knew that something was wrong. There was a chill in the air. Her father wouldn't have left the window ajar. Someone else must have visited him through it. The same way she'd broken into the nob's house.

Nancy took out her dagger and clenched it between her teeth. She would need her good hand to climb. Ignoring the stabbing pain in her arm and shoulder, and the roiling of her stomach, she placed her hand on the brick. Her sore arm she forced to hold the next one. Her feet were strong and sure as she found footholds and bricks to climb until she reached the open window. With the last of her strength, she pulled herself through the frame. Her instincts kicked in; she rolled up to a crouching position and took the dagger from her teeth. Ready to strike.

But the only person in the room was her father.

His body was on the floor in a puddle of blood. Her fingers went cold and chills ran over her body. She tried to swallow, but couldn't. Her greatest fear had come true. Her only family was dead and her gang that she had considered to be family had betrayed her. Nancy's eyes filled with tears, but then she saw his chest rise up and down slightly.

He was still alive!

Dropping her dagger, she grabbed a blanket from the bed and pressed it down on the wound. She had to get the bleeding to stop.

Her father placed a bloody hand on hers. 'It is no use, darlin',' he said, with a cough. 'I'm all out of cards to play. I am a dead man.'

Nancy's heart squeezed and tears fell down her face. 'No, Papa. It is only a scratch. I'll take you to a physician and he'll patch you up.'

'No,' he croaked. 'You'll be killed too. Heap's men are looking for you.'

Her breath hitched. There were few men in London that were more dangerous than Harry Heap, the money lender. Fear crept down her spine as her world fell apart. 'Papa, I love you. I can't leave you here to die.'

He grimaced a smile. His hand slid from hers. 'You must. I'm already a dead man, but you can live. You deserve a better life. Go to your grandfather. He…he will help you now. Remember. Remember, never trust—'

Her father's head fell back. His eyes were still open, but he was dead. Nancy gently closed his eyelids and placed one last kiss on his forehead. Her hands were shaking and her body felt numb. No one would be waiting up for her any more. No one would care if something happened to her. She was truly all alone. Nancy stifled a strangled sob; Heap's men could still be nearby. Wiping her nose, she shuffled to her feet.

'Anyone,' she whispered, completing her father's last sentence.

Chapter Two

Matthew was summoned for a second time to visit Lord Brampton at Horse Guards on business. The secretary of state for war and the Colonies insisted again on doing business with him and not his grandfather. Matthew might be the son of a duke, but the chances of him inheriting the Hampford dukedom were very small. His elder brother, Wick, Lord Cheswick, and sister-in-law, Louisa, had just welcomed their second son into the world. The babe was red-faced and red-haired and the sweetest little baby Matthew had ever held. Possibly because they had named his nephew after him. Holding little Matt, he had even thought that it might be time to find a wife and have a son of his own.

But once he'd returned to London and been stopped on his ride in Hyde Park by no less than eight matchmaking mamas in carriages with their debutante daughters, he'd decided that he was in no rush to be caught. He was only six and twenty years old after all and had no desire to be wed for his money or his title. Despite being a savvy businessman, he believed in love matches. He'd grown up with two parents who were very much in love with each other and had always wanted the same for himself. Even his elder brother, Wick, who had sworn to never marry, met his match with Louisa. Matthew decided that true love was worth waiting for.

The lord secretary, however, was not. He had waited for nearly a half hour outside of Brampton's office. Matthew's temper and patience were growing thin by the time the older man opened the door. He was a tall, slender man with a wizened face and a shock of white hair. The lord secretary didn't apologise for keeping him waiting, but Matthew didn't expect him to. Nor did he want him to. Because if he did, Matthew might have felt guilty for overcharging the government for supplies the last month. Lord Brampton showed no signs of civility and Matthew could happily add extra charges to the contract for shipping, handling, holding, snobbery, and even waiting.

Lord Brampton cleared his throat. 'You may sit down, Lord Matthew.'

Matthew took a chair by one of the windows. 'Thank you, Lord Secretary.'

'I called you in because I would like to double the army's spring order for supplies and food.'

Matthew let out a low whistle. 'I am happy to accommodate you, my lord. However, to have twice as many supplies completed within less than a month's time would be very difficult. My employees will have to work through the night. I'll have to charge you twice as much for the second half and receive a substantial down payment before I begin production.'

The older man's eyes narrowed. 'Are you not a British citizen?'

'You know very well that I am.'

'And do you not want us to win the war against France?'

He shrugged. Matthew was not particularly interested in politics. Nor in wars fought on the Continent. 'I should infinitely prefer Britain to win, rather than lose to Emperor Napoleon.'

Lord Brampton hit his fist on the desk. 'Then will you not help us?'

'I am willing to provide the majority of your army's supplies and victuals, Brampton,' Matthew said. 'Without donning a scarlet uniform, I cannot imagine what more I could do for my country.'

'Charge less!'

Matthew forced himself not to smile. He was not a philanthropist, nor a patriot—he was a businessman. 'I won't come down on price. However, this once, I could waive all the handling fees.'

Including the fee for snobbery.

The secretary of state huffed. 'I suppose if that is the best you can offer your country.'

'It is.'

'Then let us shake hands on it,' Lord Brampton said, standing up. 'I'll expect those supplies to be on boats headed to Spain by the end of the month.'

Matthew took the older man's hand and squeezed it a little harder than he needed to. 'You can depend upon it, Brampton. And I shall expect a bank draft by the end of the week. Good day to you.'

Tipping his hat, Matthew left the stuffy office and the even stuffier government cabinet member.

Nancy hadn't slept all night. It wasn't safe to close your eyes on the streets of London. As soon as the sun began to rise, she ducked into an alley and rewrapped her wound. She had no money and nowhere else to go. There was no one to turn to but her grandfather, who had refused to assist her when she was fourteen years old. Nancy was too proud to beg, so she would bring the stolen papers and blackmail him. He would have no choice but to help her this time.

The soldiers who were guarding the gate to the Horse Guards gaped at her. Nancy supposed that women did not often come to the British army headquarters. She would have tried her grandfather's house, but she'd done so once before and been dismissed at the kitchen door as a beggar. Nancy ignored their ogling and walked up to the first guard.

'I am here to see Lord Brampton. I am his grand-daughter.'

One of the guards whistled at her.

'And I'm here to see the Queen of England,' another guard said with derision. 'If you're a real lady, where are your maid and your footman?'

Nancy clutched the bag that held all her worldly possessions before walking closer to the nearest guard. He leered at her.

Pointing, she exclaimed, 'Oh, no! That poor woman is being robbed.'

The soldiers brushed past her to get a better look. Slipping through the gate, she all but ran into the nearest building. She'd only temporarily distracted the guards and they would be raising the alarm or come for her soon. She walked hurriedly down the dark wood-panelled hall and then up a marble staircase. Gasping in pain, she stumbled up the steps. Her wounded left arm was smarting something dreadful.

At the top of the stairs, Nancy paused and looked in both directions.

'May I be of any assistance, miss?'

Nancy turned, her breath catching as she looked into the blue eyes of the most handsome man she'd ever seen. He was tall, with blond hair, and dressed expensively in a grey suit. His boots were polished until they shone. On instinct, she looked at his purse and guessed it had at least ten pounds in it. If her arm wasn't wounded, she could have picked his pocket easily. His eyes met hers and he smiled at her showing perfect white teeth, then he tipped his hat to her. Nancy's whole body hummed with interest, but she had to ignore it. Her slipping past the guards had attracted too much attention.

'Thank you,' she said with her most coquettish smile. 'I seem to have become turned around. Could you direct me to Lord Brampton's office?'

'Of course,' he said, offering his arm and smiling.

Nancy took it with her weak hand and the hum of attraction escalated to a buzz that she felt from her fingertips to her heart. He smelled divine—like cedar-wood, fresh paper, and musk.

'May I take your bag for you?'

'No.' She clutched it tighter with her good arm. This man was truly a gentleman. 'I mean, I prefer to carry it myself.'

'As you wish,' he said with a smile that turned the buzz in her blood to a trill. She had never been so physically aware of another person in her life. Even her wounded arm seemed to fill with a warm glow.

He led her down a series of halls, before knocking on a dark oak door.

'Enter.'

The gentleman escorted Nancy inside an opulent room with a large marble fireplace and a dark mahogany desk the size of a bed. Everything reeked of wealth. He released Nancy's arm. 'Lord Secretary, a young lady to see you.'

The Earl of Brampton stood at their entrance and looked at Nancy and her companion forbiddingly. She had never seen her grandfather before, but he did not look at all like she had imagined. He was a tall man with dark eyebrows, a long nose, a thin mouth, and a great deal of white hair. He was dressed in a distinguished black suit, with a black waistcoat, and an intricately tied cravat. Lord Brampton had no adornments besides a signet ring on his right index finger and was not carrying a purse.

'Thank you, Lord Matthew,' he said, in a drawling voice. 'I shall take it from here.'

The gentleman bowed to her and then left the room, closing the door behind him. *Oh!* He'd been a lord.

'Was I expecting you, *miss*?' Lord Brampton enquired, with a slight sneer. As if he doubted that she was a lady.

'Not precisely, my lord,' Nancy said, forcing her lips into a smile. 'But I am pleased to meet you, Grandfather.'

His face paled to the white of his fine shirt. 'My granddaughter is dead.'

'I am Nancy Black. The only child of your late daughter, Lady Susan.'

With her good hand, Nancy pulled out the gold memorial medallion from underneath her gown. Inside of it was a lock of her grandmother's hair artistically curved over a funerary urn and plinth with the initials DC: Dianetha Chambers. The hair was brown and straight, wholly unlike Nancy's black curls. She took off the medallion that she'd worn her entire life and handed it to the older man. He brought it close to his face, as if he didn't believe what his eyes were seeing.

'Your wife's hair,' she said, touching her own curls. 'According to my father, this locket was the only valuable that my mother refused to sell after she eloped with him.'

Lord Brampton stepped closer to her and gazed at her face like he was seeing it for the first time. 'What is your father's name, pray?'

'My father's birth name was Felix Black, but he went by many different surnames.'

Lord Brampton swallowed heavily and his Adam's apple bobbed. 'You spoke of your father in the past tense. Is he dead?'

A vision of her father's body surrounded by a puddle of blood caused bile to rise in her throat, but she swallowed it down. To save herself, she had left his body. She hoped when the landlady found it, that the parish would bury him in a pauper's grave. But she would never know where he was left to rest. There would be no stone with his name or alias. No place for her to visit. Her lips had difficulty forming the small word, but she managed to whisper, 'Yes.'

'And I daresay he has left you nothing to live on.'

His words were more painful than any physical slap or strike she'd ever received. There was no pity or sympathy for the man who had raised her. Who had urged her to save herself over him. Nancy forced her lips upwards. 'Oh, I wouldn't say nothing. Papa left me these official documents which are worth a fortune in the right hands.'

Taking out one of the papers she'd stolen, Nancy handed it to the stern older man.

Brampton took the paper from her and he gestured for her to sit. Nancy took the nearest chair and clutched her bag, feeling for her dagger. Brampton walked to the window. She watched as he pulled out his quizzing glass and read through the paper slowly, peering closely as if to study the handwriting.

Nancy realised she was holding her breath and released it slowly.

Lord Brampton's dark eyebrows rose until they met his white hair. 'Is this the only government document in your possession, Miss Black?'

'No, Grandfather. How much are they worth to you?' Nancy asked, and without giving him time to answer continued, 'For I am certain that the French government would give me a fortune for them.'

'Be that as it may,' he said, his jaw tight, 'you might find it difficult to reach France whilst we are at war.'

She shrugged one shoulder. 'Not as hard as you'd like to think. I could find a French agent by this afternoon.'

His jaw went slack and a supercilious look replaced it. She was a fool to think that anyone in her family would have helped her without wanting something in return. 'Only if I allow you to leave this room.'

The hairs on the back of her neck stood up, but Nancy forced herself to laugh, clutching her bag with the dagger and the papers even tighter. 'Precisely why I didn't bring the rest of the documents with me. If you try to keep me against my will, an associate of mine will sell them to France.'

He turned away from her, as if she was unworthy of his gaze. 'Ten thousand pounds.'

Her sore arm throbbed, but she forced herself to continue to smile. 'And how precisely would you give me the ten thousand pounds, Grandfather? A bank draft would simply be a letter for my own arrest. No. I want twenty thousand pounds in jewels.'

Lord Brampton glanced up from the memorial medallion in his hands to Nancy's face.

She blushed a little under his scrutiny. She guessed that he was trying to see his daughter in her features. 'Papa always said that I don't look like my mother, but my Scottish granny. The only thing that I inherited from my mother was her eyes.'

'Susan's blue eyes.'

The colour of her eyes had got Nancy into trouble many times. They were too memorable. Her blue eyes were bright and stood out against her fair skin and ebony hair.

Rubbing her wounded arm with her other hand, Nancy said, 'Give me the jewels and I'll disappear. You'll never see me again. I promise. No one will ever know of our relationship and your government will avoid another scandal.'

His gaze didn't waver from her face. 'Why do you assume that I would never wish to see you again?'

Nancy scoffed. 'You're welcome has hardly been warm, *Grandfather.* And the fact that you have refused to acknowledge my very existence for the last three and twenty years.'

'Your father was alive,' he said in a voice barely above a whisper. 'Now that he is dead, that changes things.'

Chills ran over her body, but she shook her head. 'Not for me it doesn't.'

Lord Brampton nodded his head forward slowly. 'I understand. What if I offer you a different bargain for the stolen government papers? Something better?'

Nancy stuck out her chin, her heart beating irregularly. 'I won't take nothing less than twenty thousand pounds in jewels.'

'I'll give you the twenty thousand pounds,' he said in his whisper-like voice. 'As your dowry when you marry a man of good birth.'

Snorting, Nancy shrugged her shoulders and looked down at her finest gown. He must think her an easy mark. Even in the dress Alastair had purchased for her role as his bride, not even the guards believed that she was a lady. There was no way she could pull off that sort of charade long-term. She'd be caught out and disgraced in society. 'Clever, but I won't fall for that trick. No gentleman would marry me. Unless he wanted the money more than I do, and then in that case, I wouldn't want him.'

He handed her the memorial medallion like it was a hot potato burning his fingers. Was it the memory of his dead wife or cast-off daughter that affected him so much? She couldn't read his emotions.

'If you were properly introduced to society by my

daughter-in-law, Viscountess Delfarthing, you would be accepted in the finest homes and families in all of England. Your aunt can teach you how to conduct yourself. Her husband is dead and her sons are grown. Think of it, Miss Black. Instead of a life on the run amongst the lower scum of society, as my granddaughter, you would be a part of the *ton*.'

Nancy snatched back her mother's medallion with her right hand and put it over her neck. She inhaled slowly, thinking. Unless she had a jeweller with her at the exchange, she would have no idea if the gems he gave her were worth the actual twenty thousand pounds. And if they were, she would have to find a way to get them and herself out of the country without the jewels being stolen. There was no guarantee that she would find a better life. A home of her own.

But if she accepted her maternal grandfather's outrageous bargain, she would be guaranteed a dowry of twenty thousand pounds. An enormous amount of money. She could marry a gentleman who owned his own house and probably an estate. She would never be homeless again. She needn't be hungry or scared. Nancy would be able to live the sort of life her mother had given up when she'd eloped with her father. Lady Susan had wed for love, but Nancy had no such delusions. If she married, it would be for money, safety, and security. Only spoiled debutantes believed in love. Her mother had died in childbed nearly nine months after marrying, having already fallen into poverty. Papa's success with cards never lasted long.

And now, he was dead.

A fresh wave of pain swept through her heart and

body. He'd wanted Nancy to beg her grandfather for his assistance. That had always been their plan if something happened to him and it chaffed her soul. This lord with all his money and privilege had never once made any effort to financially assist his only granddaughter. Maybe, if he would have helped her sooner, she wouldn't have been tricked into signing a contract with a madam for a roof over her head. Nor would she have been forced to become a criminal for her own protection and to afford a room to rent and something to eat. She hated Lord Brampton with every hair on her head.

She rubbed the medallion with her thumb. 'I won't give you the government documents until my wedding and when my husband is in possession of the twenty thousand pounds. And if anything happens to me before then, my associate will sell them to the French.'

He bowed to her. 'Very well, Granddaughter.'

Nancy got to her feet and walked to the door. 'I will meet you at your house in Berkley Square. Shall we say four o'clock?'

'Don't you need the address?'

She snorted and shook her head. She'd been there before and was shooed away like vermin.

Chapter Three

Matthew had his own bachelor rooms in London, which he preferred. But since his parents were in town for the debut of his little sister, Lady Frederica, he headed to the Hampford townhouse in Berkley Square. He was met at the door by their dignified butler, Mr Harper, and ushered into the front parlour. Frederica was pounding the piano as if she was trying to harm its keys. The melody was harsh, dissonant, and positively fascinating to hear. His sister's music usually reflected her mood. Clearly, today it was a dark one.

Frederica hit one last discordant note. 'So, I see you've come to gawk at me in all my misery?'

Matthew took a seat. He leaned back and placed his hands behind his head, interlocking his fingers. 'Yes. Been waiting years for it.'

His little sister was nineteen, two years older than most debutantes. And her mature figure, combined with her dark brown eyes and hair made her look older than her age. That, or her air of confidence. Matthew thought that his parents had waited a little longer with Frederica because of his sister Mantheria's disastrous marriage at seventeen, that ended in a separation at twenty. Her husband, Alexander, had been more than twice her age and had kept his mistress after the marriage. The only good thing to come out of their brief union was his nephew Andrew.

Or possibly his mother had decided to let Frederica debut later because she had already arranged a marriage with Lord Samuel Corbin, heir to the dukedom of Pelford. The said heir was only a few years older than his sister and for a man he was still a bit young for marriage.

'Where are Mama and Papa?' he asked.

Frederica shrugged one shoulder nonchalantly. 'Papa is actually attending Parliament today. He's proposed a bill on animal rights and Mama is at her perfume factory and intends to inspect her shop on Bond Street, as well.'

Matthew nodded. Even though his father was a duke, he rarely took his seat at Parliament. He simply wasn't interested in running a country, but he was passionate about the welfare of animals. He purchased exotic creatures from travelling companies and other peers only to release them back into the wild. The animals that were too domesticated to release, he kept in his menagerie on Animal Island near Hampford Castle. Matthew's mother was unique among the peerage, for she owned her own perfume business. She actively administered the details of her shop and even made her own scents.

'Then we are free.'

She laughed. 'Beware, Mama is in a mood. Samuel has not returned from the Continent. He's been promoted to aide-de-camp to General Lord Wellington in Spain.'

Matthew raised only his right eyebrow. 'Isn't the poor fool aware that he is supposed to be proposing marriage to you?'

Frederica burst out in laughter. 'I know, right? A war shouldn't stop him. Besides, you would think that he has taken a positive dislike of me, since he hasn't set foot in England in nearly five years.'

He fiddled with the chain of his quizzing glass, before looking at his sister through it. 'There was the little incident with the bear cub.'

His sister smiled. 'I was only playing.'

'But I am not sure that you explained that to the bear, or poor Samuel. As I recall, he seemed to think his very life was in danger.'

'The pigeon-hearted fool.'

Matthew couldn't help but laugh. 'Already coming up with pet names, are you?'

'Yes, that and Lord Dunderhead.'

'The sorry fellow,' he said. 'I believe you scared him out of his wits on his last visit to Hampford Castle five years ago.'

Frederica snorted and grinned. 'So much that he asked his father to purchase him a commission in the army.'

'He can't be too much of a dunderhead or Lord Wellington wouldn't have Samuel on his staff.'

His sister shook her head. 'No, he's a dunderhead and as stupid as an emu.'

'Perhaps he's improved with time, as I must admit, have you. You seem to have grown into all your long limbs. You no longer look like a stork.'

Frederica picked up the peasant figurine from the

piano and hurled it at him. Matthew caught it deftly with one hand. He had a great deal of experience with projectiles being thrown at his head. He did have four younger sisters after all.

She intertwined her fingers with a devious look. 'I suppose if you're going to be so disagreeable, I won't warn you about Mama's plans.'

Matthew groaned as he set down the figurine on the table beside him. 'Oh, no.'

'Oh, yes,' Frederica said, leaning forward, her face a picture of unholy glee. 'She has decided that since Samuel is not here to woo me, that she will focus all her efforts this season on finding you a wife… Feel free to send me a card of thanks.'

He covered his face with his hands and groaned. He did not want to be forced into a *ton* marriage transaction. A young lady of good birth, breeding, dowry, and family connections, in exchange for his honorary title, inheritance, and ducal connections. Matthew was a businessman and he knew that love could not be bought or traded. True love did not come from contracts, but was freely offered by both parties. He was looking for that sort of love and doubted it could be found in a ballroom where everyone put on their best face. As a young man, he'd been tricked by a calculating debutante and it was not an experience he wished to repeat.

Frederica laughed loudly. 'Mama has already sent out invitations for my coming-out ball and she intends to invite a great deal of eligible debutantes for you.'

Glancing up at his sister, he huffed. 'I bet you didn't even try to dissuade her.'

Her smile beamed back at him. 'If I must suffer at all these balls and social events, I don't see why you shouldn't have to suffer too.'

Matthew stretched out his long legs. It *would* be suffering. He had no desire to spend the evening with simpering seventeen-year-old young ladies who believed that their only purpose in life was to secure a husband of rank. No, he'd much rather pass the evening with a woman closer to his age with her own thoughts. Like the bold and dark-haired beauty that he'd taken to Lord Brampton's office that morning. Even in her simple attire, she was a stunner. 'I thought young ladies liked going to balls.'

Frederica blew a curl out of her face. 'I do. It's just, Matthew, everyone seems to know about Mama's marital intentions for Samuel. I fear that no one will even ask me to dance.'

'More will, Freddie.'

'Why?'

'You're no pressure,' Matthew said with a wave of his hand. 'Every young buck will happily dance and flirt with you knowing that they'll never be expected to come up to scratch with a proposal. You'll be the most popular and sought-after young lady at every event. Trust me.'

Covering her mouth with one hand, his sister giggled. 'I won't have to trust you. Remember? You'll be there to see my triumph.'

Matthew stood up.

'Where are you going?' Frederica asked, raising her eyebrows.

'To Spain. To drag Samuel back by his coat collar.'

He left his parents' house as his little sister continued to laugh at his expense. Although, he didn't plan to go as far as the Continent, but rather to his place of business. He had plenty of work to do. Matthew was barely down the steps when he nearly collided with the dazzling young lady he'd just escorted to see Lord Brampton. His body flooded with heat as a smile formed on his lips.

Matthew bowed, taking his hat off. 'Pardon me, miss. Am I following you or are you following me?'

She laughed. It was low, husky, and extremely attractive. The woman was even more beautiful than he remembered. Her bright blue eyes were arresting in her fair complexion with the blackest shade of hair he'd ever seen. She was only medium height, but her figure was very good. Matthew became acutely aware of his own heartbeat, thundering in his chest. He put back on his hat.

The young lady curtsied, clutching her left arm with her right hand. 'I promise that I am not following you, my lord. I am merely seeking the company of my grandfather.'

Her voice was also low-pitched and he could almost hear a trace of an accent that he couldn't quite place. Matthew had received a double first at Oxford and rarely forgot anything he read. But in this moment, in Berkley Square, his mind moved more slowly than an ox-cart. He'd met this beautiful young woman after his appointment with the Earl of Brampton, the secretary of war. Ergo, he must be the grandfather. Matthew was a little surprised to see how she was dressed, her blue gown was inexpensive and sturdy. Quite middle-class. Her straw bonnet simple and adorned with only one ribbon. No flowers or feathers. But the part of her appearance that was most out of place were her boots. They were scuffed and dirty as if she'd been traversing the slums of London.

'The Earl of Brampton?'

She nodded, her expression wary. 'I am to meet him at four o'clock at his home.'

Brampton House was only five row homes down from his parents', but Matthew's mind still had difficulty reconciling her words with her appearance and her lack of escort. She should have been with a chaperone, a maid, or a footman. Possibly all three. She wasn't in her first blush of youth, but she was by no means an antidote.

He pulled out his pocket watch on its gold chain and saw that the time was half past two. 'You're early.'

The woman gave another low, husky laugh. 'Yes. But I had nowhere else to go. My father has died and I am to live with my grandfather.'

Matthew's mind turned more slowly than the gears of a clock. He hadn't known the earl had a granddaughter. Only two grandsons. 'I wasn't aware that Lord Brampton had another son.'

She shook her head slightly, causing her ebony curls to bob up and down. He longed to reach out and touch them to see if they felt as silky as they looked. 'He did not. He had a daughter, Lady Susan Chambers, who died three and twenty years ago. I am her daughter.'

He had a vague recollection of this scandalous Chambers family story. His mother was no friend of the earl's daughter-in-law, Viscountess Delfarthing, who vocally disapproved of her role in trade. Duchesses weren't supposed to be successful businesswomen. 'May I be so bold as to enquire after your name?'

'Nancy Black.'

'*Miss* Nancy Black?' he repeated with a question.

She grinned at him and Matthew's fingers ached with the need to touch her. Her hair. Her skin. The pad of his thumb against her generous bottom lip. The curves of her body.

'Yes, and you are?'

Instead of touching her, he tipped his hat again. 'Lord Matthew Stringham. My parents are the Duke and Duchess of Hampford. I am, alas, a second son, therefore my title is only a courtesy one. And you're welcome to just call me Matthew.'

'Nancy,' she said.

Matthew repeated her name stupidly. His once keen mind was a complete wreck. Oh, how his brother, Wick, and sisters would tease him if they could have seen him at the present time. He'd never before understood how strong attraction could make people stupid. Humbly, he did understand it now. 'It is only a few steps away, but I would be honoured to escort you to your grandfather's house.'

Her face paled a little and he heard her stomach rumble; her right hand moved back to her left arm, just below the shoulder. 'My grandfather is not expecting me yet.'

'Wonderful,' Matthew said and she blinked at him. 'I…I mean, why don't you come into my parents' house for some tea whilst you wait until four? My sister Frederica is there and she can play gooseberry…if you listen carefully, you can hear her pounding the keys of my parents' pianoforte.'

He watched her lift her left hand to her ear and her eyes widened when she heard the music.

'Your sister is a talented musician.'

'I'll introduce you,' Matthew said, unable to resist the urge to touch her left elbow to escort her.

Nancy gasped and pulled away from his light touch, cradling her left arm, the colour draining from her face. He glanced down and saw that there was blood on her sleeve.

'Are you injured? What happened? May I help you?'

She didn't speak, only nodded, her expression pained.

'I won't touch you this time,' he said apologetically, 'but why don't you come into my parents' house and Freddie can patch you up and I'll have Cook get you something to eat.'

'Please,' she said in a voice barely above a whisper. Her beautiful face pinched with pain.

Matthew felt a surge of protectiveness, even though there was something smoky about her visit to the Horse Guards and the fact she remained unchaperoned. Nancy clearly wasn't raised a lady and she was injured, but he was too fascinated by her to care about the proprieties. He went back up the steps to his parents' house and Harper opened the door. How the butler knew he was still there boggled his already slow wits. Matthew ushered Nancy into the front parlour.

Frederica stopped playing, her back still turned away from him. 'You can't have gone to Spain and back yet.'

She swivelled on the seat and her eyes widened when she saw Nancy. 'And she is most certainly not Samuel.'

'Stop being a ninny and go and get your new red soap,' Matthew said, fussing and trying to stay in control of the situation. 'Nancy's injured.'

His sister sprang to her feet and dashed out of the room. Matthew gestured to the sofa, careful not to touch Nancy. He didn't wish to hurt her again. Pinching the skin at his throat, he asked, 'Do you want me to stay until Frederica returns, or shall I go and fetch you some tea and something to eat?'

Nancy's stomach grumbled and a little colour stole into her cheeks. 'I suppose my body has already answered that question.'

'I shan't be long.'

Matthew left the parlour and went down the hall to the back of the house, down the stairs to the kitchens. He wasn't very helpful in dire situations, but he knew how to procure food. At his entrance, the maids froze like statues, but Cook, Mrs Jones, went around the large cutting table and hugged him. The older woman was like a grandmother to him. She had short curly grey hair, and a plump, comfortable figure.

He hugged in return. 'Cook, it has been too long.'

She stepped back and gave him a playful swat on the arm. 'Harper said you'd come and gone without so much as a hello.'

'I am a reprobate,' Matthew said, theatrically hanging his head.

'Oh, nonsense, handsome,' Cook said, with a wave of her hand. 'I'll get you some biscuits and cake.'

He touched his heart and thought of the mysterious

young woman in the parlour. 'You are truly my favourite person, but my guest requires something with a bit more sustenance and some tea.'

Cook blinked at him.

Matthew swallowed and pulled at his collar. 'I'm afraid she's been injured and is bleeding, but Frederica's going to patch her up.'

Mrs Jones pointed at one of the kitchen maids. 'Molly, start two kettles to boil. One for the tea and one for the cleaning of the wound. Kitty, you go and fetch some bandages, a needle, thread, and talcum powder.' She snapped her fingers. 'Be quick about it.'

Matthew watched as Cook took out bread, ham, cheese, fruit, and nuts and generously plated them. Then set the platter on a silver tray. She took out a teacup and saucer and placed them on it, as well. He waited until Cook had filled the silver teapot with hot water and tea leaves, before he offered to carry the tray.

Mrs Jones pointed her ever-ready finger at him. 'Now, don't you go and drop it, my lord.'

'I won't.'

Cook put down her finger. 'I'll follow you in a minute or two with the bandages and a water basin.'

Matthew's hands shook a little as he carried the tray out of the kitchens and up the stairs to the ground floor. He realised that he'd never done this before. Harper or another servant had always brought his food to him. Keeping the tray perfectly level was actually more difficult than he supposed. Happily, he managed to arrive in the front parlour without any major incident and carefully set the tray on a table beside Nancy. Her bonnet was on the sofa next to her.

Frederica was already back and helping Nancy take off her blood-soaked spencer. He watched her cut off the sleeve of Nancy's dress. He saw that there was a bit of cloth tied above the lesion as a tourniquet. The wound was an angry red around the skin and looked swollen.

'What happened?' Matthew couldn't help but ask.

Nancy bit her lower lip as Frederica untied the tourniquet. 'I got shot last night. I was in the wrong part of town.'

Frederica gasped. 'You poor thing! Did you see a physician?'

The pale young woman shook her head.

What had she been doing in the wrong part of town? This woman was more dangerous and intriguing than anyone he had ever met. And it was more than simply base attraction. Perhaps he was so interested because she was a puzzle. A lady. But not a lady. Something nebulous and in between, not unlike his own existence in society. She piqued his mind as well as his body. He wanted to understand her piece by piece.

'Good heavens!' Mrs Jones said from the door to the room. She carried a larger tray with a water basin, needle and thread, a roll of bandages, and bottle of talcum powder. 'Step aside, Lady Frederica, this is no job for a delicately nurtured young lady.'

Frederica stepped back from Nancy, but gestured to the red bar of carbolic soap that she had invented. 'But my—'

'I'll clean the wound with your newfangled soap, my lady,' Cook assured her.

Matthew and Frederica watched as Cook cleaned

the wound with the hot water and the cake of soap that Frederica had made. His sister wanted to expand their mother's perfume business to include scented soaps. Cook scrubbed the wound and the area around it with soap and water, before threading the needle and puncturing it into Nancy's skin. Bile rose in Matthew's throat and he had to turn away as Cook stitched her lesion together. Next, she applied the talcum powder and wrapped Nancy's arm with the new bandages. She placed all the soiled rags and even Nancy's spencer on the tray, then she stood up. 'Best get this cleaned up before Mrs May gets back from her shopping.'

Mrs May was their housekeeper and a wonderful woman, but she would feel obligated to tell his parents about this misadventure.

'Thank you,' Matthew said, nodding. He didn't think Mama would find any relative of Viscountess Delfarthing beautiful or intriguing, especially if she were introduced whilst bleeding in their sitting room.

Cook pointed at Nancy. 'Drink your tea and eat some food, miss. You'll feel better for it.'

Then the good lady left the room.

Matthew cleared his throat. 'Cook is a bit bossy, but she means well.'

Nancy gave him a shy smile as she picked up the teacup with her right hand and Matthew felt something entirely new inside his chest. His body felt weightless. This feeling was more than base attraction, it was something he had never experienced before.

'I am not offended,' she said. 'I am merely overwhelmed by all your kindness.'

Frederica chuckled and sat in a chair by Nancy. 'Oh,

we Stringhams are always overwhelming. I'm Frederica, by the by. I think Matthew called you Nancy. Shall I do the same, or would you like me to call you miss?'

Chapter Four

Nancy took a sip of her tea, making sure that everything was real. A handsome gentleman, nay a lord, had invited her into his family's home. And what a home it was. The furniture was stylish and expensive in shades of green. Antique paintings were on the walls; Nancy would guess that she could have sold each of them for over five hundred pounds to the right dealer. And the largest pianoforte she had ever seen was in the middle of the room. It had been the perfect place to stash the documents when they'd left her alone. This was the sort of house that she'd only been in as a thief, never a guest drinking tea.

'Nancy is fine. It's nice to make your acquaintance, Lady Frederica.'

Frederica grinned and stared at her brother. 'She said it's nice to meet *me*, but not *you*, brother.'

Matthew shook his head slightly. 'That is because *nice* is too mild a word for the pleasure of meeting me.'

She listened to the two siblings' banter while she ate her food. The last time she'd had a proper meal had been at a pub, weeks ago. Before her father's luck at the tables turned. Thinking of her father caused another wave of pain to rush over her. She could not go back and bury her father. It was too dangerous. She might be caught by a money lender, a Bow Street runner, or a member of her former gang. None of whom would show her mercy.

Nancy would make Giselle pay for betraying them, but not yet.

She ate until her stomach protested that it was too full. Nancy took one last sip of the tea. It was the finest that she'd ever tasted.

'Can we get you anything else, Nancy?' Matthew asked.

Nancy felt her blood warm with each of his words. He was treating her like an equal. He didn't look down on her like Lord Brampton had.

'I couldn't eat another bite.'

Frederica got to her feet. 'But you'll need a new spencer, your last one is quite ruined. As is the sleeve of your dress. We'll have to cover it. Shall I fetch one of mine? You needn't bother returning it. This particular spencer has become too small for me.'

'Excellent notion,' he said.

'Give me one moment,' she said, leaving the room.

Swallowing the lump in her throat, Nancy felt overwhelmed again. This time by their charity. 'I don't know what to say. Your generosity… I'll ask my grandfather to repay you. I am to be staying with him for the season.'

Matthew laughed. 'Oh, you don't need to repay us. But please do tell your grandfather. I can't think of anything he'd hate more than to be indebted to the Stringhams.'

The young lord was even handsomer when he laughed, if that were possible. Nancy felt her whole body warm at the sight.

'Lord Brampton doesn't like you?'

He shook his head. 'He can't stand me or my family. He flatly refuses to do business with my grandfather who is a cit and one of the most powerful businessmen in the city. He insists on meeting with me to purchase supplies for the army. I charge him extra for snobbery.'

'Then everyone in the city will have to pay it,' Nancy quipped, causing him to chuckle again.

Touching his chest, he grinned at her. 'I am sure you did not mean to include my humble self in your comment.'

She thought Matthew was much too wealthy and good-looking to be humble, but he was the kindest gentleman she'd ever encountered. 'You are very self-*less*.'

'Which is much better than self-*ish*.'

Nancy licked her lips. 'But less tasty than shell-*fish*.'

'And certainly preferable to oaf-*ish*.'

'Or off-*ish*.'

He winked at her. 'But not wolf-*ish*.'

His smile was certainly *wolfish*, which made her feel light-headed. She'd never met such a clever cove before. 'You're making me feel waif-*ish*.'

'And me huff-*ish*.'

'If we don't stop now, our conversation might become raff-*ish*.'

Before he could respond to her *tawdry* comment, Frederica entered the room with a beautiful light blue spencer of figured silk. 'Here, let me help you put this on.'

Nancy got to her feet rather unsteadily. She'd never

been waited on before and certainly not by the daughter of a duchess. Frederica was gentle as she helped Nancy pull the spencer over her wounded arm and then her good one. She even buttoned it up and put on the bonnet, tying the ribbon to one side of Nancy's face.

'Good as new.'

Glancing down at the garment, Nancy realised she had never worn anything so fine. 'I can't thank you enough, Lady Frederica.'

'Just Frederica, but please not *Freddie*.'

'I like the name Freddie,' Matthew said, getting to his feet.

His sister placed her hands on her hips. 'Because you're a boy.'

'Well spotted.'

Nancy felt her lips quirk up.

Matthew held out his arm to her. 'Shall I escort you to your grandfather's now? I'm dying to see his face.'

Smiling, Nancy placed her hand on the crook of his arm. She had never voluntarily touched a man before and she felt rather weak in the knees. He was even more handsome up close. But what amazed her the most was that he made her feel safe, as if she could trust him. She bowed her head to his sister. 'I hope to see you again, Frederica.'

'Of course,' she said. 'And I shall personally send you over an invitation for my coming-out ball.'

Matthew led her out of the house and down the front steps where they had run into each other for a second time. Nancy almost wished that her grandfather lived farther away from the Stringhams, for the walk was all too short for her liking.

'Thank you again for the meal and patching me up. I have never known such altruism.'

'What did you say?' Matthew said, holding his free hand to his ear. 'I'm feeling a bit deaf-*ish*.'

A chuckle escaped her lips. 'You had to get the final word. Didn't you?'

'Always.'

'Or rather, all-*ish*.'

'That's not a word or an animal. Trust me, I know. My father is a famous naturalist,' Matthew protested as he lifted the knocker on her grandfather's front door. A nob like him would never think of going to the kitchen door or a servant's entrance.

A male servant that she supposed was the butler opened the door.

'Miss Black and Lord Matthew to see His Lordship,' he said.

The butler bowed. 'His Lordship is not yet home, but has sent word for his granddaughter to be placed in the care of the housekeeper, Mrs Melbrook.'

Releasing her hold on Matthew's arm, Nancy had not realised how much she'd been leaning on him physically and emotionally. 'I suppose this is goodbye then, Matthew.'

He shook his head. 'Goodbye-*ish* for now, Nancy.'

'Would you like me to assist you in dressing, Miss Black?' the housekeeper asked in an uppity tone.

Nancy grinned ruefully as she remembered her father's favourite maxim: *Smile first. Stab second.* 'I would be delighted to have your assistance.'

Twenty minutes later, Nancy thought that she had

never looked better. She had always arranged her own hair and her black curls were unruly. Mrs Melbrook managed to confine her ringlets and arrange them becomingly around her face. Nancy picked up her reticule.

'You don't bring your reticule to dinner,' the housekeeper said.

Nancy clutched the bag tighter with her dagger inside of it. 'I am afraid I would feel quite undressed without it.'

The Earl of Brampton stood by the fire and his tall, slender body seemed elongated by his shadow. His mouth was in a tight line so that his lips could barely be seen. Nancy was surprised to see his bright blue eyes were identical to hers in shape, size, and colour. She'd been too nervous in his office to notice. And she could tell at a glance that his clothing was of the very finest cut and style and had been made by a fashionable tailor.

Nancy stared at her grandfather, and he in return scrutinised her, as well. She bobbed a schoolgirl curtsy and then stood up like a soldier before his general. She felt half tempted to salute.

'You may sit down.'

She obeyed immediately and marvelled at the proportions and elegance of the library. Bookshelves lined the walls from the floor to the top of a twelve-foot ceiling. Above the fireplace hung an old family portrait. Sitting at the feet of her parents was a young girl playing with a pair of white kittens. It had to be her mother, Lady Susan. She had soft brown hair that curled prettily around her perfectly oval face. Nancy took in every line and curve, and memorised them to keep with her always.

'Have you always lived with your father?' Lord Brampton asked in a flat voice.

'Since I was eight, my lord.'

'And you have no other family on his side?'

'None,' she said crisply. 'My Scottish grandmother cared for me until I was eight years old. Then she died of a fever. After that, it was only my father and me.'

The earl's thin lips curled. 'Why the devil did you bring your reticule to dinner?'

Nancy pulled out her dagger from it. 'I don't go anywhere without a weapon.'

Her grandfather blinked, appearing surprised for the first time that evening. The old earl had no idea what she was capable of.

'Am I to understand that you know how to use it?'

She pointed the blade at him. 'I am more than happy to give you a demonstration of my skills.'

'What other *skills* have you?' Lord Brampton asked in a soft, mocking voice.

Nancy gritted her teeth. 'I'm a pretty good shot with a pistol up to twenty feet. Beyond that, I will hit my mark with less precision. But I'm better with a dagger or knife in a close-range fight.'

'And have you been in many fights?'

It was her turn to scoff. 'I grew up in the slums of Edinburgh and London. So yes, I have put my skills to good use many times.'

He tapped his long fingers on his desk. 'Your father should never have taken you there.'

Nancy twirled the dagger between her fingers of her left hand. An intricate trick that had taken her years to master and resulted in many cuts. Her wounded arm stung from the effort. 'Never. Talk. About. My. Father. Like. That.'

To her astonishment, the earl laughed. 'You did not exaggerate your skill.'

'I never exaggerate. Exaggeration will get you killed.'

Lord Brampton nodded, slowly. 'May I ask what happened to him?'

'He was betrayed and shot,' she said, lowering her dagger and cradling her wounded left arm with her other hand.

An awkward silence followed.

'I take it that your living conditions were poor?'

'You know nothing about me or my life.'

'No, I don't,' he said. 'Tell me about yourself. What sort of education have you had? Employment? Or has blackmail been your main source of funds?'

She forced herself to smile sharply. 'You are the first person I have blackmailed, Grandfather. I learned how to read and write in English from my father. To speak Gaelic and Irish from my granny, and commoner's French from a courtesan. Also, I would say growing up on the streets of London was an education in itself. One of our many landladies taught me how to sew. A madam who runs a fancy house, taught me how to walk, curtsy, dance, and talk flash. I believe she thought I'd be an excellent addition to her girls, but my father broke out from jail and I was able to escape from her.'

Nancy couldn't help but give a full-body shiver in remembrance. The fear. The bile that rose in her throat when Madame Sweetapple said what her position would entail. What if Alastair had come for her a day later? What if he had not helped both herself and her father escape? She didn't want to think what would have become of her.

Her grandfather blanched. 'How old were you?'

'Fourteen,' Nancy said, willing her cheeks not to blush. There were younger prostitutes on the streets. 'Then my father and I joined a criminal gang for protection from slum bosses and the pimps who run the stews. For the last nine years, we've done countless jobs. At first, I was the lookout. Then the decoy. And finally, the thief. I can scale a three-storey building in less than two minutes. I'm an excellent picklock, as well.'

'As fascinating as those skills undoubtedly are,' he said, his nostrils flaring. 'I don't think any of them will be of use in procuring you a suitable husband in society. So, I have written to my daughter-in-law, Lady Delfarthing, your aunt Marianne. She will be coming to live with us. She will see that you are suitably behaved and dressed for your new station in life. You are to obey her.'

'Yes, my lord.'

Obedience was a small price to pay to live in such a house.

Chapter Five

The butler opened the door to the library and Nancy entered. She saw her aunt-by-marriage's face for the first time. Viscountess Delfarthing was handsome rather than beautiful. She had brown eyes, a hook nose, and a small mouth. She looked aristocratic and distinguished. The older woman eyed Nancy coolly, appraising her like a captain-sharp. Nancy bobbed a curtsy and sat in the chair adjacent to her aunt.

'Marianne, may I introduce you to my granddaughter, Miss Nancy Black?' Lord Brampton said in a formal voice.

'I am delighted to meet you, my lady.'

A look of hauteur overcame her sharp features. 'You may call me Aunt Marianne. You are pretty, that's something. And your accent isn't terrible. I daresay you have no accomplishments. But do you dance and play cards?'

Lord Brampton coughed, but Nancy did not show any embarrassment, instead she laughed. 'You are correct. I do not have the typical female accomplishments of netting screens, water colours, or playing the pianoforte. But I do know most country dances and I'm rather good at cards.'

The correct term was a card sharp. Not that Nancy always cheated. Only when she was hungry and had to. Most of the time, counting cards was the easiest and safest way to win any game. And she did not consider that cheating. If only her father could have learned that particular skill.

Aunt Marianne stood up from the settee and walked to the window, grimacing. She turned back to her niece and said in a flat tone, 'Nancy, if someone asks you about your accomplishments you must answer as vaguely as possible. Let them assume that you know more than you do. Not that I wish you to tell falsehoods, but in most cases, the less you say the better.'

'Very well, ma'am—Aunt.'

Nancy glanced at her grandfather who was smirking. He obviously appreciated this delicate duplicity. And she almost liked him for it.

Almost.

Aunt Marianne missed the exchange between them and continued, 'There is no time to waste. London is still pretty thin on company, but come the first of April, the season will be in full swing and your ball shall be one of the first events. We will hire you a dancing master, write out the invitations tomorrow, and have the ball three weeks from today. But first, we shall go to my modiste tomorrow morning and order you some proper clothes.' She looked at Nancy's attire and wrinkled her nose. 'Then we can cast in the fire what you are wearing now, after we incinerate that ridiculously large reticule.'

Nancy clutched her reticule with her dagger inside it even tighter. *Over my dead body.*

'Once you are properly attired and your hair cut in a more modish style, we will make morning calls and procure you vouchers to Almack's. I am sure Lady Sefton will be quite happy to oblige me, she is a dear friend,' her aunt continued haughtily. 'I shall take my leave of you both. There is much to do and time is of the essence.'

Her aunt arrived at her grandfather's house the next morning with her two grown sons. Nancy guessed that both men were in their midtwenties, but their appearances couldn't have been more opposite. The elder was tall and slender, verging on gaunt. His suit was made of fine cloth, but simple in cut. His light brown hair and blue eyes reminded her of their mutual grandfather. Cousin Peregrine, Viscount Delfarthing, gave her a clumsy bow and said not a word. Nancy didn't know if he was stuck-up or shy.

Cousin Basil was his brother's opposite in all ways. He was short and rather portly. His hair was dark and curly, his nose hooked, and his lips so red they looked as if they had been painted with carmine. But it was his clothing that caught the eye. He wore a lilac-striped waistcoat with a matching lilac coat with overlong tails. His tight yellow pantaloons were adorned with an intricate pattern of loops and applied braid decorates. His tall Hessian boots had tassels and gleamed in the sunlight as if they'd been freshly blackened. His cravat was tied in an intricate style with more folds than

Nancy could see or count. And Basil's shirt points were so high that they reached his chin.

'Coz! I am so happy to meet you.'

He grinned at her, before sweeping her into an un-expected embrace. Nancy stiffened like a stone statue. She wasn't used to being touched. Men were danger-ous if you allowed them too close. Her cousin, how-ever, didn't seem to notice that she hadn't returned his embrace. He stepped back from her a foot or two and looked her up and down like she was a horse for sale. Nancy felt herself blushing.

Then Basil's eyes met her own and she realised that his appraisal had not been amorous.

He grinned at her. 'I am going to have so much fun dressing you! Please, oh, please say that I can help se-lect your wardrobe. Ask Mama. I have an eye for co-lour. Don't I?'

Basil turned to his mother whose resting haughty face softened as she smiled at him. 'My son is an arbi-ter of fashion. I do not purchase so much as a reticule without garnering his opinion first.'

Her cousin beamed, touching both of his red cheeks with his hands. 'Oh, Mama! You are too kind. I am not yet as influential as the great Beau Brummell, but I hope in time to be worthy of such high praise.'

Cousin Peregrine finally opened his mouth. 'You are a credit to us, brother.'

'Who is Beau Brummell?' Nancy asked. She couldn't help wondering who this august person was.

Basil's red lips formed a perfect O. He squeaked out a few unintelligible noises before he was able to speak real words. 'Thunder and turf! He is only the most powerful and influential fashion leader of the *ton*. He is the pinkest of pinks. A tulip among the thorns. The ultimate Bond Street Beau. He has snubbed duchesses and belittled royalty. With one lift of his eyebrow, he can make or break a debutante's season. You must earn his approval, Cousin Nancy.'

Her lips twitched. 'I'll do my best, Cousin Basil.'

Basil took her hand. 'You'll have to do better than your best. Come, we must order you an appropriate wardrobe at once. Mama, there is no time to waste.'

Pulling her across the room like there was a fire, Basil yelled to the butler to call for the carriage. Then turned back to his mother. 'Should we cover Cousin Nancy with a hooded cape? I should hate for anyone to see her before we've made her presentable.'

Aunt Marianne smiled and took her son's other hand. 'We will be extra careful not to meet anyone that we know.'

This seemed to mollify her son, for he nodded. 'We should pull down the curtains over the carriage windows. As an extra precaution.'

Sticking to Nancy like glue, Basil shielded her from the sun and from others' view with an umbrella until they entered the carriage. He helped Nancy and then his mother inside before closing the curtains until not even a sliver of light could be seen in the now dim compartment.

'Is Cousin Peregrine not joining us?' Nancy asked.

'Not today,' Aunt Marianne said.

Basil squeezed his eyes shut and lowered his head, before confessing in the most serious of accents, 'My brother cares nothing for fashion.'

'Oh, no!' Nancy said in a mocking tone.

Her cousin missed her sarcasm completely. He patted his mother's hand. 'Alas, no one is perfect. But my good brother has paid my tailor's bills more than once when I've outrun my quarterly allowance. He's a good 'un.'

Despite being a bit of a fop, Nancy thought that her Cousin Basil was a *good 'un* too. And that her Aunt Marianne was a different person with her sons. A kinder, more loving one.

Chapter Six

Cousin Basil and Aunt Marianne did not waste time in procuring a proper wardrobe for Nancy. They had her measured for chemises, day frocks, pelisses, spencers, riding habits, and gowns. Basil hurried them to a prominent milliner, where her aunt purchased no fewer than fifteen hats for her. Next, Aunt Marianne took Nancy to a stylish bazaar where she purchased ten pairs of gloves, five parasols, two pairs of stays, and two dozen silk stockings. Nancy's feet were measured for kid boots and dancing slippers. Her hair was cut into a more modish style and a lady's maid was hired who did not look down on her like Mrs Melbrook. Miss Arnold was about the same age as Nancy and her hair was the bright gold of guineas. She had a sweet countenance and treated Nancy like she was a queen and not an unwanted granddaughter.

Nancy rarely saw or spoke to her grandfather. He never seemed to be at home the entire fortnight before her finished wardrobe arrived.

Despite only being five houses down from Matthew

and Frederica, she had not seen either of them since the day they bandaged her arm. Which had healed quite nicely. Nancy longed to see Matthew again, but was content to wait until she was properly dressed.

Once her new gowns were delivered, Marianne informed Nancy that they could now start to make morning calls. *Morning calls* as it turned out, did not happen in the morning, but between the hours of three and five o'clock. And as they trundled round London in the carriage that morning, Nancy realised she and Aunt Marianne didn't actually *call* on people. They stayed in the carriage while a footman rang the bell and handed the butler Viscountess Delfarthing's card. They left nearly thirty cards at different residences, but not one at Hampford House.

'Are you not acquainted with the Duke and Duchess of Hampford?'

'Lady Hampford is nothing more than a tradesman's daughter,' her aunt said between clenched teeth. 'The *woman* even owns her own perfumery. How vulgar! And she only gives individual scents to her particular friends.'

Disappointed, Nancy realised that Aunt Marianne wasn't one of those friends. Although her aunt was certainly high in the instep.

Nancy felt surprised when the footman opened the door of the carriage and assisted both ladies out. They were actually going inside a house.

'Who are we meeting?' Nancy asked.

'Lady Sefton,' her aunt said. 'She is one of the patronesses of Almack's Assembly—the most exclusive club in town. Only the best of the best in society receive vouchers to attend. Therefore, it is crucial that you gain her approval, so that she will give you a voucher to attend there. I expect your very best behaviour. No slips of the tongue.'

Her stomach turned with nervousness, but Nancy couldn't suppress her grin. Nothing irritated Aunt Marianne more than when she talked slang. 'Of course. I won't say that I'm as sick as a cushion. Or that I'm feeling as queer as Dick's hatband.'

The grey stone terraced house was very fine and she and her aunt were ushered into a yellow drawing room. The golden chairs looked like royal thrones.

'Your Ladyship, Lady Delfarthing and Miss Black are here to see you,' the butler droned.

Maria Molyneux, Countess of Sefton, was an attractive woman with large eyes, and a heart-shaped face. Her brown hair was mostly covered by a white cap. She stood, giving a languid smile to Aunt Marianne and gestured towards a pair of chairs. 'Do please sit down, dear friends.'

Nancy sat uncomfortably on the edge of her seat, desperate not to make a mistake. Her aunt took the throne chair beside her.

'Maria, allow me to present my niece, Miss Nancy Black,' Aunt Marianne said majestically. 'No doubt you have received the invitation to her coming-out ball.'

'I have,' Lady Sefton said.

Nancy had to bite her lower lip to keep from laughing. On the table next to Lady Sefton, there was a stack of cards and invitations as high as a vase. The Countess then turned to look at Nancy who sat up straighter.

'You do not favour your mother,' Lady Sefton said,

eyeing her closely. 'We came out in the same season, but you do remind me of her—no doubt it is the way you bite your lower lip when you try not to laugh.'

Nancy gave a genuine chuckle at this and to her surprise, so did Lady Sefton.

Aunt Marianne grimaced more than smiled. 'Maria, I hope I am not too presumptuous in assuming you will send my niece a voucher? I would be most grateful.'

Lady Sefton inclined her head. 'Of course. I look forward to seeing you both at an Almack's Assembly very soon.'

'And may my niece waltz during the season?'

The Almack's patroness folded her arms. 'I suppose, but I will consider the debt I owe you paid in full.'

Her aunt tapped the side of her hooked nose. 'There are no debts between friends such as ourselves.'

But clearly there were. Nancy couldn't help but wonder what sort of debt Lady Sefton owed her aunt. She felt surprised that Aunt Marianne was using it to help her. Perhaps her supercilious aunt was fonder of her than she'd originally thought. She had been kind to Nancy, but most of their conversations were criticisms or corrections. She supposed that her aunt had only weeks to prepare Nancy for society, whereas most mothers spent years.

The butler opened the door and announced another guest. 'Lord Matthew Stringham, my lady.'

Turning, Nancy licked her lips in anticipation.

Matthew walked confidently into the room. His golden hair seemed to shine and he was taller and more handsome than she remembered. Unlike her Cousin Basil's flamboyant fashion, Matthew's dark suit was exquisitely cut and understated. His necktie arranged in a different style than Basil, but just as complicated a knot. She felt the familiar hum of desire from just being in the same room as him. He bowed to Lady Sefton and handed her a small oval box. 'With my mother's compliments, my lady.'

The countess tilted her head, accepting it. 'My very own scent. Lord Matthew, I believe you are acquainted with Viscountess Delfarthing.'

Her aunt gave him a cold nod, but gestured to Nancy with one hand. 'Lord Matthew, may I present my niece, Miss Black?'

He took Nancy's hand and all further thoughts fled her head. The hum turned again to a tingle she felt from her head to her toes and a strange warmth deep in her belly. Bending over her hand, Matthew's lips gently brushed her glove. Her heart beat wildly. She wished his mouth had touched her skin. 'A great pleasure, Miss Black.'

Nancy desperately wanted to say something witty or charming, but all she managed to do was smile at him. He returned her smile and her body flushed in delight. Matthew released her hand. 'I bid you all a very pleasant morning.'

The countess raised a finger. 'Oh, no, Lord Matthew, you are not escaping our society so easily. Sit down and speak with Miss Black whilst I have a little chat with my dear friend, the Viscountess.'

Nancy could barely believe her luck as Matthew took a seat on the settee beside her. He flashed her another grin and she assumed that he didn't mind being commanded to stay.

'I've been hoping I might run into you,' she admitted, blushing. 'And your sister, Frederica.'

'Haven't seen much of her either,' he admitted, raking one hand through his hair. 'I've been busy overseeing a large supply order from the government. As well as monitoring my investments in other speculations.'

Nancy blinked in surprise. She thought that gentlemen and lords did not sully their hands with real jobs. 'You work?'

His lips twitched upwards and his eyes danced. 'Did I not already tell you? I am a lowly second son. We do not inherit our fortunes, so we must earn them.'

Like her old criminal boss, Alastair, Matthew would not inherit the family's estate because he was not the eldest male heir. Alastair had taken care of primogeniture by poisoning his cousin and acceding to his title and estate.

Could a second son offer her the security that she so badly desired? Or was he only flirting with her and needed to find a young lady with enough money to support them both? She'd learned from her aunt that marriage among the upper classes was primarily a financial transaction. Matthew already knew more about her than was prudent. He knew that she'd been shot. That she had a lower-class background. He also had seen her appearance and dress before Basil's transformation. But he didn't know her most incriminating secret and she doubted she could ever tell him, or any other toff, the truth.

Honestly, she truly liked him and enjoyed his clever company. It would be better for her to trick a less intelligent gentleman that she had no feelings for into marriage. That way, if or when, things went sour and her past was revealed, she would not be hurt. She'd learned from her father that love only brought pain.

Forcing herself to smile, she said, 'You could always marry a fortune.'

'Gold would be a cold bedfellow,' he said in a low voice that the two matrons could not hear. 'I would prefer a red-blooded woman.'

A shiver of pleasure ran down her spine. Nancy understood his witticism, but the mention of a bed had made her even more aware of him. His spicy and intoxicating scent of cedar-wood and leather. His broad shoulders and muscled torso that his well-fitting jacket highlighted to admiration. She was a woman. And her own blood was both red and hot.

'Not a cold *fish*,' she quipped.

He flashed his teeth in a grin. 'Or any other variety of fish. Too clammy.'

Nancy had to be a *cold fish*. She'd shivered and been hungry enough nights to not let her body or her heart make the decisions. 'If I may speak with *clam*-our, gold never changes. Nor loses value. There is safety in a fortune.'

Matthew leaned closer to her. She could feel the warmth of his breath on her ear. 'Not to be *clam*-like, but there is no excitement in coins.'

Nancy had already experienced enough excitement in her life; she now longed for safety. A steady home and a family of her own. To want love or anything more than security would be greedy and foolish. 'I suppose coins on a mattress would be rather uncomfortable for sleeping and *clam*-orous.'

He laughed and she thought she saw admiration in his eyes. But there was a world of difference between attraction and affection. She'd seen that look before from men who wanted to make her their mistress. Desire was dangerous when one was seeking security. Nancy did not know if Matthew was fairly flush in the pockets. He must not be, if he was employed. And whilst the twenty thousand pounds in her dowry was a fortune to a girl from the streets, it wasn't for the *ton*. She'd seen the bills from her wardrobe. Life among the upper class was expensive and she feared that a man raised in privilege would expect the comforts of life.

Nancy reminded herself that she did not want to love her prospective husband. She wished for simple things: clean clothing, warm food, and a roof over her head. Loving her husband would invariably lead to disappointment. She'd loved Papa and he had failed her time and time again. She had learned painfully that the only person she could rely on was herself.

Aunt Marianne got to feet. 'Come, Nancy. We have more calls to make.'

Matthew stood quickly and offered Nancy his hand to help her up. 'I should be delighted to escort you to your carriage. Good day, Lady Sefton. If you'll *clam*-p your hand here, Miss Black.'

Nancy put her hand on his left arm and he offered his right to Aunt Marianne who took it with a small harrumph that made Matthew's face form into a knee-melting smile. Nancy didn't bother fighting her own grin as he led them out of the house. A light flirtation would not hurt either of them. There was no need for her to *clam* up.

The door to the house closed behind them with a thud, causing her to jump a little. Goose bumps formed on her arms. It felt as if someone was watching her. She glanced around and saw no one as Matthew led them to the carriage. He assisted her aunt into the vehicle first, something Nancy did not think was accidental.

'If you'll forgive my pro-*clam*-ation, I hope we will meet again soon,' he said, grinning down at her. He lifted her gloved hand to his lips and brushed a kiss that burned through the material all the way to her skin.

'You will not hear my dis-*clam*-ation.'

Matthew helped her into the carriage and closed the door. Behind him she saw only a glimpse of a lad with a shock of red hair. She recognised Mick. Even at his young age, he was Alastair's best tail. Her old boss would know that she hadn't disappeared or died. If she wasn't careful, her past would ruin any chance at a future with any gentleman.

'I am afraid that I will not be able to come to Frederica's ball,' Matthew said, lifting his wine glass to his lips. He was at his parents' house for dinner. 'Lord Brampton has doubled his supply order and I must oversee its quick completion.'

Frederica snorted into her napkin, in a poor attempt to hide her mirth.

Sisters!

Father nodded absent-mindedly. His eyes always glazed over when Matthew tried to talk about business matters with him. He only paid attention to conversations about animals.

His mother cleared her throat. 'Am I to understand, Matthew, that you intend to be at your canning factory until the wee hours of the morning? Surely, it is unsafe to work machines by lantern light?'

He wished that Mama was like other society matrons and knew less about how factories were run. Schooling his face to show no emotion, he said, 'I'm sorry, but we must, Mama. Old Brampton wants it completed within a fortnight and we will have to burn the midnight oil to meet the deadline in time. He wants them crated and on a ship by the end of the month.'

'I hope the lord secretary is paying you adequately for the trouble and extra hours you are working,' she said, her eyes still on him watching for a weakness.

'Yes, Mama. I'm charging him double.'

'Good.' She set down her fork with a clatter and he jumped in his seat. 'I completed my own business arrangements early today and I stopped by my father's house to check in on my stepmother. I was pleased to find Papa there, as well.'

Matthew couldn't help but squirm as he brought his own fork to his mouth. Grandfather Stubbs was notorious for his honesty and he wouldn't bamboozle his daughter even to help his favourite grandson.

'And how is Grandfather?' Frederica asked archly, her eyebrows raised.

'He is in excellent health, although, the wet has certainly caused the rheumatism in his bad leg to act up,' Mama said, dabbing at the corners of her mouth with a napkin. 'Strangely enough, he mentioned that he could not attend Frederica's coming-out ball as well, because there was a large supply order that he had to personally oversee… I can't help but wonder why both of you must be there? I even had the forethought to ask Papa and he said that there was no reason for you to be at the factory. And that you had never stepped a foot inside it since you both bought it last summer.'

Matthew was in the basket now. 'Well, uh, you see... Grandfather Stubbs isn't getting any younger and, I, well, I was going to try to take a more hands-on approach to the production side of the business before he retires.'

His mother lifted her wine glass at him. 'I applaud your resolution. I have found in my own company that it is essential for me to oversee not only the shops, but the entire manufacturing of the product, to ensure only the highest quality for my customers. But since you are so new to the process, I am sure that the factory can spare you for one night. Stepmother assured me that it could spare Papa, as well.'

Matthew's father laughed and pointed at him with his fork. 'She's dished you.'

Frederica giggled behind her napkin. The traitor.

He sighed. He'd been caught in his lies. 'Very well, Mama. I suppose I can come late to the ball.'

Mama picked up her fork and pointed it at him like a sceptre. 'Nonsense, Matthew. You will be one of the first guests here. For I have had the inspired idea of securing your partners for the entire evening. Every young lady on the list would make you an excellent wife. They all possess good birth, breeding, and respectable dowries.'

Matthew groaned and Frederica laughed loudly, no longer trying to hide her mirth behind her napkin. Both of his parents smiled at each other from opposite sides of the dining room table. His entire family seemed to find joy in his discomfort.

'I thought society frowned upon a fellow taking multiple wives since Biblical times,' he said blandly.

Papa barked an even louder guffaw and Frederica giggled.

His mother gave him the I-am-not-amused look and picked up her wine glass. 'You know very well that I only wish for you to marry *one* of them.'

One of the many debutantes that wanted his fortune or connections, like Lady Annabelle Lindsay. In his salad days, he'd fallen for her beauty and charms. He'd mistaken the look of avarice in her eyes for attraction. She had used his courtship to snare a greater matrimonial prize. His heart had smarted like the devil at the time, but he'd recovered quickly enough to be sure that it wasn't true affection he'd felt. Merely infatuation. What had stung the most was how little he had truly known Lady Annabelle. Or she him. If anything, he'd learned to be wary of feminine wiles.

All debutantes and their ambitious matchmaking mamas were on the hunt for a buck of the first stair. Together they worked to secure the best match they were able to socially; they would care nothing about his heart or hopes. It was like a game of cards. Every debutante was eager to get the highest-valued suitor. Preferably a peer with all his teeth and a fair amount of his original hair. Along with the entailed estate and family fortune. Only a desperate few on their third or fourth seasons wanted a second son. He had no desire to be anyone's consolation prize.

'I hope you've selected Frederica's partners as well,' Matthew said. 'I should hate for her to be left out as a wallflower at her coming-out ball.'

His mother touched her glass for the butler to add more wine to it. 'Indeed, I have.'

Matthew smirked at his sister. She responded by holding up her knife. It wasn't a victory, but not a complete loss either.

'Harper, please hand Lord Matthew the list,' his mother said.

She seemed determined to ruin the meal for him. Matthew accepted the piece of paper with a brief thanks and carefully studied the list of his partners. He groaned when he saw the names of both single Ashton sisters. At least, Lady Rebecca was now married. She had been the worst of the three and couldn't speak without giggling. He cringed. He actively loathed every proper young lady on this list. Even the new seventeen-year-old debutantes that he hadn't met yet. They were too young and coltish to capture his interest. He was nearly ten years their senior and had no desire to 'train them' to be the perfect wife. Matthew already had four younger sisters, and he wanted an equal in his marriage partner.

He set down the list. 'Fine, but I will be saving a waltz and the supper dance for Miss Black.'

One of his mother's eyebrows went up. 'Who is Miss Black?'

Frederica let out a low whistle. He often wished that his little sister did not know him so well. It made a fellow dashed uncomfortable.

Matthew cleared his throat. 'She is Lord Brampton's granddaughter. Frederica sent her an invitation. I believe her aunt, the Viscountess Delfarthing is her dragon—I mean, chaperone.'

His mother's upper lip curled. '*Her.* I cannot endure that Friday-faced woman. And it seems foolish of Lord Brampton to try to foist his granddaughter of low birth onto the *ton* after ignoring her for over twenty years.'

Frederica dropped her knife in apparent surprise. 'That's harsh, Mama.'

Matthew shook his head, slowly. 'It seems pretty rich for us to look down upon Miss Black, Mama, when our fortune is derived from trade. Both you and I work each day. And Grandfather Stubbs is very proud of his common heritage.'

'You know that I hate that family,' she said, her face turning red and her nostrils flaring. He'd never seen his mother so worked up before. Snubs rarely got underneath her skin. 'I have already prepared an extensive list of suitable young ladies for you to court and all of their dowries are excellent. At least, forty thousand pounds. I daresay Miss Black's dowry will be paltry, for the Earl of Brampton is a miserable miser.'

Matthew folded his arms. 'As you well know, I am fairly flush in the pocket and I have no intention of making my marriage a business transaction. If and when I marry, it will be for someone whom I love. Money will not be a part of the equation.'

His mother exhaled slowly as if trying to control her temper. 'Money is not the only consideration. All the young ladies on the list are of excellent birth, from noble families.'

'You wouldn't have been on that list, Mama,' Frederica said, holding up her glass of wine. 'Or do the daughters of merchants now count as noble families?'

Papa snorted. 'You can't bamboozle our children, dearest. They're too clever.'

Their mother stiffened in her seat. 'I am sure you are unaware, but there were rumours that Lady Susan was forced to elope with an Irish gambler because she was already expecting his child. He had nothing more than a glib tongue and a way with the cards to recommend himself. Whatever her parentage, Miss Black's birth is not respectable.'

'And rumours are always true, aren't they?' he said sardonically. 'Like the ones whispered about it being Mantheria's fault in her failed marriage. Again, I don't see that Miss Black has done anything disgraceful by being born or by choosing to attend the London season. That's just the sort of snobbery that I cannot endure.'

Mama touched her heaving chest. 'I shan't say another word, for it would only encourage you to pursue her. And if you knew half of the slights that Lady Delfarthing has given me over the years for my *common* heritage, you would have nothing to do with either her or her niece.'

Matthew exhaled, nodding. Despite being a duchess for nearly three decades, some members of the *ton* had never quite let his mother forget that she wasn't born one of them. Viscountess Delfarthing with her hooked nose and blue blood came from one of England's oldest families. She was proud of said aristocratic nose and her noble heritage.

'Just think, Mama,' he said persuasively. 'Lady Delfarthing will hate her niece dancing with me even more than you do.'

Frederica sniggered, but covered her laughter with a napkin after their mother shot her a dagger glance.

Papa was less circumspect. He guffawed loudly and freely.

'I won't have the viscountess in my house and that is final,' Mama said. 'We've already sent over three hundred invitations and there is simply not room for additional guests.'

His sister put down her napkin. 'Too late, Mama. I've already had Harper deliver my personal invitation to Miss Black.'

'She can have my spot,' his father offered from the head of the table. 'I hate balls. They are dead flat. Unless I am dancing with you, my love.'

Mama huffed. 'Now don't you start, Theophilus.'

Papa was undeterred. 'You always want me to wear a new suit, when I should infinitely prefer to show up in my leathers and riding boots.'

'I'd rather you came in nothing at all,' Mama snapped, no longer trying to rein in her ill-temper, 'than dressed in shabby old clothing.'

Papa raised his glass of wine to her. 'I will wear nothing, if you insist, dearest.'

Matthew and his sister broke out into laughter. He couldn't help but think that this ball might be entertaining after all.

The next morning his secretary, Mr Howitt, met him at the door of his place of business. The man was a few years older than himself, but was still young. Not more than five and thirty. He was a slight man on the shorter side, but he held himself so erect that he appeared taller than he was. His black hair was always slicked back and there were a few distinguished grey hairs at his temples. Mr Howitt's clothing was always neat and precise. Never a scuff on his boots. Or a wrinkle in his coat. His secretary applied that same level of neatness to his work. He never left any report or contract undone or without perfect grammar. He opened and replied to all of Matthew's letters. Even to his little sister Helen, who often wrote demanding that he send a specific book, scientific journal about snakes, or magnifying glass. His secretary would then purchase the required item and put it in the post. Helen, always a bit of a rascal, had started to address her letters to Mr Howitt directly instead of himself.

'I have proofread the contracts, my lord,' he said, 'and I have a few suggestions on tightening the phrases and replacing a word or two.'

'Put them on my desk and I will get to them this morning,' Matthew said, taking a seat behind his desk. 'Today, I have a rather different sort of job for you. I should like you to gather any information you can on a Miss Nancy Black, granddaughter of the Earl of Brampton. I believe she grew up in the London slums. Her age is between twenty and twenty-five. She is extremely pretty with dark hair, blue eyes, medium height, and quite a good figure.'

Mr Howitt pulled out his little brown book from his jacket pocket and wrote down what Matthew had said. 'Am I looking for personal or financial information, my lord?'

'Anything and everything,' Matthew said, picking up the contract on top of the pile. 'I believe that her father was an unsavoury character with possible criminal connections. Pay the informants well, but not too well that you are told lies.'

Chapter Seven

Nancy's feet ached in her current boots and Cousin Basil and her aunt showed no signs of tiring during yet another day of shopping. 'Perhaps, I can wait for you in the carriage?'

'Nonsense,' Aunt Marianne said. 'The next shop is only a step away. Come Thomas. I may not approve of Lady Hampford being involved in business, but her perfumes are the best on the market.'

At least Nancy didn't have to trail behind her aunt like the unfortunate young footman. Thomas was nearly six feet tall, but still told to fetch and follow like a dog. She did not know how the young man endured it.

Basil squealed. 'I see Lord St Erth across the street! He is on the strut. May I be excused to go and say hello, Mama?'

Sighing, Aunt Marianne said, 'Very well, but do catch up with us after you've said your greetings.'

Her cousin gave another high-pitched squeal before crossing the street to meet two men walking on the other side. Both gentlemen were dressed very finely and unlike her enthusiastic cousin, their manners appeared to be reserved and their demeanours lofty. She could well believe that they were dandies.

Her aunt took her elbow and continued their forced march. They stopped in front of a sleek shop with the sign Duchess and Company. Thomas moved to open the door, but before they could go inside a loud voice called out, 'By Jove! Lady Delfarthing, you are looking more lovely than ever.'

Nancy's knees felt weak and her mouth fell open. She didn't need to turn around to recognise the familiar voice of Alastair—the head of their criminal gang. Except he was speaking like a fine gentleman and not a slum boss. Aunt Marianne tipped her chin in acknowledgement of his greeting.

Alastair knew her aunt!

Her stomach fell. Sweat formed on her forehead as she examined the transformation of her former ally into a gentleman. Alastair was a tall, but muscular figure, with a rather narrow nose, lines around his green eyes, and dark brown hair that looked black, swept into curly disorder under a beaver hat jauntily tilted a little to one side. He was expensively rigged out in a salmon jacket with a matching waistcoat, a white shirt with collar points, and an intricately tied cravat. His raiment rivalled Basil's in ostentatiousness. He wore a black band on his right arm and carried an elaborate cane that Nancy knew encased his sword-stick. Even smiling, he was dangerous.

He'd only recently inherited his cousin's title and seemed to be already well-known in aristocratic society. She wondered if he too was blackmailing prominent members of the *ton* to help with his ascension. She wouldn't put it past him. But then she wouldn't put anything past him.

Walking up to her aunt, Alastair put his left foot forward and swept her a magnificent bow, doffing his hat. 'Your humble servant, my lady.'

Women of all classes usually tittered at Alastair's exaggerated compliments, but Aunt Marianne stared him down like the dowager she was. 'Sir Alastair Lymington.'

Nancy swallowed down her surprise and tried to keep her countenance blank of recognition. He had taken his cousin's title as well as his estate, Addington Hall in Buckinghamshire.

Undeterred by her cold greeting, Alastair offered Aunt Marianne his arm. 'Allow me to escort you inside, Lady Delfarthing. It is rather sunny out.'

She watched her aunt place her fingers delicately on the sleeve of Alastair's coat and he led her inside the perfume shop like he was bringing her to meet the queen. Her former criminal boss certainly had the audacity to do it. Nancy couldn't help but wonder if Alastair truly was the new baronet. She'd heard him call himself by at least a dozen different surnames and she'd seen him play twice as many roles. He was ten years her senior, and in the decade that she'd worked with him, he'd always had the manners and tastes of a gentleman. He rarely did the unpleasant or violent parts of a job, rather, he sent Peter or Bones to do it. She had often wondered if he were the disappointing son of a vicar or the second son of a squire, for he'd clearly been educated for a higher life than the slums he ruled. She might not know his true origins, but Nancy did know where his money came from: blackmailing, stealing, and occasionally passing sensitive information to the French.

Alastair didn't actively run the lower criminal networks of the rookery, Bones did that, but the slum bosses paid him for protection. He was not a man to cross. He knew too many secrets. Including hers.

The inside of the perfume shop was as finely furnished as the exterior. It was decorated like a fancy parlour, but there were shelves of perfume on every wall and colognes on the tables. Nancy walked up to the nearest display.

'Lady Delfarthing, would you do me the honour of introducing me to your young friend?'

Aunt Marianne's eyes narrowed as if only her good manners were stopping her from snubbing the man. 'Of course. Sir Alastair Lymington, may I present my niece, Miss Black.'

Alastair took Nancy's gloved hand in his, tightening his hold, and then brought it to his lips. A frisson of fear worked its way down her spine at his touch. 'Miss Black, a great pleasure.' In a lower tone that her aunt couldn't hear, he added, 'Our dear friend Mrs Sweetapple was asking about you only yesterday. She has not forgotten you.'

His meaning was all too clear. She was no longer under his protection and Madame Sweetapple was not a person to be crossed. There was still ten years left in the contract Nancy had signed with her. With a sharp intake of breath, Nancy pulled her hand free from his. 'Your grip is still bruising.'

'Sorry, Nance,' Alastair said, his tone anything but contrite. 'Perhaps I could persuade the madam to forget her claim, if I were in possession of certain documents that should have been sold a fortnight ago.'

She couldn't give him those documents. The trust between herself and her grandfather was new and fragile. He had promised her a financially secure marriage and a new life. In return, she had agreed to return the stolen papers.

Rubbing her sore hand with the other, Nancy forced herself to smile and say in a loud voice, 'I am delighted to make your acquaintance.'

'You shall see more of me,' he said with a sinister smile that set her heart racing in fear. 'Much more of me.'

His presence would be disastrous to her chances of finding a suitable husband and the security of her own home. If Alastair dropped one word, one hint about how she'd nearly become Haymarket ware, she'd be ruined. And he wasn't one to forget a debt owed. But if she gave in to him now, he would blackmail her for the rest of her life. There was nothing Nancy wanted more than to be free of her past. But like a ghost, it haunted her present. Robbing her of the safety she so badly desired.

Doffing his hat once more, he left the shop as another gentleman came inside. He took off his black hat and Nancy immediately recognised his golden curls: Matthew. Relief and warmth washed over her.

'What luck,' he said with a devastating grin. 'I was passing by and saw you two and thought I would stop in and say hello. Lady Delfarthing, Miss Black.'

Aunt Marianne bowed her head slightly. 'Lord Matthew.'

He held out his arm to Nancy. 'May I show you 'round the shop? I've been coming here since I was in leading strings.'

She glanced at her aunt who gave her a small nod, before Nancy placed her hand on his arm. The slightest touch caused her body to begin the familiar hum and tingle of awareness of him. Of want. He led her to a table where there were jars of ground coffee and strips of paper in a basket.

'Does your mother sell coffee as well?'

Matthew shook his head, picked up the bottle, and unscrewed it. He smelled the ground coffee beans deeply before handing the glass jar to Nancy. 'You sniff coffee to clear your olfactory senses between testing perfumes.'

He pointed to small pieces of paper in a basket. 'Most customers prefer to dip paper into the bottles to test the scent, rather than testing it on their skin. Once it is on your body, it's almost impossible not to get traces of it and it will quite ruin your ability to choose the right one.'

Nancy shook her head, slightly shrugging her shoulders. 'I had no idea how involved choosing a scent could be. I've only ever used rosewater before.'

'A sturdy scent, but you deserve something more sophisticated.' Matthew handed her a bottle. 'A truly excellent perfume will enhance your natural scent and must be carefully selected.'

Nancy dipped the piece of paper into the bottle of perfume that he gave her. She took a whiff of coffee, before placing the paper beneath her nose and breathing in deeply. She recognised a hint of citrus from the one time she'd eaten an orange.

'A good perfume typically has three notes, or three main elements,' Matthew explained, counting off on his fingers. 'The top notes, which are the strongest, and the first ones that you smell. The most popular are lemon, orange, bergamot, lavender, rose, and basil.'

Nancy sniffed again. 'This one is orange.'

'Very good,' Matthew said with a wink, holding up two fingers. 'The base note adds depth and resonance to the perfume. It's often composed of cedar-wood, sandalwood, vanilla, amber, or musk.'

'And the last note?'

He held up a third finger. 'It is actually the middle note which makes up the majority of the scent. It is called the *heart* note and it lasts the longest,' he said, his dark blue eyes searching hers. 'It continues after everything else has faded.'

Her chest fluttered, almost painfully. Did love ever truly last? She'd seen many people in love or at least, in relationships, but she'd rarely observed a couple that were happy long-term. Giselle fell in love frequently and out of it nearly as quickly, but perhaps that was only part of her profession. Nancy loved her father, but his love had not been dependable. Sometimes it felt like he cared for the cards more than her. He'd certainly gambled away her earnings more than once and stolen all her hopes for security.

No, it was better not to love. Not even the heart note of a perfume could be trusted to remain for ever. It would fail her like her father. Or simply fade away over time. Love did not last.

Aware of the sound of her own organ beating loudly, she tried to joke, 'How *heart*-ening. What makes up a heart note?'

'There is nothing *heart*-ier than a full-bodied, aromatic oil,' he said slowly, somehow making the words sound titillating.

Nancy was sure now that he wasn't only talking about perfume. And she was certain that *she* would be thinking about this conversation long after. The tingles in her limbs had turned into a slow burn. She wanted to kiss him desperately. To trace the lines of his lips with the tips of her fingers. Then to do the same with her tongue and finally her own mouth. Nancy wanted to throw herself in his arms. Now. In the middle of his mother's shop on Bond Street. But desire did not last and she would not wager her new life on love.

His eyes dipped down to her lips. Did he feel the pull to her as well? She stepped closer and felt his sweet breath against her forehead. The scent of his body. Trust the son of a perfumer to smell intoxicating. Matthew would make for a delicious dalliance.

'Niece,' Aunt Marianne said in her loud, commanding voice. 'Come and advise me which perfume to select.'

Recalling herself, Nancy moved from Matthew's side and went across the room to where her aunt stood by a glass shelf. She wasn't a girl from the slums any more who could kiss any man she'd liked. Now she was a lady and ladies didn't embrace gentlemen in public. Or in private, unless they were married to them. And no matter how much Matthew might be attracted to her, or even care for her, he did not truly know her. Who she was and what she had done. All of Nancy's life, she'd played different roles with different names; she could not endure a lifetime pretending to be someone she was not. Nancy was not worthy of Matthew's admiration and she feared the day he would realise that and despise her. Such a gentle love was not for the likes of a girl from the gutters.

Nancy heard his footsteps before she felt his presence behind her.

'Allow me, my dear soft-*heart*-ed, Lady Delfarthing,' Matthew said, taking the two perfumes from her. He sniffed both of them deeply, before returning to the first one. 'This would flatter your natural scent the best, my lady.'

He handed the bottle to Nancy and she smelled it. She caught the note of lavender, something citrus, and then the woodsy base note. It was subtle, yet pleasant. It grew more appealing over time. Not unlike her aunt's personality. Prickly at first, but warm underneath.

'It's perfect.'

Aunt Marianne's lips twitched as if she was fighting a smile. There was a slight colour in her cheeks which made Nancy think that her aunt liked Matthew against her better judgement.

'I shall accept your suggestion, Lord Matthew,' she said with an imperious nod.

'How *heart*-warming. I would rather you accepted it as a gift from myself,' he said, then picked up another scent from the highest shelf. 'And one for your niece.'

Matthew bowed his head as he gave it to Nancy. A

lord bowing to *her* as if she were someone special. A lady of importance. She only wished it were true.

Harumphing, Aunt Marianne could no longer suppress her smile. 'Very well. I suppose we will accept, since you are courting us both.'

Matthew grinned broadly. 'I am delighted and whole-*heart*-ed. I did not think I had a chance with such a handsome and distinguished lady.'

Nancy couldn't help but giggle as her aunt's cheeks darkened into a blush.

Aunt Marianne offered her hand to Matthew, who took it in his and formally bowed over it. 'You are a saucy young man. You know I meant as my niece's chaperone.'

He released her hand and pressed his own against his chest. 'Now I am down-*heart*-ed. You wound me deeply. To the very core of my being.'

Aunt Marianne chuckled. 'I suppose I shall send an acceptance for your sister's coming-out ball, after all.'

Matthew turned to look at her and Nancy felt warm all over. Another sweeping of desire for him. 'With the fear of being *heart*-broken, may I be so bold as to ask for the first waltz and the supper dance?'

Her aunt had explained that one's partner for the supper dance was also the person that you sat by at dinner. Matthew wanted to spend as much time with her at the ball as he could. She should refuse him, but couldn't find the strength to do so.

'You pull at my *heart*-strings. I will reserve them for you.'

Smiling at her aunt, he asked, 'And shall I escort you lovely ladies to your carriage? Or shall I play the role as your footman at another shop? What I lack in experience, I make up in *heart*-iness.'

Nancy almost suppressed her giggle. If only he wasn't so witty and likeable. If only she didn't have a dangerous and disreputable past. If only—

Aunt Marianne took both perfume bottles and handed them to Thomas, who snickered at Matthew's joke. 'You may accompany us to our carriage. My son Basil is our escort. I daresay we will meet him outside.'

Matthew held open a fancy oval box with papers in it for Thomas to place the perfumes inside. Once he did, Matthew secured the lid and handed the package to the young man. 'I do think I would make a fine footman. Eh, Thomas?'

The young man nodded.

Matthew offered his arm to her aunt first and then to Nancy. Her whole body shivered with pleasure as she touched his muscular arm, pressing the side of her body against his. Holding him was as dangerous as cradling a burning candle in her bare hands. She was going to get burned and be left alone in the cold.

They walked slowly down Bond Street. Nancy half smiled as she thought that the three of them were 'on the strut.' Her Cousin Basil bounded towards them with an energy that he only seemed to have while shopping.

'Mama, you didn't pick the perfumes without me?' he said, sounding disappointed.

'I can assure you, Basil,' Matthew said with a nod of his head. 'That I personally selected the very best scents for your mother and cousin. If only I had known you were among the party, I would have picked a *heart*-some cologne for you, as well.'

'Truly, Lord Matthew?'

'I will have my man send a *heart*-shaped bottle to your rooms, sir.'

Nancy squeezed Matthew's arm and whispered in his ear. 'How *heart*-felt. Does that mean you are now courting the three of us?'

He turned and gave her a smile that made her insides feel soft and gooey. 'I would do anything for you, my *heart*.'

Oh, how she longed to believe that were true. That one person in her life could prove trustworthy. Her father had lied to her. She had once trusted Alastair more than anyone else in the world and now he was blackmailing her. And he would not hesitate to destroy her if she did not do as he said. Nancy would not allow Alastair or her past to destroy Matthew too.

Thomas opened the door to the carriage and Matthew helped her aunt inside. He then took her hand and lightly kissed the top of her glove. 'Don't forget the *heart* note.'

Breathless and blushing, Nancy was in no danger of that.

Chapter Eight

Happily, for both Matthew and his mother, Papa decided to wear clothing to Frederica's coming-out ball and he did not go through with his threat to appear in nothing at all. He wore a plain, but expensive black suit from Weston that fit like a glove. It would have met the dandy Beau Brummell's approval. But not the Honourable Basil Chambers. Nancy's cousin would have wished for more frills and furbelows. Still, Matthew's father would have been an intimidating figure of a duke, if he didn't pull at his collar every minute or so, rumpling his cravat. Papa seemed to think his very clothing was a cage, like the enclosures he kept his animals in.

He stood next to Mama in the foyer. She was dressed in a purple silk gown with a matching turban. She looked beautiful and commanding, like a queen. Her dear friend, the Prince Regent, had promised to come to the ball, ensuring its success as one of the most popular events of the season. Matthew personally didn't care much for the regent or his cronies. Matthew couldn't help but wonder why he had to scrape and bow to a dandified buffoon who just happened to have the luck to be born a prince. And if he was caught in a conversation with the prince, Prinny would suggest Matthew get a good cupping and then unfortunately detail his own medicinal bleedings. But no matter how much Matthew loathed the prince and his politics, he had been a good friend to his mama.

'Do you have your list?' Frederica asked from behind him.

Matthew turned to see his little sister decked out in white lace with clustered silk rosettes. She resembled their mother the most out of all his sisters. Frederica was a tall, curvaceous, brunette with a commanding personality.

He patted the pocket of his suit. 'Yes. And you?'

'What lists are you two talking about?' Mantheria asked, coming up to them.

His sister Mantheria, or rather the Duchess of Glastonbury, was only three and twenty. She was the beauty of the family with golden hair, a slim figure, and sparkling blue eyes. She had married for social position and been miserable. He would not make the same mistake. No amount of money or titles could make up for a cold marriage. And unlike the Duke of Glastonbury, Matthew intended to keep his wedding vows.

Frederica grinned as she linked arms with her elder sister. 'Mama has made us both lists of whom we must dance with tonight. Isn't that a lark? Matthew has to dance with both of the Ashton sisters.'

Flipping out her fan, Mantheria waved it at herself a few times. 'I am only offended that I did not receive my own list. What if I have no partners?'

'I am sure Sunny will dance with you,' Frederica said, winking. 'He always does.'

Matthew was sure of it, as well. The Duke of Sunderland was hopelessly in love with his sister Mantheria, but whilst her husband lived, nothing could ever come of it.

Mantheria took Frederica's sheet and glanced down at it. 'I see Sunny is on your list as well for the quadrille. You are starting out with a duke. That is good luck.'

'The first dance,' Matthew said, consulting his own paper. 'Ah, I have the privilege of dancing with Lady Eliza Ashton. Oh, goody. What a treat is in store for me.'

'I don't think she likes men,' Mantheria said, snorting.

Then both of his sisters laughed at his expense. He loved all his family dearly, but that didn't stop any of them from teasing each other mercilessly.

Frederica and Mantheria were still smiling as he led Lady Eliza out on the dance floor to form the set for the quadrille. She was not an unhandsome woman, but she wore a perpetual scowl which would have put any young man off. Or an old one for that matter. She had a willowy figure, dark eyes, and her blond hair was practically white. The more Lady Eliza scowled at him, the more his sisters grinned over the shoulders of their own partners. Like Frederica had predicted, Mantheria did not lack a partner. To his great surprise, Matthew was actually enjoying himself at the ball. He usually assiduously avoided marriage marts since his salad days and infatuation with Lady Annabelle, but this evening had already been amusing and he looked forward to dancing with Nancy. To touching her beautiful curves and holding her close. Or as close as she'd let him. He could tell that she was keeping something back from him.

Nancy intrigued him greatly. He wondered who had shot her the night before they met and why. Despite several discreet enquiries, his secretary could find no history of her at all before the day she arrived at the Horse Guards and he escorted her to see Lord Brampton, her grandfather. She was hiding something, but what?

Nancy was certainly a mysterious young lady. There was a world-weary look in her blue eyes, as if she had few illusions left. Whatever her past had been, it wasn't the gently bred experience of most debutantes. She was also more beautiful than any woman or courtesan he had ever seen. He loved her dark hair and fair skin; they made her blue eyes striking in her face. He wanted to know her better. To know her in every possible way.

Mostly, Matthew wanted to discover if she was interested in him or in his money. His entire life he'd been either snubbed for his trade background or toad-eaten for being the son of a duke. Both types of people were insufferable. Few people seemed to wish to learn about him as a person. He hoped that Nancy would be one of them. That the feeling between them could grow into the true love he'd searched for his entire life.

But he couldn't forget her words about money: *'Gold never changes. Nor loses value. There is safety in a fortune.'*

He did not wish to be a safe choice of husband. Despite being a man of business, he wanted a love worthy of the words of the poets. He'd received a double first in the classics after all. He didn't want an aristocratic alliance for social position and prominence. Nor did he desire to fall victim to a fortune-hunter. Even to a beautiful, clever-tongued, mysterious dark beauty like Nancy. He wanted a marriage like his parents'. One where they put each other's needs first. They sacrificed for the other. They supported one another. His parents were the reason that he believed in love and any relationship that was inferior would be a disappointment.

The musicians finally played the last notes of the never-ending quadrille. He could hardly wait to escort Lady Eliza to her mother, Lady Ashton, even if it meant that he would have to take her little sister's hand for the country dance. If her daughters were not interested in his fortune, he knew that Lady Ashton was. Matthew preferred not to be courted for his bank account. By the mother or the daughters.

Lady Ashton fluttered her eyelashes at him. 'What a handsome couple you two make. You are both so tall, so blond, and so—'

'Serious?' Matthew supplied, causing the matron to flush with colour and her daughter Lady Eliza to smile for the first time all night. He bowed over her hand. 'Thank you for the dance, my lady… Lady Caroline, I believe I am fortunate enough to be your partner for the next country dance. Shall we?'

He held out his hand to Lady Caroline who paused, squinting at it. He assumed the poor girl must be very short-sighted. She stretched out her hand and it was several inches from his own. Matthew easily took it and carefully led her to the dance floor. He now understood why she was such a terrible partner. He didn't think she could see much past her own nose. She should have been wearing spectacles, but no doubt her lady mother was afraid that they would scare suitors away. The matchmaking matron should have been more concerned about gentlemen's feet. Lady Caroline stepped on his several times. Each time he could hear his sister Frederica laugh. He would have found it amusing too, but didn't wish to offend the young lady's sensibilities. Matthew had been laughed at enough times as a boy at school that it had taught him empathy.

He made good his escape, searching around the crowded rooms for Nancy. The musicians were striking up a waltz and he didn't intend to miss a moment of it with her. He spotted Viscountess Delfarthing first. The blue plumage in her hair would have been the envy of any strutting peacock. Nancy did not have feathers in her hair, but she didn't need them. White flowers had been artfully placed and contrasted beautifully with her black curls. She wore a celestial blue dress with a white lace overlay and matching blue gloves. Around her neck was a gold memorial medallion that looked to be an heirloom.

He bowed deeply to them. 'Lady Delfarthing, Miss Black. How privileged we are that you were able to attend our ball. May I have the honour of claiming your niece's hand for the waltz?'

Viscountess Delfarthing gave him a piercing glare over her hooked nose. 'Very well, my lord. But keep to the dance floor and mind the liberties you take with my niece. She is under my protection and that of her grandfather, the lord secretary.'

For all her snobbishness, she was a downy old bird. Matthew would have liked nothing more than to take Nancy to a secluded corner of the garden and kiss her senseless. And the way that the other gentlemen in the room were eyeing Nancy in her finery, he was not the only one thinking it.

'Of course,' Matthew said, taking Nancy's hand to lead her to the dance floor, his pulse quickening. He'd held many women's hands. It was a gentleman's job to lead a lady to and from the dance floor. Holding hands was often a part of dancing itself, but no other women had dazzled him like she did. Nor had touching them made him feel hot under the collar and everywhere else. With Nancy he was on fire. He could have yanked at his cravat like his father. Yet, he was certain that removing it would not relieve his burning for her.

When they reached the dance floor, he easily spun her into his arms. She was medium height, but he unfortunately, was taller than most footmen. The top of her head barely tickled his chin. He had to wait for her to look up at him. It was a sort of torture to hold her in his arms but not see her face. Nancy was an elegant dancer. She followed his lead with the smallest of touches. He longed to pull her closer. To kiss her. Which was quite impossible in the middle of a dance floor. Matthew forced himself to think of something else. The poor spotted sod dancing with Frederica was not an accomplished dancer and nearly ploughed into them. Matthew was forced to do a quick turn to protect Nancy from the other man's feet, placing his body between her and Frederica's partner. The man bumped into him slightly, but continued to drag his annoyed sister around the dance floor. Matthew was certain that man's name would not be on his sister's dance card again.

Nancy finally glanced up at him. 'You saved me.'

'You have a face,' Matthew said, his voice low and tender. 'I thought I was waltzing with only a head of hair.'

His silly jest brought a smile to her thick lips. The urge to kiss them heightened. Suck on them. Bite them.

'This is my first dance at a *ton* party and I was minding my steps,' Nancy confided. 'My aunt assures me that if I make the smallest of mistakes, it will end in my censure and exclusion... Because of my low birth.'

'Your father is Irish, I believe?'

She licked her lips. 'And half Scottish.'

'No wonder you are not another milk-and-water miss,' Matthew said. 'May I ask what his name is?'

'Felix Black,' she said, her dark eyelashes lowered. 'Our surname often changed, depending on who he owed money. He liked picking different colours...but he died, not long ago.'

It was no wonder that his secretary's previous enquiries had met with no success. He'd been chasing the wrong name.

His eyes fell to her healed arm. 'I am so sorry for your loss. Was it the same night that you were shot?'

'You don't miss much do you, Matthew?'

Any other time he would have been pleased by her words, but he could hear the pain behind them. See the sorrow in her eyes. 'Was he shot as well?'

'By a moneylender's henchmen.'

Mr Black must not have paid his debt, but for him to be killed the sum must have been a large one. 'Was your father a gambler?'

He watched her inhale slowly. 'A dreamer. Always sure that his salvation was in the next hand of cards or the roll of the dice. And that his fortune would be made on the next job.'

'Despite what the poets say, dreams are hard to live on.'

'Dreams do not exist in the London slums. One can only focus on survival.'

Nancy's background was darker than he had imagined. His chest tightened; whatever she was hiding from him must be very incriminating indeed. Through his work at his grandfather's factories, he'd been through plenty of rookeries. He knew how dangerous they could be. Desperation hung in the very air the people breathed. How could Lord Brampton have allowed his granddaughter to grow up in such an environment? He was a colder and prouder man than Matthew had previously guessed.

'I suppose your father's employment opportunities were not precisely legal,' he said softly, trying not to offend her.

'My father always said that a man is only a criminal if he gets caught,' she said. 'And he was imprisoned only once, when I was fourteen. I tried to go to my grandfather's house, but I was turned away like a beggar at the kitchen door.'

As Matthew twirled her in the waltz, he pulled her closer to him, as if to protect her. 'Where did you go?'

She blushed and her eyes no longer met his. 'A kind woman let me into her grand house—at least, I thought she was being kind. She taught me how to walk and talk and dance. She gave me fine clothes. She was trying to turn me into a courtesan. I barely made it out in time—before. Well, I learned not to trust anyone.'

The heat in his blood turned from desire to anger. Nancy was lucky to have escaped a worse fate. Most poor young women did not. The madams made the bulk of the money because prostitutes were easily replaced. He respected the women, but hated the trade. If one approached him in the street, he offered them a different job. At one of the many factories his grandfather owned and he oversaw. Some took him up on his offer, many didn't. Madams and pimps didn't let the women go easily.

'Yet, you are trusting me with your secrets,' he whispered. 'I am honoured.'

Nancy smiled at him and it was striking in its intensity. Matthew was grateful to be wearing gloves, for he felt his hands moisten. The desire to hold her closer was overwhelming. His heart thrummed with warmth. He wanted to shield her from the horrors of her past. To love her as she deserved to be loved. If only Nancy would let him in, rather than dropping small pieces of her past for him to collect and put together haphazardly.

'Most of your peers would have run away by now. If you were wise, you would too.'

Unable to stop himself, he pressed her closer to him. 'I am not running.'

'No, you're dancing.'

'We're dancing,' he corrected her as she spun around in his arms. Despite their proximity, Nancy felt far away from him. She made Matthew feel protective and he wished to wipe away the crease in her brow with gentle kisses. But first, he would have to earn her trust. Something she would not give away without a struggle. 'And are you trying to frighten me away? For I must warn you, I am a businessman and I don't frighten easily.'

Nancy shook her head. 'I wish this waltz would never end.'

'I'll speak to the musicians.'

She laughed as the music ended. It sounded like the tinkling of a cymbal.

Matthew bowed over her hand, reluctant to release her from his hold. 'I suppose I shall have to return you to your dragon now.'

'Aunt Marianne?'

He nodded.

Nancy graced him with another grin. 'If she is a dragon, then I hope you are a brave knight.'

'The bravest.'

'And humble,' she quipped.

'The humblest. That goes without saying, but feel free to say it as often as you choose.'

She giggled and Matthew's whole body thrummed with desire for her. It was a good thing that they weren't playing the word game tonight, for his mind had only one thought: Want. Want. Want.

They stopped in front of Viscountess Delfarthing and it was as if the entire room quieted and held still as he kissed her hand. But Nancy's aunt's eyes were not on them, but someone behind them. He released her hand and saw that Mama's dear friend, the Prince Regent, had arrived and was soaking in his subjects' attention.

'Bow to your future king,' Viscountess Delfarthing whispered to her niece.

Matthew and Nancy both bowed as the Prince Regent passed them with his new favourite gambling friend, Sir

Alastair Lymington, on his arm. Rumour around town was that Sir Alastair had newly inherited the title from a cousin. There was an air of mystery about the man and no one in the *ton* seemed to know who or what he was before his inheritance. The man's past was clearly smoky and he gazed at Nancy like she was Haymarket ware. For the first time in his life, Matthew wished that he hadn't let his elder brother, Wick, fight all his battles. Not that Wick had given him much choice in the matter as a boy. He wanted nothing more than to punch Sir Alastair on his pointy nose and teach him some manners.

Viscountess Delfarthing fanned herself. 'What a compliment for your sister, my lord, for the prince to attend her coming-out ball.'

'The compliment is entirely for my mother,' Matthew said drily. 'The Prince Regent is her friend. He can't keep our names straight.'

With the mention of his mother, Matthew was recalled to his dancing partners list. Bowing, he left to claim his next partner. He would not be able to speak to Nancy again until the supper dance.

Chapter Nine

Fanning herself, Nancy couldn't believe how honest she'd been with Matthew. So much for her aunt's demands that she be discreet about her past. She could have lied to him, but didn't want to. Partly because she liked him so much and partly because she didn't think he would have believed her. There was a shrewd, knowing air about Lord Matthew. She knew that he was employed in business and one did not get very far in that world without being able to size up the competition accurately.

But he was also the son of a duke. His courtesy title was 'my lord'. Everything about his birth and breeding was impossibly above her own. Through his mother, he had a connection to the Prince Regent. A personage she had never seen before and Alastair had been on his arm, the sight of which had nearly knocked her off her feet. Since his cousin's death and inheriting a baronetcy, her former criminal boss had certainly started mixing with more elevated members of society. She doubted that the future king realised that his new friend had a long and illustrious history of selling English military and government secrets to France. But she couldn't expose him without proving her own guilt. Maybe she could use Alastair's relationship to the Prince Regent to delay delivering the stolen documents that he demanded. Documents that she'd already promised to her grandfather.

Not that she saw her grandfather often. He was either at Horse Guards or one of his many clubs. She ate every meal with only her Aunt Marianne, and sometimes Basil. Her aunt scolded and fussed, but Nancy thought that she was fond of her. They'd received Nancy's voucher to Almack's Assembly and countless other invitations to balls, routs, Venetian breakfasts, and soirées. Aunt Marianne was certainly doing her part to introduce her niece to the very best of *ton* society.

Her aunt took Nancy's elbow into a tight grip and turned her around. 'Mr Ackerman, may I introduce you to my niece, Miss Black?'

The man before her was not precisely handsome, but pleasant looking with light brown hair, tawny eyes, a rather large nose, thin lips, and a pointy chin. He smiled at Nancy and gave her a little bow. 'It is a pleasure, Miss Black. Might I have this dance?'

Before Nancy could answer, Aunt Marianne gave her a shove in the middle of her back towards him.

Nancy put her hand in his. 'Delighted.'

Mr Ackerman was a good partner, if not a great conversationalist. He barely spoke three sentences to her during the entire half an hour of the country dance. He returned her to Aunt Marianne who had another gentleman ready to dance with her. Lord Jeremy, the third son of an earl, with auburn red hair and a great deal of freckles. He spoke nearly the entire dance, never pausing for a breath. Or for her response.

Winded and thirsty, Nancy would have preferred to go to the refreshment table instead of back to her aunt. Her partner, however, did not pause in his speech long enough for her to ask him.

Lord Jeremy bowed over her gloved hand. 'Splendid dance, Miss Black. You have such a light step. Such form and grace. And you are quite the conversationalist, as well. I don't recall a set where I have been so entertained. So amused. I shall certainly seek your hand at the next ball that I see you. Yes, I shall.'

Even in his farewell, he didn't let her get a word in.

Aunt Marianne stepped back and Nancy saw that Alastair was by her side. He looked older, handsomer, and more menacing than ever. Nancy swallowed, her throat dry and scratchy. He was the last person in the world that she wanted to dance with. He represented everything from her old life that she wished to forget.

Bowing, Alastair held out his hand. 'Miss Black, your aunt has assured me that you are an excellent dancer. Shall we join the set?'

Refusing him was not an option. Aunt Marianne had taught her that a lady at a ball must accept every partner who asks her, or no one.

Her hand was shaking as she placed it inside of his larger one. She'd seen him kill with those hands. She would have been a fool not to be afraid. Nancy was no longer under his protection.

The dance was a Roger de Coverley: a light, happy tune that was incongruous with her current emotions.

Alastair preformed the dance with the same precision that he did everything in his life. One did not become a crime boss by making mistakes. If Nancy hadn't known better, she would have thought he was as fine a gentleman as his green velvet suit suggested.

'Days have passed, Nance,' he said, using her father's nickname for her. 'Even a week and I have yet to receive those papers. If it had been anyone else, they would be dead by now. Because of our former friendship, I have been lenient. But my patience is running out.'

She spun away from him in the dance. Her pulse thundering and her head pounding. She could barely follow the steps of the figure. Their hands met again and his grip was bruising. He meant to leave his mark on her.

Nancy glanced down at their hands. 'I don't have the papers in my possession.'

'Oh, but I know you took them and therefore, you have an inkling as to where they are now,' he said, his voice cold and barely above a whisper. 'My associate reported them being stolen and no one but your father or you could have them. I have already searched your last rooms in the rookery, what a place of squalor, and your fancy yellow room at your grandfather's house with a four-poster bed, yellow flower coverlet, and no less than seven pillows.'

She gasped. Someone had been inside of her bedchamber where she slept. Nancy schooled her features to blankness, but Alastair knew that he had landed a hit. 'And one word from me to my grandfather and your royal friend will drop you faster than a hot coal. And you will have your own room at Newgate. I hope you'll get a good view of Tyburn where they do the hangings.'

'Tut. Tut. Tut, my sweet,' he said, shaking his head. 'I would hate for you to meet the same fate as your father.'

They separated in the dance. Nancy's eyes filled with tears and her hands trembled. She tried in vain to compose herself before they met again in the figure. What if it wasn't Heap's men? 'Did you kill him?'

Alastair shook his head. 'No. It must have been one of his many creditors. Despite my objections, your father borrowed money from dangerous men.'

'He was under your protection.'

'Alas, we had parted ways only a week before his untimely death. Felix had become too much of a liability from the money lenders. How pleased Harry Heap would be if he knew of your existence.'

She gritted her teeth. 'Then how did my father know about the job?'

'It was supposed to happen the next night,' Alastair said. 'Your father learnt about it from Giselle. You two were never meant to be involved. Bones and Peter were supposed to have broken in. Stealing those papers was your father's final betrayal. The last card trick in his hand.'

A gambler and liar to the end. And yet Nancy still loved him. Grieved for her father. He was the only person she could wholly trust, her only family, and even he had not been trustworthy. He had lied to her. Again. Even after promising her that he wouldn't any more.

The music ended and Alastair took her hand in the same bruising grip. He whispered in her ear before they reached her aunt, 'You have three days to get me those papers and don't think that your grandfather can protect you.'

Nancy sighed in relief when he stepped away. Alastair bowed to Aunt Marianne and gave her a smarmy smile before returning to the Prince Regent's side.

'There's something about that man that I don't like,' Aunt Marianne said in an undertone to Nancy. 'Watch yourself with him. There is a great mystery surrounding his cousin's death and the estate Sir Alastair inherited from him. No one rises as quickly in society as he did without either a great deal of money, or knowing damaging secrets.'

Flinching, Nancy nodded. Alastair knew almost as many damaging things about her as she knew about him. At least he didn't use his sword-stick at balls.

Her aunt introduced her to a shy young man named Mr Jackson for the next dance. She did not hear him articulate even one word. He only nodded when she spoke. Which was perhaps for the best. Her nerves were shot from her dance with Alastair. A quiet partner helped Nancy regain control of her emotions and her fears. The pace of the country dance was more sedate too. Her heartbeat slowed to a normal rate by the time he brought her back to Aunt Marianne's side. She was speaking to Lady Sefton.

'Ah, Miss Black,' Lady Sefton said, bowing her head slightly. 'What an accomplished dancer you are and you look very pretty this evening too. Your mother loved to dance. We used to tease her that she could go through a pair of dancing slippers in only one night.'

Despite the sword of Damocles hanging over her head, Nancy found herself smiling. She hadn't known that about her mother, who she often thought of as *Lady*

Susan. This unknowable person from her past. But bit by bit, a story from Aunt Marianne, a remark of a friend like Lady Sefton, Nancy was piecing her mother's personality together. Creating a picture to hold in her heart.

'I did not know that,' Nancy said, curtsying. 'Thank you, my lady.'

Lady Sefton's eyes focused behind Nancy. There was a smile in them. 'Lord Matthew, here I assume to take away Miss Black for the supper dance.'

Turning, she saw Matthew sweep a bow to Aunt Marianne and Lady Sefton. 'As always, Lady Sefton, you are precisely correct. Miss Black, shall we?'

He held out his gloved hand and she put her own shaking fingers into his. They had danced once before this evening and she'd told him little truths, but not the worst thing she'd ever done. Did he regret having reserved this second dance with her? Now that he knew she was a girl from the slums? A young woman with no accomplishments who had nearly become a courtesan. Yet still he seemed interested in getting to know her better. Could Matthew ever love her? Could she ever trust him enough to love him in return? To tell him all her darkest secrets?

Shaking her head, Nancy knew she was a fool. She'd already learned that she couldn't trust anyone. How many times would she have to learn the same painful lesson?

If he were disappointed with her as a partner, he did not show it in his demeanour as they weaved through the figures. She felt his hand holding hers, firm, yet gentle. He was a good leader. She followed his steps without question. She trusted him not to lead her astray in the dance, but could she trust him with more of her secrets?

'Dancing with you makes all the waiting worth it,' he whispered in her ear as their hands clasped during a turn.

Nancy felt breathless. 'I thought perhaps you regretted reserving this dance with me.'

He released her and followed the gentleman in front of him. When he took her hand again, Matthew spun her around in a circle. 'Never.'

'I am not a proper lady.'

Stepping closer to her, Matthew said. 'I'll let you in on a little secret... I'm not a proper lady either.'

A laugh escaped her throat. Her whole body felt lighter. More joyful. She closed her eyes and surrendered herself fully to the joy of a country dance. To following his gentle touches and enjoying his whispers against her cheek. The dance ended all too soon for her liking, but instead of returning Nancy to Aunt Marianne's side, he led her to the supper room. Matthew nodded to Frederica and her partner, but sat away from them at the end of the table. His seat close to hers.

Nancy looked down at the food on her plate. Her stomach rumbled, but she was not hungry. She was too worried about Alastair's threats. He was like a spider. His criminal arms stretching in so many directions that she had no idea how he'd known the colour of her room in her grandfather's house. Had he bribed one of her grandfather's servants? She assumed it was Mick who had given her location away. She'd caught a glimpse of him that day.

'Something has changed since our first dance,' Matthew said quietly. 'You're paler and your hands are shaking.'

She tried to stop her hands from moving, but it was

like trying to stop a river. They kept trembling. She tucked them underneath her napkin. 'Don't make this a *shake*-down. I am simply nervous about being at my first *ton* ball.'

He took a few bites of food, before his blue eyes rimmed in black swallowed her whole. 'I don't want this to sound earth-*shaking*, but I was watching you. And I noticed that you grimaced the entire dance with Mr Jackson. And you paled when he spoke. Does he know something about you? About the bullet hole in your arm?'

Her hands trembled worse than ever. Matthew had guessed the wrong man. Nancy took a calming breath, but it didn't help her thundering pulse or the quivers that seemed to spread from her hands to her entire body. 'I am only a little *shake*-n. He merely held my hands too tightly.'

Matthew nodded, but his countenance did not look convinced. He continued to eat, while she used a fork to stir the food around her plate, pretending. Her throat felt too thick to swallow anything. All she could manage was a few sips of wine.

Lifting his glass, Matthew gestured towards where her aunt was sitting across the room. 'I know that we are new acquaintances and that I have yet to earn your un-*shake*-n confidence. But know that I will always help you if you ask me to… Also, I am sure you can trust the Nose with any or all of your secrets.'

Balling her napkin in her lap, Nancy asked, 'Did you just call my un-*shake*-able Aunt Marianne, *the Nose*?'

His lips twitched into a *heart*-melting smile. 'That's Lady Delfarthing's nickname in society. Did you not know? Everyone calls Lady Jersey *Silence*, because she doesn't stop talking. And everyone calls your aunt *the Nose*, because she uses that aristocratic hooked feature for intimidation. Also, she seems to be in the *know* about everything and everyone. But unlike Silence, the Nose is not a gossip.'

She leaned towards him. No longer playing their word game. 'Then how do people know that she knows?'

Matthew moved closer to her so that their shoulders touched. 'The Viscountess Delfarthing keeps her cards close to her chest, but I would guess that Lady Sefton sent you that voucher to Almack's because of something your aunt knows.'

'Are you accusing my aunt of social blackmail?'

'Yes,' he said, his eyes dancing. 'No one dare snub her for fear of what she could tell about them. I admire her style greatly. In business, I would call it leverage.'

She took a sharp breath and tested his affection. 'What if I told you that the only reason that I am here, is because I blackmailed my grandfather into providing me a season and a dowry of twenty thousand pounds?'

Nancy expected him to frown. To look at her in disgust. Not to throw his head back and laugh loud enough for half the room to hear him.

Sobering, Matthew wiped a tear from his eye with his napkin. 'I would have said that you should have asked for twice as much. Never accept a person's first offer. I always counter for twice as much as I'm willing to take. You'd be surprised how many times a person will pay the outrageous sum. It's all about supply and demand.'

Unexpectedly, Nancy found herself fighting a smile. 'Then you're not appalled by my blackmailing?'

He lifted his wine to his lips and sipped. 'I daresay many a gentleman would be. But I am a businessman. It is wise to use whatever you have at your disposal to get the best terms possible in a contract. And in my opinion, your grandfather owes you a great deal more than twenty thousand pounds. You deserve a lifetime of recompense.'

She felt her throat opening and managed to take a bite of her food. Then another. Matthew had finished his own plate, but he watched her eat hers. He seemed in no hurry to leave her side. She wished that she was brave enough to tell him about Alastair and the stolen government documents. But she was not a damsel in distress. Nancy had survived on the streets of Edinburgh and London since she was eight years old. She knew how to take care of herself.

Chapter Ten

'Are there any flowers left in London?' Matthew asked, entering his parents' drawing room which resembled a flower shop. Every table was filled with vases of different coloured blooms.

Frederica peeked her head over some peonies. 'None!'

Picking up a rose, he smelled it. 'Any of your beaux of interest? Who is this one from? Ah, the young and nearly bankrupt Earl of Edgewell. Is he the spotted fellow that kept running you into other couples?'

His sister blew a curl out of her face and shrugged one shoulder. 'Yes, it was the most horrid of all dances. And no, I am not interested in any of the beaux from Mama's list. Still, it's nice to receive flowers.'

'Nicer than an ice at Gunter's?'

Frederica popped up faster than a daisy in spring. 'Nothing is better than an ice at Gunter's.'

'Then fetch your bonnet,' he said, clapping his hands together. 'I thought we'd stop by Mantheria's to see if she or Andrew would like to come with us too.'

'Vying for Wick's position as favourite uncle?' she asked, tying the ribbon of her straw hat.

His elder brother bribed their nephew with ices whenever he came to visit.

'I haven't a chance. Wick has provided two male cousins and entirely eclipsed me.'

Matthew held open the carriage door for his sister and they made the short trip to Mantheria's house in Mayfair. Technically it belonged to her husband, the Duke of Glastonbury, as it was a part of the Glastonbury estate. However, Alexander let Mantheria use it exclusively. While in London, he lived with his mistress, Lady Dutton. The butler took them up to the nursery where Mantheria and her five-year-old son, Andrew, were battling with two toy armies on the table.

'You're having a battle without me?' Frederica said, placing a hand on her heart as if she'd been deeply wounded.

'And me?' Matthew said, doing his best imitation of his sister's voice.

Both Mantheria and Andrew laughed.

Their nephew was the son of a duke and even though he was only five, he already knew proper social manners. He stood up and bowed. 'Uncle Matthew, Aunt Frederica, I should very much like it if you would join my battle.'

Frederica took a seat on a precariously small chair. 'After such an invitation, how could we refuse?'

Matthew took the seat beside her, his knees reaching above the height of the table. Still, he picked up a little cannon that was very like its larger counterpart. 'Detailed little piece. I wonder where it was manufactured?'

Andrew grabbed the cannon and put it back in its place on the battlefield. 'Why are you here?'

Mantheria cleared her throat. 'A gentleman never demands why someone has come to call. If you would like to cut to the chase, you might say: to what do I owe the honour of this visit?'

His nephew wrinkled his button nose. 'To what do I owe the honour of this visit?'

'I was hoping to invite you for a drive and a visit to—'

Andrew didn't allow him to finish the sentence. 'Gunter's!'

Matthew tapped the end of his nephew's button nose. 'The very same.'

His nephew flew out of his chair, presumably to fetch his hat and coat.

'He's lying,' Frederica said flatly to their sister. 'I think his real reason for inviting me, and visiting you, was to find out more about your acquaintance with Lady Delfarthing.'

Mantheria's eyes widened and her lips curled. 'Why would you want to know about the Nose? Have you done something indiscreet?'

Before Matthew could respond, Frederica did it for him. 'He's not interested in the aunt, but in the niece. Miss Nancy Black is very beautiful and has a most mysterious background. The first time I met her, she had a gunshot wound on her arm and was dressed like a middleclass housekeeper.'

Matthew elbowed his sister. 'Hush, Freddie. I thought you could keep a secret.'

Frederica elbowed him right back into the stomach. 'I

have kept the secret. Mantheria's our sister. She doesn't count.'

'She's a duchess. She always counts.'

Mantheria cleared her throat, moving a red-coloured soldier to a different spot on the table. 'Your battle is much more interesting than Andrew's little soldiers, but perhaps we should go to Gunter's before you two come to blows.'

Grumbling, Matthew knocked down her piece. 'I have never struck any of my sisters.'

Frederica shook her head. 'I'm afraid that I can't say the same.' She held out her right arm and showed scars that looked like thin scratches. 'I'll never know if Helen or my cat gave me these marks.'

'They're both feral,' Mantheria said.

He folded his arms across his chest. 'I daresay you deserved it and that Helen has similar scars.'

Matthew half expected his sister to turn mutinous, but instead she laughed. A dangerous sign.

Frederica opened her big mouth again. 'As you know, Mama can't abide Viscountess Delfarthing and refused to invite them to my coming-out ball. I did anyway. I quite like the niece. Matthew is now hoping to convince you to invite Miss Black and Lady Delfarthing to a small dinner party or perhaps to be a part of a group for the theatre. So that he can spend some one-on-one time with Nancy.'

Matthew grumbled. His little sister even had his wording correct.

Mantheria gave him the sly smile of all matchmaking mamas. 'I did receive a calling card from Lady Delfarthing only last week. I suppose I could invite her to a small dinner and her sons too. Both, I believe are quite eligible.'

Grinning, Matthew elbowed Frederica again. 'Two eligible young men for you. How lucky! Do you prefer tall and silent? Or short and fashionable?'

'I never said anything about coming,' Frederica protested, pinching his arm. He could well believe that her fingernails had left scars.

'How could you not come?' Mantheria said, grinning wickedly. 'It was your idea after all.'

Entering the door, Andrew placed his hands on his little hips. He had his coat and a straw hat on. 'No more boring stuff, I want an ice.'

Mantheria clicked her tongue. 'Dearest, that is hardly the correct way to speak to guests, especially to your aunt and uncle.'

Frederica held out her hand to Andrew. 'I agree. No more boring stuff. Should we race your mama and Uncle Matthew to the carriage? Last one there has to ride backward!'

His nephew squealed and laughed as he and Frederica dashed out of the nursery. Matthew got to his feet and offered his hand to Mantheria.

'I was rather stuck in that little chair,' she said with a laugh. 'Even Andrew is getting a little big for this set.'

'I hope my request doesn't put you out.'

Mantheria grinned. 'Not at all. I assure you. In fact, when we return from getting our ices, I intend on writing to our little sisters and Louisa. They'll all be agog to know that Matthew, the confirmed bachelor, is smitten at last. Although, she already seems to me a much better choice than Lady Annabelle.'

Exhaling, Matthew said, 'You knew?'

'You were quite young and obvious,' she said. 'Nor would you listen to my suggestions that she was a mercenary creature and only after your fortune.'

They began to walk down the grand staircase to the foyer. 'I was such a fool. Distracted by her beauty. Flattered that she singled me out. I thought you were jealous of her popularity.'

Mantheria gave him a cat-like smile. 'I can't help but feel with Lord Trent, that she got exactly what she deserved: a title and little else. Despite her much-needed dowry, Lord Trent has found himself on the rocks again.'

'Not all of us can find the perfect wife by mistaking her as an errant governess,' he quipped. For that was how their elder brother, Wick, had found his wife and they were extremely happy together. The sort of happiness and family life that he craved for himself. Not that he wanted a wife like Louisa, although he loved his sweet sister-in-law. She was too saccharine for his tastes, but the perfect complement to his brother's personality.

At one and twenty, Matthew had been infatuated with Lady Annabelle, but it wasn't the tragedy that his sister thought. He'd been embarrassed, shocked, and a little hurt. But it hadn't lasted for longer than a month or so. He realised then that the feelings he'd harboured for Lady Annabelle were not love. At least, not the sort of love his parents shared and what he wanted. He'd never thought of himself as a confirmed bachelor. He simply doubted that true love could be found in a ballroom or at a dinner party and he had been content to wait until both his heart and his mind were engaged. He would never have guessed he'd meet her at the Horse Guards and bump into her again on his parents' street. If only he could know if Nancy felt the same way towards him? Did she try to scare him off because she cared about him too? Or because she was not interested in him and his position as a second son?

He stopped abruptly. 'How do you know if a young lady is interested in you or your fortune?'

His sister stepped down another stair and glanced back at him. 'You have to trust your own judgement and trust the person to whom you are offering your heart. It is possibly the hardest thing you will ever do—but you cannot find love without showing your own vulnerability.'

Matthew needed to trust, not simply lust. 'Then what happened with Sunny?'

Mantheria took a deep breath and slowly released it. 'He refused my heart and I married Alexander. I am glad that you didn't marry immediately after the Lady Annabelle debacle. You deserve to love and be loved.'

Matthew shook his head, unsure. Which was a feeling he rarely experienced in his business life. 'Perhaps, I am moving too quickly. She's guarded. I don't know if she returns my preference. Maybe it would be better if I met her again at a larger event. Perhaps at Lady Duncannon's Venetian breakfast next week.'

His sister laughed and patted his arm. 'You're too late. I wouldn't miss throwing this little dinner party for the entire London season.'

He groaned and she laughed harder as he helped her into the carriage. Matthew and Mantheria sat with their backs to the front.

Mantheria arranged her skirt. 'Now that you owe me a favour, I should like to collect on it.'

'You haven't done anything yet.'

His sister sniffed and held up her nose at him in an excellent imitation of Viscountess Delfarthing. 'I will send the invites this very afternoon. What I should like in return is to be able to purchase fifteen percent of your shares in the railroad venture.'

Rubbing his eyes, he exhaled slowly. 'You know that Mama and Grandfather both think that it is not a good investment.'

'Yes,' she said, raising her eyebrows. 'They're traditional in their attitudes. But I heard you explaining why holding a majority of the shares will eventually make you one of the richest men in England, once the steam locomotive and track reach London and other port towns. I agree with you that it will revolutionise how goods are delivered and how humans travel the world.'

'Five percent, at current value,' Matthew countered. He couldn't help but be a little pleased that *someone* had been listening. Papa had fallen asleep during the conversation.

'Ten percent at the original price you paid for the shares is my final offer,' Mantheria said. 'You'll still own fifty-five percent of the company and a majority.'

Huffing, he said, 'Fine. But I am going to charge you a fee for writing the contracts.'

'Then I'll send you a bill for penning the dinner party invitations.'

His sister drove a harder bargain than their mother, who was even more ruthless than he was in business. 'All right.'

Mantheria elbowed him. 'A pleasure doing business with you.'

Matthew only harrumphed in response and did not speak another word until he ordered their ices. He was risking more than his capital in the railroad on Nancy. He was risking his heart. But Mantheria was right. One did not gain a fortune without danger and chance. Or the love of a mysterious woman. He had to trust his own instincts and they were all pointing towards her.

After escorting his sisters to their homes, he returned to his office. There was much business he still needed to accomplish that day. He was not a gentleman of leisure but a businessman. Reading Mr Howitt's responses to his letters, Matthew signed his name to the bottom of the pages.

Ringing the bell for his secretary, Matthew sat back in his chair. Mr Howitt did not keep him waiting long.

He bowed. 'Are the letters ready to be mailed, my lord?'

Matthew nodded. 'Yes. And I should like you to arrange for the sale of ten percent of my railroad shares at their original price to my sister, the Duchess of Glastonbury.'

'Very good,' Mr Howitt said, taking out his little leather book and making a notation inside of it.

'And how are things coming on your other assignment? Any findings on Nancy Black? Or Mr Black?'

His secretary heaved a great sigh.

Matthew gestured to a chair. 'It sounds like you'll need to take a seat. Tell me everything you have discovered so far.'

Chapter Eleven

Aunt Marianne held an invitation in her hand and offered it to Nancy. 'The Duchess of Glastonbury has invited us to dinner. She has included my sons in the party, as well as her brother, Lord Matthew, and her sister, Lady Frederica. It is flattering, if short notice.'

Nancy tried not to grin too widely as she took the invitation from her aunt and read the words written in an elegant law-hand. Her own penmanship wasn't nearly as fine. Even the paper was thicker and nicer than she'd ever held before. Lord Matthew and his sister, the duchess, belonged to a different world than hers. A life that she had only seen by peeking through the curtains. One that she had wanted so badly her entire life.

'How kind of her.'

Her aunt raised one eyebrow. 'I doubt kindness has anything to do with it. The invitation is clearly Lord Matthew's doing. However, Lady Glastonbury's approval will help smooth your way into the *ton*. But whether or not I accept, is entirely up to you.'

Nancy gulped. 'Why would it be my choice?'

'Lord Matthew is signalling to us that he is serious in his courtship. If we are to accept, we would be encouraging him,' Aunt Marianne said. 'To be honest, Lord Matthew would be a higher match than I could have hoped for you.'

Her neck felt hot and so did her cheeks. He was higher than her in every way and she cared more for him and his good opinion than was safe for her heart.

'He's the son of a duke,' her aunt continued, 'as well as his Grandfather Stubbs's heir. I daresay he will have more money than nearly any peer in England. And I assume that once he marries, he will buy his own estate. He is well connected with royal, political, and business ties. But none of that matters if you do not like him.'

Nancy moved a hand to her neck and she found her tongue. 'I do like him. I have never liked anyone so much before…and he said that I should confide in you.'

'Then I shall send a card of acceptance to the duchess,' her aunt said briskly.

She hadn't expected her aunt to care for her opinion. Or to let her choose whether or not to allow someone to court her. Her personality was no-nonsense, and she had a stiff upper lip, only softening up for Basil. She did not expect her aunt to consider liking or loving in the finding of a suitable marriage partner.

'Did you love my Uncle George?'

Aunt Marianne stiffened and peered down at Nancy over her famous nose. The look was as cold as ice, but then Nancy saw tears in her aunt's eyes. 'Not at first. He was the heir to an earl and a very suitable match for me. Your grandfather arranged it with my parents. George was handsome enough and kind. We had two children and rubbed together well enough until your mother eloped… Your grandfather was pressuring her to accept a marriage proposal from a much older man. The Marquess of Slough had already buried his first two wives. Susan didn't like him, and by chance, she'd met a young Irishman with a clover tongue. I never knew whether she eloped with Mr Black because she loved him, or because she saw him as a way to escape Lord Slough.'

Nancy did not move. She did not speak. She wanted—no, needed—to hear the end of this story. 'Please tell me more.'

'Your grandfather cut her off without a penny and refused to have anything to do with his daughter. He demanded George do the same and threatened to disinherit him if he didn't…my husband simply shrugged his shoulders and said, "Do what you will, Father, I am my own man." I could have cheered. And I began to more than respect him. I admired your uncle. And I slowly came to realise that I loved George for every single thing that your grandfather criticised in him. George was both giving and forgiving. He never held a grudge. He was not unkind to anyone no matter their station. And I knew how lucky I was to be married to him and I have never forgotten it.'

Nancy thought how different her uncle must have been from his own cold and standoffish father. She was grateful that Uncle George had stood by her mother for the short time of her marriage. 'I wish I could have met him.'

'You did twice,' Aunt Marianne said, her voice cracking with emotion. 'We both held you after you were born. George arranged and paid for your mother's funeral. It was a small affair. Only us, our sons, your father, and the paid mourners. George held on to you so tightly. He didn't want to let you go. He offered your father a small fortune to give you up, but Mr Black refused and I didn't see you again until now.'

Nancy's knees shook and she managed to get to a chair to sit down before she fell to the floor. Her mother's family hadn't completely abandoned her. Her Uncle George had wanted her. He'd even been willing to pay to adopt her. Why had her father never told her that? He'd only ever said that her grandfather had refused to be bled for money. The one time he'd mentioned her Uncle George was to say he was an easy pigeon to pluck. Never once had her father told Nancy that her uncle had wanted her. Loved her.

'Papa said that Uncle George gave him money a few times.'

Her aunt sat down, nodding. 'That he did. He hoped that it would help you, but we never knew if it did or not. Your father refused to let us see you. Then my husband died quite unexpectedly and I never heard from Mr Black again.' A tear fell down her aunt's cheek. 'So many times over the years, I have thought of you. I've wondered what it would have been like if you had become my daughter. I am not naturally a warm woman, but I like to think that we would have been close. I would have hoped that you could have shared anything with me.'

Matthew had been right. Her aunt *knew* something. The nickname the Nose was apt after all. Nancy couldn't decide if this was more comforting or terrifying.

'My father was a criminal,' Nancy whispered. 'And I helped him on his jobs.'

Aunt Marianne didn't so much as blink. 'Did any of those criminal activities include Sir Alastair Lymington? There are rumours of his unsavoury background and your behaviour around him felt studied and unnatural.'

Nancy blanched, but nodded. 'He was the head of our nine-person crew. He ensured that my father and I were safe. Alastair has connections with several rookery bosses. I knew that he spoke flash, but I had no idea he was a proper gentleman.'

'There's nothing proper about him,' Aunt Marianne said with asperity. 'What hold does he have over you?'

Her aunt certainly didn't miss much. Gulping, Nancy steeled herself. 'The night my father died, I performed one last job. I stole government papers from a lord. My father was going to sell them to a French agent, but when I arrived back at our rooms, he was shot.'

'By Alastair?'

'No,' Nancy said, biting her lower lip to compose herself. 'By one of the money lenders. Papa was a gambler and could never stay ahead of the bills more than once or twice a year. He stole the job from another person in Alastair's crew.'

'And were you successful?'

Nancy lowered her head and her voice. 'The papers are stashed in the Hampfords' front parlour in their pianoforte. I couldn't keep them with me. It would have been too dangerous. Alastair has already had someone search my room here. I don't know who or how. But he knew the colour and every detail about it.'

Aunt Marianne tucked a curl behind her ear. 'I'll speak to the housekeeper and whoever it was on the staff will be immediately dismissed. What do you intend to do with the documents?'

Focusing on her hands, Nancy felt her face go red. 'I used them to blackmail my grandfather. I needed money to start a new life. He countered with an offer of a dowry of twenty thousand pounds and a season. I didn't plan to give them to him until after I was married and he could not go back on his word.'

Her aunt stomped one foot and huffed. 'The old fool will not go back on his word. I shall see to that. You are his granddaughter and you should not have needed to stoop to blackmail for him to do his duty by you.'

Nancy dropped her face into her hands. 'Alastair has demanded that I give him the papers in three days, or he threatens to either expose me as a thief or kill me. Today is the third day.'

She felt a hand on her back and saw that Aunt Marianne had moved to sit beside her. Her aunt rubbed Nancy's back in circles as she whimpered and finally cried. Nancy sobbed for her father who loved himself more than anyone else. For all the lies he had told her. She wept for Alastair, who had once been her hero. Tears fell down her cheeks for her own misdeeds and poor choices. For her past that precluded any hope of a brighter future with Matthew or any other gentleman.

'Has your grandfather seen all of the documents?'

Nancy sniffed and Aunt Marianne handed her a monogrammed handkerchief to dry her nose and eyes with. 'No. Only the first paper, but I told them that there were more.'

'How many of them are there?'

Wiping at her eyes, Nancy whispered, 'Twelve.'

Aunt Marianne rubbed one more circle on Nancy's back and then patted her shoulder. 'Then we will send half of them to Sir Alastair by a footman and give the other half to Lord Brampton. Neither of them will be any the wiser.'

'Isn't that treason? I know that Alastair will sell them to his French contact.'

Her aunt cleared her throat. 'What the bad-mannered baronet does with them is entirely his own affair. We do not need to take responsibility for his choices. And if your grandfather had taken care of his family as he ought to have done, you would not be in this mess to begin with. Now go and wash your face and have Arnold fetch your finest day dress. We are going to pay a call on the Duchess of Hampford and get those documents back today.'

Sniffling, Nancy stood up on trembling knees. 'I thought that you were not friends with the duchess.'

'I am not,' Aunt Marianne said, lifting her nose in the air. 'We are about to eat humble pie, so we must be dressed in our very best.'

The yellow sprigged muslin with matching ribbons was Nancy's favourite dress. She liked it even better than the more expensive and formal evening gowns. It was bright, light, airy, and made her feel happy. She dabbed a little of the perfume that Matthew had given her on the inside of her wrists and the back of her neck. She couldn't pick out all three notes yet, but she'd deciphered that the heart note was lemongrass. Miss Arnold helped her put on a white spencer and a matching white chip bonnet.

Thomas, the footman, followed Nancy and her aunt as they walked the five houses down the street to Hampford House. It was identical on the outside to her grandfather's London mansion, but having been inside of it once, she knew that the interior was decorated quite differently. She had never seen a pianoforte as large as the one in their front parlour. It had seemed the most logical place to hide the stolen papers.

The footman lifted the knocker and then waited for a servant to answer the door. Thomas handed the butler her aunt's card and they were ushered into the front room with the grand pianoforte. Thomas remained in the foyer, waiting to escort them back home.

The butler bowed to her aunt. 'I shall let Her Grace know that you are here.'

He closed the door behind him.

'Quick, Nancy,' Aunt Marianne hissed at her, waving one arm.

Nancy didn't have to be told twice. She leaped the few steps to the pianoforte and retrieved the stack of papers that she'd hidden underneath its lid. Tucking them safely into her reticule with her dagger, she made her way back to the sofa where her aunt sat. Her backside had barely touched the fabric when the butler opened the door and announced, 'The Duchess of Hampford.'

She'd met the woman briefly at Frederica's ball, but they had not exchanged any dialogue. Frederica was a younger version of the duchess. They had the same full figures, brown eyes, glossy brown hair, and their countenances radiated intelligence. The duchess's figure was a little fuller than her daughter's and a few grey hairs could be found in her locks, but age had been kind to the older woman. Matthew did not take after his mother in looks, but he did have some of her mannerisms.

Nancy and Aunt Marianne stood and curtsied to Lady Hampford, who returned the gesture.

'Please do be seated,' she said in a cold voice, sitting down like a queen on her throne. 'How fortunate that I was home when you called.'

'We are the fortunate ones, Lady Hampford,' Aunt Marianne said in an equally cool tone. 'I assume that you are often at your perfume shop or factory.'

Wrapping her arms around herself, Nancy was pretty sure that Aunt Marianne had just both complimented and insulted the duchess.

'You have been to my shop recently,' Lady Hampford said. 'I can smell one of my fragrances on your niece.'

What a refined nose the duchess had. It was no wonder that she was a famous perfumer. 'You are correct, Your Grace. Lord Matthew selected it for me.'

If Nancy thought her words would have softened the older woman, she was mistaken. The duchess sat up even straighter in her chair. Her face could have frozen water. It possessed none of Frederica's natural warmth or uncontainable energy.

'It appears that your son and my niece have formed a friendship,' Aunt Marianne said, folding her hands in her lap. 'Perhaps we should do the same and let bygones be bygones.'

Before the duchess was forced to give her answer, the door to the parlour burst open and Frederica and Matthew came inside. Frederica all but jumped into her chair. Matthew followed behind her at a more sedate pace and took the seat closest to Nancy. A detail that made her heart skip a beat.

'Lady Delfarthing, Miss Black,' Lady Hampford said in the same cold voice. 'I believe you are acquainted with my children?'

'Nancy and I are already the best of friends,' Frederica said with exuberance, placing her hands on her bouncing knees.

An awkward silence followed. Both older women looked indignant and Nancy could see that Matthew found the meeting humorous. His lips were twitching. He appreciated the ridiculous.

'I should love to hear you play the pianoforte again,' Nancy said, filling the uncomfortable silence.

'Of course. And I should be delighted to entertain you,' Frederica said, bouncing out of her chair. 'Come and turn my pages.'

Nancy left her reticule with the papers near her aunt and sat on the piano bench next to Frederica.

Her new friend began playing the pianoforte without any sheet music. Her fingers flew over the keys faster than Nancy's eyes could keep up with them.

'I rarely read music, but I wanted to have a chat whilst I play a little Chopin.' Frederica pressed her fingers more firmly against the keys and Nancy was fairly certain that no one else in the room could hear their conversation.

'I am glad to have a private word with you too.'

'How is your arm doing?' her friend asked. 'I have been so worried about you.'

Unconsciously, Nancy covered the white scar with

her opposite hand. Once the wound healed, Miss Arnold had cut out the stitches. 'It is all better, thanks to your expert care.'

'And my red soap. It's going to make me a fortune someday.'

Nancy didn't have to fake a smile. She liked Frederica immensely. And the fact that she was a young woman, a daughter of a duke, and had invented something useful and lucrative only increased her value to Nancy. In the world that she had grown up in, most women were too busy making ends meet to invent anything new. Nor had Nancy known that women could successfully fulfil positions typically held by men. The women in Matthew's family were certainly inspirational. Even his toplofty mother.

'I am sure you shall.'

'I hope you're coming to my sister's dinner party,' Frederica said, casting a look at her brother. 'Poor Matthew had to agree to sell Mantheria railroad shares to arrange it.'

Nancy had never heard that word before. 'What is a railroad?'

Frederica lifted one hand from the keys and crossed it over the other before continuing to play. 'A road for a steam carriage on wheels. Matthew's obsessed with them and Mantheria made him sell ten percent for this party at its original price—not the higher current value. Everyone says that I am the most like my mother, but I think Mantheria takes the cake.'

'And the railroad shares,' Nancy said.

Her friend laughed and completed her piece. Nancy didn't know what to think. Or how to feel. No one had ever sacrificed anything for her before. Not her father. Or Alastair. Everything they gave her came with a price. Oft-times a hidden one. She could scarce believe that Matthew would do such a thing for her. A man she barely knew and thought about entirely too much.

After the music, Aunt Marianne stood and said her goodbyes. Nancy picked up her reticule and reluctantly followed her out of the room, casting one last longing look at Matthew.

'Please allow me to escort you home,' he said, grinning at them.

'Our footman is waiting,' Aunt Marianne said in her imperious way.

'Alas, poor Thomas appeared bored fiddling his thumbs in the foyer and I sent him home ten minutes ago,' Matthew said, offering his arm first to Aunt Marianne. 'You'll have to let me play the footman in his place, Viscountess. I can provide you written references. Should you require them.'

He offered his other arm to Nancy and led them out of the house and slowly back towards Brampton House. Nancy breathed in his presence. The familiar hum of attraction that began in her chest and radiated through her entire body. She felt tingles from just touching his arm.

'You seem to like to play the footman,' Nancy said, smiling up to him. 'This is your second time.'

'Only when the ladies are as lovely as you two.'

Aunt Marianne shook her head, but there was a hint of a smile on her lips. Matthew spread out his charm lavishly, like butter on bread. She longed to lean her head against his shoulder and weep out her woes. But she didn't. Her aunt would have probably had an apoplexy if she did. Besides the documents were in her hands and with the help of the real footman, half would be delivered to Alastair this very afternoon. She prayed that he would leave her alone after he received them. But criminals were not known for keeping their words.

Matthew bowed over her aunt's hand and then took Nancy's into his, bringing it to his lips and brushing a soft kiss on her glove. How she wished it had been on her skin. 'I look forward to our next meeting, Miss Black.'

''Tis better than back-*ward*.'

'Or down-*ward*.'

Beaming, she revelled in his witty wordplay. 'That would be co-*ward*-ly.'

'And awk-*ward*.'

Aunt Marianne huffed. 'Lord Matthew, please let go of my niece's hand. It is quite untoward. She'll have need of it later and we shall see you tomorrow night at your sister's party.'

Turning Nancy's hand over, he brushed one more kiss against the delicate skin of her wrist before letting go. His lips were like a brand, searing his claim on her. 'You are my re-*ward* for attending.'

Nancy could only smile back at him. Words refused to form inside of her brain or her throat. She was made up entirely of flames. She watched him walk away, before her aunt herded her into the house. Gripping her reticule tightly, she poked herself on the tip of her dagger. Blood pooled on her index finger and she remembered the important documents that she carried. There was no time to listen to her way-*ward* heart. Her life was on the line.

Chapter Twelve

Matthew circled back to his parents' home and checked the pianoforte. The packet of government papers was gone. Nancy must have retrieved it during the visit with her aunt. Not that it really mattered. Matthew had already copied the documents in his own hand and quite interesting he'd found them. They included the locations of the British Army platoons, the names of their officers, estimated number of soldiers, and the routes of their supply lines in Spain. None of the sensitive information was new to him. His company had received similar instructions from Horse Guards to provide enough victuals and supplies. The French, however, would probably pay a great deal for such details on the enemy army. He had a shrewd idea that they were the blackmail that Nancy had used to bluster her way into her grandfather's house and the *ton* for the season.

He'd thought Nancy exceptionally clever to hide them in his parents' house instead of the Earl of Brampton's. But it was curious for her to take them before she was successfully engaged and married. Something was afoot.

At Frederica's ball, one of her partners had caused her to pale and shake. Matthew had encouraged Nancy to confide in her aunt. Then the Viscountess Delfarthing had called on his mother and offered an olive branch, giving them the perfect opportunity to retrieve the stolen government documents. Something must have gone wrong with Nancy's original plan and it only irritated him a little that she'd gone to her aunt instead of him. Matthew tried to find solace by pointing out that *he* had suggested that very thing. Still, it would have been rather amusing to play the knight in shining armour coming to the rescue of the fair maiden. However, if weapons were involved, Nancy would inevitably have had to rescue him.

'Taken up the pianoforte?' Frederica asked from behind him.

He lifted his hat. 'Merely forgot my hat.'

His sister took a seat on the piano bench and began to play a Chopin prelude. 'I wonder what sort of trouble Nancy is in?'

Leaning against the pianoforte, Matthew asked nonchalantly, 'Why do you think she's in trouble?'

Frederica rolled her eyes and her Chopin volume increased from pianissimo to forte with her emotions. 'Matthew, I'm not completely stupid. She had a bullet hole in her arm only weeks ago and now she's been taken into the bosom of the *ton*. She's not the typical debutante. There's no smoke without fire.'

Shrugging, Matthew saw Thomas, the Earl of Brampton's footman, walking past the house carrying a parcel. He left the parlour without a word and jogged out the front door to meet up with the young man.

Matthew purposely bumped into the lad, who was

only an inch or two shorter than him, but nearly half his width. 'Oh, I am so sorry. Ah! If it isn't my fellow footman. How do you do, Thomas?'

The tall, thin young man rubbed his rather large nose with his free hand. The expression on his face was disgruntled. 'Well enough, my lord.'

Smiling, Matthew gestured to the parcel in his hand. 'And where are you off to? More shopping for the Viscountess?'

He shook his head. 'No. Just a delivery *on my afternoon off* for Sir Alastair Lymington on Half Moon Street.'

Matthew didn't miss the young footman's emphasis. He was clearly put out to be running an errand on the one afternoon he had off. 'But what a happy coincidence. I am going that way. Shall I take it for you? A small favour from one footman to another.'

Thomas rubbed his nose again. 'I shouldn't wish to cause you any trouble, my lord.'

'Or yourself, I assume,' Matthew said, tapping the side of his nose with one finger. 'I promise not a word of this will ever cross my lips. Here, I'll take it. Go and enjoy your afternoon off.'

The young footman didn't hesitate a second time before handing the parcel to him. Matthew touched his hat and watched Thomas scamper away. He probably had family to visit and pubs to drink at. Maybe even a young maid to court.

Matthew resisted the urge to open the parcel right away. He made his way towards Half Moon Street and slipped into a pub for a drink at a corner table. It was dark and a little dank, but it was perfect for what he wanted. He carefully untied the strings and opened the parcel to see six of the documents inside of it. Half of the original number and only half the needed information. These papers were worthless to the French without the first six. They included details about the size of the platoons and their leadership, but nothing of their locations or supply lines. Clever Nancy. She would still have something to blackmail her grandfather with and she was able to give the rest to Sir Alastair Lymington. The newest baronet and the Prince Regent's favourite since Beau Brummell had fallen out of his grace. There were whispers in society that Sir Alastair had murdered his cousin to inherit the baronetcy and that he was involved in some shady business dealings.

Clearly, he was. Stolen government documents were not for the innocent.

Nancy had paled after dancing with Sir Alastair. She'd appeared shaken and scared. He must have some sort of hold over her. He mused that Nancy or her father, perhaps both, must have been in league with Sir Alastair at one time. And now thanks to Thomas, he knew where to start his enquiries.

Carefully folding the parcel back up, Matthew tied it before finishing his drink. He walked to Half Moon Street and paid a street-sweeper a shilling to deliver it to Lymington's kitchen door. He watched the lad hand off the parcel, before heading back to his office. He had another lead for Mr Howitt.

Matthew tugged at his collar. He had tied his blasted cravat too tightly around his neck. His sisters laughed at him.

'Hot already, Matthew?' Frederica teased.

'Overheated and nervous to be precise.'

'Lady Delfarthing and her niece are not even here yet,' Mantheria said, looking very pretty and as cool as a cucumber in a green silk gown.

He felt a trickle of sweat fall down his neck, hidden by his tall shirt points. Already regretting asking his sister to host a dinner party. 'You may be in high gig now, Frederica. But you won't be after you sit at dinner by the deadly dull Viscount Delfarthing. I was at school with him for seven years and I don't think I ever heard him say a word. And his little brother the Honourable Mr Basil Chambers, is a fop.'

She leaned forward, as if intrigued. 'Is he the one who wears the bright coats with all the spangles?'

'And frills and furbelows.'

Frederica looked nonplussed. 'Why does he never dance at the balls?'

Matthew's neck and face were both hot as he tugged at his collar once more. 'Basil's more interested in fashion than females. Show him a new snuffbox and he'll keep you talking for an hour.'

Frowning, Frederica nudged her sister with a sharp elbow. 'You can sit by him, Mantheria. I'll suffer by the silent brother.'

Mantheria raised one eyebrow and said drily, 'How thoughtful of you, dearest.'

Their conversation paused, as the butler opened the door of the drawing room to announce, 'Lady Delfarthing and Miss Black.'

Matthew and his sisters bowed to their guests.

The Viscountess Delfarthing looked magnificent

and haughty. Her dark green turban and matching gown were fit for a queen. She lifted her nose up at him, putting Matthew in his place.

The last person to enter was the one he'd been waiting for, Nancy. She was even more beautiful than he'd remembered. She carried a small reticule with a sharp point—could it conceal a weapon? The blue evening gown she wore clung to her lush figure. And the colour brought out her bright blue eyes. Matthew couldn't have imagined a more beautiful woman.

Bowing, Mantheria smiled. 'Lady Delfarthing and Miss Black. I am delighted that you could accept my invitation on such short notice.'

Before Mantheria could ask everyone to be seated, her butler opened the door again and announced the Chambers brothers and Lord Sunderland. Lord Delfarthing bowed, but did not open his mouth. He was tall and skinny, whilst his little brother was short and round. Their suits could not have been more opposite. Lord Delfarthing's plain dark coat was rather loose on his gaunt figure and Basil's velvet green coat appeared to have been sewn onto his skin. Matthew counted no fewer than six tassels.

Sunny entered behind them and surreptitiously took his place by Mantheria's side as if he were her husband instead of a dear friend. Matthew thought that Sunny must care for Mantheria still or he would never have accepted a last-minute invitation of such an ill-assorted group of guests.

Basil brushed past his brother and proceeded to kiss the hand of every lady in the room, starting with Mantheria and ending with his own mother. He was all smiles like the hostess of the party. 'What a pleasure it is to be in the company of such beautiful women.'

Frederica turned her snort of laughter into an unconvincing cough. Matthew nudged his sister and she elbowed him right back. Sunny smirked at them.

Mantheria exchanged pleasantries before they all went to dinner. She sat at the head of the table with Sunny at the opposite end. Frederica had a Chambers brother on each side of her. As he predicted, Delfarthing did not speak at all and Basil never shut up. Matthew suffered marginally less. He had Viscountess Delfarthing on his left side and Nancy on his right. Every time he opened his mouth to speak to Nancy, her dragon of an aunt would ask him a question and force him to converse with her.

Happily, the fifth course seemed to capture the dowager Viscountess Delfarthing's fancy and he was finally able to turn his attention to Nancy.

'Was your grandfather unable to join us?'

'Yes,' she said with a brilliant smile. 'He is kept very busy at Horse Guards… I don't know if I ever properly thanked you for helping find my grandfather's office that day.'

'I must admit my motives were not entirely noble,' he said, returning her smile. 'The lord secretary and I rarely agree on politics or people. I thought bringing you to his office would infuriate him.'

Nancy set down her fork. 'I believe it did, but now that I live with him, he has successfully avoided being in my presence for nearly a month.'

Sipping his wine, Matthew looked around the room. 'His loss. Besides, my parents aren't here either.'

'But your sisters are.'

He laughed softly. 'Not all of them, thank the heavens. I have two additional sisters who are still at home, Helen and Becca. They are both a bit of a handful. Helen is obsessed with snakes and Becca is fond of mice, they carry their reptiles and vermin everywhere they go… I blame my father. He is a naturalist and delights that two of his offspring share his passion. They are his favourites.'

'But you do not.'

'No, nor does my elder brother, Wick. Uh, his courtesy title is Lord Cheswick, so we all call him Wick.'

Nancy took a drink before asking, 'Is your brother in town as well?'

'Wick hates *ton* parties and the entire season,' Matthew said, cutting his beef. 'And being the father of two boys keeps him very busy. I stayed with him last month and every time I looked for him, he was in the nursery holding his new son. Who happens to be named after yours truly.'

She gave him another dazzling smile. 'What an honour.'

Matthew remembered holding his little namesake and thinking that perhaps having a little one of his own might not be the worst idea he'd ever had. Unlike little Matt with his flaming red hair, if he and Nancy were to have a babe, the child would probably have her dark curls. This thought both pleased and embarrassed him. He lifted his glass up. 'Not one I necessarily deserve, but I am honoured all the same.'

'I envy your close family,' she said. 'I lived with my Scottish granny until I was eight and she died. In her cottage, I felt as if I belonged. Unfortunately, I do not feel the same in my grandfather's house. Aunt Marianne is loving in her reserved way and Basil has quite taken me under his wing, but Cousin Peregrine never talks to me. And my grandfather seems to want nothing to do with me.'

'Believe me, you are not missing much.'

Nancy chuckled and Matthew hoped that his voice had not carried.

The footmen served the dessert course and Matthew could barely taste it. He was so absorbed with Nancy. He'd always liked women and respected them, but no lady before had ever had this effect on him. She licked her spoon and all Matthew could think about is how much he'd like to be licked by her lips. Anywhere. Everywhere.

She caught him staring at her and she flashed him a little smile. 'Do you know if there'll be cards after dinner?'

'I believe so.'

'Good. You can be my partner and we'll fleece my cousin together,' Nancy said. 'It will teach Peregrine a lesson for ignoring me.'

A laugh escaped him. 'Are you good at cards?'

Nancy paused, as if deciding what to tell him. 'My father once owned a gaming house in Edinburgh. Once his own debts became too great, we moved to London and he changed our last name.'

A gaming hell was a dangerous place for anyone. Particularly a young girl. But it seemed that her father had gambled with her safety as much as he had with their fortunes. 'Are you telling me that you are a captain-sharp?'

She laughed, a sound that would haunt his dreams

that night. 'I have been known to count cards, but I rarely cheated. Unless I needed the money.'

He paused at her words. Matthew, himself, had grown up with an abundance of everything. Food, estates, siblings—he had seven—and even friends. He'd never known need of any kind. Or desperation. He wouldn't have judged her harshly even if she had cheated.

'Have I finally succeeded in shocking you?' she asked, her black eyebrows raised.

'Nonsense. And your confidences are always safe with me,' he said and meant it. 'I am very much looking forward to seeing your card skills.'

She slid the hilt of a dagger out from her reticule, before slipping it back inside. 'I'm good with cards, but I'm better with knives.'

Matthew was entranced. 'I look forward to seeing those skills, as well. Perhaps after Frederica pounds the pianoforte into submission.'

'Aunt Marianne doesn't consider them skills that a young lady should possess,' Nancy admitted. 'And how are you going to entertain me?'

He gave her a sheepish grin. 'Words. I can make the twenty-six letters in the English language do whatever I wish them to.'

'*Word*-play must come in very handy with your business and legal work.'

Matthew nodded, smiling. 'I am definitely a *word*-monger.'

'But *word*-smithing would be very boring to watch,' Nancy said, teasing him.

'I shall try to come up with a new and interesting *word*-less talent to display for you when we next meet.'

Her eyes lowered to focus on her lap. 'I hope it is not a swear *word*. When will that be?'

'I could escort you and your cross-*word* to the park tomorrow morning.'

Nancy's eyes darted to Viscountess Delfarthing on his other side. 'I am not sure my aunt would approve of us going alone together. I should hate to become a by-*word*. Especially since I have yet to officially come out.'

'Therefore, you must *stay in*?'

She chuckled again. 'I suppose.'

'We could *stay in* at my parents' house. They have a large conservatory and I'll make Frederica and Mrs May, our housekeeper, remain with us for the proprieties. My sister loves pistols. I daresay she'd be pleased as punch to learn how to use a dagger.'

Her mouth opened and she leaned her head closer to him. 'Is your sister a good shot?'

'Best in the family.'

'I am rather good with a pistol, as well.'

Matthew grinned. What an interesting life Nancy must have lived. He longed to hear every story. 'I am not surprised. I only wish I could accompany you both to Manton's shooting range and have a match. I would love to see Frederica brought down a peg or two. I am not very good with a gun.'

'It could be me who is brought down,' she said with a coquettish smile.

'Nothing could bring you down in my esteem.'

And by Jove, he meant it.

Chapter Thirteen

The next morning in the Stringhams' conservatory, Nancy laughed so hard that she cried. The room was a large greenhouse that attached to the back of their London mansion and took up nearly all the garden space. The walls were made up of windows. There were plants of every variety in pots. The Stringhams' housekeeper, Mrs May, sat on a wicker chair in the corner of the room with her basket of sewing repairs. She glanced up occasionally from her needle, but her gaze was on Frederica, not Matthew.

His 'interesting *word*-less talent' was balancing his hat upside down on his nose. He was doing rather well, until his little sister blew upon it. Matthew and Frederica had her constantly in stitches. They began by verbally sparring and then physically with her dagger. Glancing up from the corner, the housekeeper only shook her head as if familiar with their antics. She felt a pang of envy as sharp as a dagger to her skin. How much she would have given to grow up with a large and loving family.

Recalling herself, Nancy held up her hand again. 'No,

no. You're holding it wrong, Frederica. That is a reverse grip. It is only good for stabbing people unawares or in the back.'

Matthew sniggered. 'That sounds like your style.'

Frederica wrinkled her nose at her brother. 'Et tu, Brute?'

Nancy held up her own dagger and gripped it tightly with all five fingers, the blade closest to her thumb. 'This is the forward grip. Your thumb needs to have contact with your forefinger. Your wrist needs to be locked and square.'

She watched her friend switch her hold on the blade and mimic the way Nancy held it. 'Is this it?'

Nodding, Nancy smiled. 'Yes, make sure that the dagger is always pointed up. You can deliver slashes and cuts at the greatest distance from your own body.'

Frederica pretended to slash and stab her invisible opponent, before handing the blade to Matthew. 'Your turn. I must use the necessary and I need your assistance, Mrs May. We shan't be gone more than a moment or two. So use it wisely.'

The housekeeper set her sewing down into the repair basket and gave a harrumph before following Frederica back into the house and closing the door behind her.

Matthew must have been watching Nancy's instruction to his sister closely, for his grip was perfect. Nancy stored her own dagger in her belt and took his bare hand in hers. She moved his thumb to the top of the spine. His grip on the knife was now open, but she didn't remove her hand. For the first time her skin was touching Matthew's for more than a brief brush of his lips. She could see the black ink mark on his middle finger from all his writing.

Nancy could feel the calluses from his driving of horses and see a little white scar on his knuckle. She ran her finger lightly over it, caressing his old pain.

'I wish I could say that I earned that scar by doing something incredibly brave,' Matthew said in a lower tone for her ears only. 'But I am afraid that it is only from a particularly mean swan who used to chase my little brother, Charles, around. I attempted to intervene and it ended poorly. I am not much of a fighter.'

She was close enough to him to inhale his spicy and expensive cologne. She wished she knew what his heart note was. Running her fingers over his scar again, Nancy glanced up into his eyes. 'I didn't know that you had a brother named Charles. You've never mentioned him before.'

The usual smile that lurked in his eyes was gone, replaced by a sadness as deep as any despair Nancy had ever felt. 'He died of scarlet fever when he was twelve. As did my little sister Elizabeth. My elder brother, Wick, blamed himself for their deaths since he was the head of the family whilst our parents were away, but it was Charles and I who brought the illness home from Eton. I teased Charles that it was the first time he'd ever shared something with me willingly. But that wasn't true. My little brother was kind and trusting. He looked up to both me and Wick and I felt like I'd let him down. Since then, I have done my best not to disappoint or fail anyone that I love.'

She knew how it felt to be disappointed by someone she loved. Still stroking his hand, Nancy shook her head. 'That's not always possible.'

'No,' he said placing his free hand on top of hers,

sandwiching their hands together. 'We humans are imperfect beings, but that doesn't mean we should not trust or depend upon others… As you are aware, my sister, Lady Glastonbury is separated from her husband. Through a great deal of negotiations, paperwork, and guilt, I was able to get her husband to return her dowry. Mantheria is the mistress of her own fortune.'

Nancy stiffened and pulled her hand away. 'I wasn't aware that a married woman had any rights to her dowry or even her salary, if she has employment. It is all legally her husband's.'

'Unfortunately, yes,' he said. 'I hate how English law renders half of its subjects powerless. However, with enough paper and leverage, and a dash of help from Chancery Court, I can make a woman's fortune her own. Even if she is married. However, it is not without its limitations. She still must have a trustee or two and Chancery Court to oversee it. And I am my sister's trustee, however, I wouldn't dream of telling her no. It would go badly for me.'

She took a deep breath. 'Why are you telling me this?'

He smiled and it completely broke down her guard. 'I am trying to get you to trust me.'

'With my future dowry?'

Matthew waved a hand. 'I've plenty of my own money. I am more interested in your secrets and the hold Lymington has over you.'

Gasping, she stepped back. 'Alastair no longer has a hold over me. I gave him what he wanted.'

'A man like that will always want more.'

Nancy held up her knife, ready to strike. 'I can protect myself.'

He held up both of his hands, as if she were a high-wayman telling him to 'stand and deliver'. 'I am certain of it. But if you ever need my help, please don't hesitate to call upon me. I would be honoured to serve you in anyway.'

Matthew was showing her that he wasn't a threat, but could she trust him? Would he still wish to serve her if he knew the truth? Or would he abandon her like her father and Alastair had?

'You are not a criminal.'

He laughed softly, reaching his hands out to her. 'Your grandfather would tell you that I am. I drive a hard bargain in my business dealings.'

Nancy put her hands into his and Matthew pulled her behind a large potted plant. 'Frederica said for me to use my time with you wisely.'

'And how do you intend to do that?' she asked, stepping closer so that her fluttering chest met his hard one.

'Kissing you,' he whispered, brushing his lips against her forehead. 'If you've no objection, of course.'

Nancy moved her hands from his grasp and threw them around his neck. 'None at all.'

Before he could kiss her, she pressed her lips to his. It was the first time that she'd ever kissed a man voluntarily. Her previous experiences with embraces had all been unwanted overtures from men who had pinched her backside and kissed her without her permission. Sometimes in a pub or the streets of a slum. She'd always responded with her dagger. No one had ever asked for her consent before. It was dizzyingly attractive. She kissed him hard with all the hunger of a lifetime without love.

Despite having been instructed on how to be a courtesan, Nancy had no real-life skills with seduction. Madame Sweetapple had planned to sell her virginity to the highest bidder. She did not know what to do other than to press her mouth to his and let nature take over.

Matthew returned her fervour, but gentled the kiss, by moving his hands into her hair and holding her a little farther from him. His lips then moved over hers with soft, drugging, movements. She felt rather than heard herself moan. Then he licked her mouth and his tongue played between her lips, before she opened wider. His tongue was as soft and caressing in her mouth as his kisses had been on her lips. She felt his tongue stroking her own and was lost in the sensation of the embrace.

Where their mouths met there were sparks.

Where their hands met there were embers.

And where their limbs met, she was on fire.

His hands moved from her hair down to her shoulders and then made a slow burn of a path to the dip in her back. Pressing her more firmly against him, he moved his mouth to her ear and gently nibbled it. Nancy's entire body was aflamed. Nuzzling her neck, Matthew pressed more kisses against the column of her throat and her thundering pulse. She had never before felt so much pleasure. Such need. She now understood why men and women tried to sell and purchase this feeling. But somehow, she knew that such a kiss could not be bought. Not even for hundreds of guineas. It was a give and take between two people who cared for one another. Any other kiss would have been a counterfeit.

Matthew made a trail of kisses from her neck back to her mouth and Nancy found that she could not think at all. She twined her fingers in his hair, tugging him closer to her. He sucked on her lips like a bee sipping nectar from a flower. Then he kissed the side of her neck and her knees shook with pleasure. She felt completely undone in his arms. Yet she held on tighter. He saw her. All of her. And he took her spark and made her burn.

The sound of someone clearing their throat loudly caused them to break apart. Frederica was standing behind them, her arms folded across her impressive chest. Behind her stood Mrs May who sighed in resignation.

Frederica shook her head. 'Amateurs. You have been caught and I opened the door very slowly and loudly. You ought to have broken apart and pretended to be doing something else.'

'I had no idea you were such an expert,' Matthew remarked sardonically. He bowed to the housekeeper. 'Forgive me, Mrs May, for becoming carried away for a moment. It shan't happen again underneath your chaperonage. And forgive me if my attentions were untoward, Miss Black.'

Nancy flushed as he bowed to her, as well. He did not need to ask for her forgiveness, he'd had her consent, and what they shared was beautiful.

Frederica grinned and brought her hands to her mouth. 'But it shall happen again. I know it will. And next time, listen for the door hinges creaking.'

Nancy was certain that her face was as red as the roses behind her. Her hands still trembled from the embrace that had shaken the very foundations of her soul. She'd felt safe and cherished. Even loved.

Frederica patted Nancy's hair that had tumbled down. 'And another helpful hint, a cold rag against your lips will hide any swelling. However, unless your aunt is a complete ninny, she'll know that you two have been kissing.'

Her aunt Marianne was not a ninny, but she refrained from commenting on Nancy's swollen lips when Matthew and Frederica escorted her home. She also gave her permission for Matthew to take Nancy driving the next day before her coming-out ball. Matthew and his sister took their leave of them. Nancy's hand stole to cover her hot neck.

'Lord Matthew appears to be serious in his pursuit of you,' she said, turning her hawk-like gaze back to her niece. 'I would not tell him anything about your past that could jeopardise his intentions. The less you say the better.'

Nancy blushed again, nodding. She cared for Matthew. It would be devastating if he were to leave her now because of the life she'd lived with her father and the terrible deeds she had done at Alastair's bidding. Yet, she could not deceive him when she cared about him so much. He deserved a better wife than someone with her tainted past. Someone worthy of his gentle and respectful attentions. 'Yes, Aunt Marianne…and there has been nothing from Alastair?'

'Not a note or calling card,' she said. 'I hope that means that the unfortunate business is completed.'

Her heart skipped a beat as she remembered Matthew's warning about Alastair wanting more from her. 'And the remaining documents?'

Aunt Marianne swallowed. 'They are secure. It is better if you do not know where. You can honestly say to Sir Alastair, or anyone else, that you do not have them in your possession.'

Her aunt's high-handed words rankled a bit, but Nancy was thankful for her help. Grateful that her aunt Marianne cared for her despite knowing about her chequered past.

'You may as well remove your hand from your neck,' Aunt Marianne said. 'It's as red as the rest of your face.'

Dropping her hand, Nancy explained, 'He only kissed me. I mean, I…I remember you telling me not to allow any liberties until I was engaged to be married, but it just sort of happened.'

Aunt Marianne put a hand on her shoulder, a slow smile building on her lips. 'Yes, that is the rule of proper etiquette. But I was young once too, even though it was in the last century, and your Uncle George was not my first kiss. Was it pleasant?'

Nancy giggled. 'Very.'

On impulse, she leaned forward and hugged her aunt.

The Viscountess hesitated for only a moment before returning the embrace. 'Tell me all of the scandalous details.'

Chapter Fourteen

Climbing up into his father's phaeton, Matthew took the reins from the groom with a thank-you. He could hardly wait to take Nancy on a romantic drive down Rotten Row of Hyde Park. Yes, they would have to nod politely to acquaintances and nearly half the *ton*. But at last, he would be alone with her, in an open carriage where everyone could see them, but no one could hear them. No dragon aunt. No obnoxious sisters. And not even his family's dear housekeeper, Mrs May.

Matthew guided the horses down the five houses. He pulled his father's blood chestnuts to a halt and then handed the reins to the footman. He did not have to wait long for the butler to open the door and Nancy to spring out of it wearing a fashionable navy riding habit with two rows of brass buttons down her bodice and a dashing military-like hat with feathers. After offering her his arm, they walked down the steps.

'You look beautiful.'

Nancy tittered. 'I know. Cousin Basil selected my riding habit. He assured me that it was *all the crack*!'

Grinning from ear to ear, Matthew lifted Nancy up into the phaeton. A thrill ran through his entire body as his hands encompassed her narrow waist and he felt a surge of protectiveness towards her. She was so slight in his arms. So fragile. He climbed in himself and sat down closer to Nancy than he'd meant to. Colouring, he waited for her to move over on the seat, but instead she kept her body close to him. Her shapely leg pressed firmly against his. And he blushed like a blasted debutante.

'How well you drive,' Nancy complimented.

'Thank you,' he said, accepting the compliment. Even though, he wasn't a very good driver compared to his brother, Wick, or his sister Frederica. They were notable whips and he was happy if the horses did what he wanted them to do most of the time. Unlike his parents, he didn't keep a stable in London. It was not cost effective. 'Do you drive as well, Nancy?'

'I am afraid I have not had the opportunity,' she admitted. 'My father never owned a carriage.'

Matthew couldn't help but glance at Nancy's face. She was smiling. At. Him. Her white teeth gleaming against her pink lips. Black curls framed her beautiful face with one long curl down her back.

'Watch out,' Nancy shouted.

He immediately looked forward and deftly steered his horses around the slower cart. If she hadn't said something, he would have crashed into it. Harming not only his father's beloved chestnuts, but possibly Nancy. The one person he wanted to cherish and shield from danger. Matthew resolved not to stare at Nancy again until they entered the park.

'I'm usually not such a bad driver,' he explained. 'You're simply distracting me from the road.'

Huffing, Nancy giggled. 'So, it's my fault?'

Matthew held the reins tighter. 'Yes. When I drive with other people, I have no difficulty focusing my full attention on the road in front of me.'

'I will try not to be such a great distraction.'

His eyes still on the road, he shook his head lightly as he lifted his whip. 'Impossible. You are the greatest distraction.'

They wound their way into the park and off the busy London roads. He slowed the horses down to a walk. He wanted to make this drive last as long as possible. Tipping his hat to Lord Norwich, he directed the horses to the other side of Rotten Row. Matthew kept the ribbons in one hand as he touched his hat to Lady Devonshire and her devoted followers. Next, to Lady Jersey, Lord Kent, and Mr George. He spotted Mantheria's landau, but carefully drove around her carriage with a brief wave. He did not want to waste his time with Nancy talking to a sister.

Once they were ahead of most of the promenade, Matthew asked, 'Would you like to try driving a team?'

'Yes, if you will tell me what to do.'

He checked the chestnuts to a slow walk and handed the reins to Nancy. He held her hands in the correct position and showed her how to spur the horses onward and to stop them, feeling her warmth through his gloves and his mouth moistened. Oh, how he longed to kiss her again right there and then. If only there were a convenient forest to hide both themselves and the phaeton.

Nancy smiled up at him before attempting to drive.

A dog ran in front of their carriage and she pulled on the reins. Causing them both to fall forward and then to jerk backward. Happily, the horses did not hit the dog, but she relinquished the ribbons back to him.

'Perhaps I can try driving the team again, another time,' she said. 'Are you very fond of horses?'

'Have you heard of *The Salamanca*?'

She raised an eyebrow. 'Isn't that in the Peninsula? Wasn't there a battle there?'

'Oh, no. I was speaking of the steam locomotive *The Salamanca*.'

'I've never heard of a steam locomotive. Is it like a steamboat on land?'

Matthew couldn't help but smile. 'Exactly like that. For my seventeenth birthday, my grandfather took me to see Sir Isaac Moulton's steam locomotive. I confess I was a little alarmed by the noise, but soon my curiosity overcame me and I could not believe that I had seen a machine propelled by steam pull a cart across a track of rails without a horse.'

Nancy grinned back at him as if she was truly interested. Unlike his family members whose eyes glazed over when he started talking about his favourite subject. 'It must have seemed like magic.'

'It did. I was fascinated and my grandfather introduced me to Sir Isaac. I returned to Oxford and completed my university work there, but I was still obsessed with machinery. By chance, I became acquainted with Aiden Richards, an inventor who wished to create a steam locomotive. I provided the capital and paid Sir Isaac a royalty for Richards to use his design for the steam engine, but Richards has vastly improved upon it. He added a second cylinder when he created our steam locomotive which he named *The Salamanca* after Wellington's victory.'

'Have you ridden on it?'

Matthew guided his horses around the turn before answering. 'Yes. Although steam locomotives are not yet built for passengers, I believe that one day steam will be the most efficient way for people to travel and firms to move their goods. And since I invested in railroads early, I shall make a fortune.'

Nancy raised her eyebrows. 'I thought you already had a fortune.'

He laughed. 'A second fortune. One can't have too many.'

The expression on her face sobered. He wondered if she was thinking that his interest in her was because of her dowry. It wasn't. 'Not that I need more money. I've already made a fortune providing supplies for the Peninsula wars. I should simply like to prove both my mother and grandfather wrong. They don't think investing in steam locomotives and railroads is worth the risk.'

There was a wariness in her eyes. 'How does the locomotive stay on the metal railroad track?'

'The steam locomotive's wheels and the metal track are both toothed rack.'

'I am afraid I do not understand.'

Matthew pulled his horses to a stop and held the reins in one fist. 'Could you hold up one hand?'

Nancy held up her gloved left hand.

He pointed to her hand. 'Imagine your fingers are the meshed rack of the track and my hand is the wheel of the locomotive, with my fingers being the toothed rack.' He kept his fingers straight and intertwined them with Nancy's. 'Like this.'

'How fascinating. I should very much like to see *The Salamanca*.'

'It is located near Leeds,' he explained, reluctantly releasing her hand, 'but someday I will take you there.'

A little colour stole in Nancy's cheeks and Matthew felt his own heat rise. Before he could say anything, they were hailed by Lady Ashton and her two youngest daughters in a landau. They briefly exchanged greetings, before Matthew could make good his escape. He continued to drive around Hyde Park, until Nancy asked if they could walk for a little while.

Matthew pulled his team to a stop and stepped out of the carriage, still holding the reins. He gave Nancy a hand down. 'I hope you don't mind if I walk the horses as well?'

She laughed. 'I didn't think you planned to leave them unattended.'

He offered his arm and led her along the edge of the Serpentine Lake.

Nancy stopped and picked up a stone. Then threw it into the water. 'Is it not beautiful here?'

'Very,' Matthew said, but he was not looking at the Serpentine.

Tucking a curl behind her ear, Nancy smiled back at him. 'It seems strange that so much greenery and even lakes exist in the middle of a city.'

'Did you never come to Hyde Park before?'

She bit her lower lip, shaking her head. 'My grandmother's stone cottage was near a river. The water was so cold, but so beautiful. When she died my father took me to Edinburgh. I played in the streets there.'

He couldn't keep himself from saying, 'That doesn't sound very safe.'

Nancy shrugged one shoulder. 'My father dressed me as a boy in Edinburgh. It wasn't until we came to London four years later that I began to wear dresses again. Perhaps it would have been better if I had stayed disguised. Then Madame Sweetapple would not have found me, but I suppose my father didn't think I could pass as a boy any more.'

Matthew's fists clenched. Felix Black had been thoughtless in the care and protection of his daughter. Yet he was still Nancy's father and he knew that she loved him. Criticising her parent would not be the best way to get her to confide in him. 'I assume the money-lender had your father killed for unpaid debts?'

She turned her face away from him, stooping to pick up another rock and tossing it in the lake. 'Yes. His past caught up with him. As it does with all of us eventually.'

He would not press for confidences she was not yet ready to give. 'You must miss him greatly.'

Nancy's eyes filled with water and she sniffed. 'I do. Every single day.'

'I don't know what it is like to lose a parent,' he said. 'But I do know what it is like to lose family members and while it doesn't get any easier, you become better at bearing the weight of their loss. I find comfort in sharing stories about them with my sisters—and even my brother, after he married. Before then, the memories were too difficult for him to discuss. Everyone grieves differently, but if I am allowed to boast about myself, I am a very good listener. It's one of my top three most charming personality traits.'

She walked towards him and put her hand on his arm. 'And the other two?'

'I should think they would be obvious to the average observer: my vocabulary and my stubbornness.'

Nancy let out a trill of laughter.

Matthew tried to stop his lips from smiling back at her. It was an impossible task, even if her laughter was slightly offensive. 'If you do not agree with my personal assessment, tell me your own.'

'You are without a doubt charming,' she said, mollifying the sting of her mirth. 'But I would say your top three traits are: kindness, patience, and intelligence.'

Sighing dramatically, he dropped his shoulders. 'I was hoping for all three of your favourites to be from my personal features. Alas, not even my eyes made the list.'

Nancy gazed into his eyes with an intensity that made him feel breathless. There was nothing he wanted more than to pull her into his arms and kiss her worries away. But her secrets and his doubts stood between them. They walked for a while in silence. Matthew couldn't help but think there was more to Nancy's father's death than she was telling him. He wondered if her grandfather knew the entire truth.

Chapter Fifteen

A servant told Nancy that her grandfather wished to speak to her in the library. She went there immediately. She had not seen her grandfather during the day since Aunt Marianne had come to live with them. Her aunt told her that he spent most of his days at Horse Guards or Parliament, and his nights at his gentlemen's clubs. And she had not been invited into his presence since the day he introduced her to Aunt Marianne a month ago.

Why did he wish to see her now?

Goose bumps formed on her arms as she opened the door. Her grandfather sat behind his desk reading some papers. He looked older and more tired than he had when he'd introduced her to Aunt Marianne.

'Hello, Grandfather.'

He glanced up at her, then back down to the paper in front of him. 'Please sit down, Nancy.'

She gave him a forced smile and took her seat. For her to marry a gentleman, society had to believe that they were reconciled.

'I have just endured a conversation with your aunt,'

he said heavily. 'I am still recovering from the unpleasantness.'

'May I ask what it was about?'

'You,' her grandfather admitted. 'She wanted to know what your dowry will be, to enable her to present your prospects properly. It appears that an eligible young man has already taken an interest in you.'

Nancy was less interested in the suitor and more in the money. This could mean her financial freedom. 'The agreement between us was for twenty thousand pounds.'

He held up the paper he'd been reading. 'Your aunt wanted twice as much as that. She gave me the government documents you had in your possession. I shall see that they are returned discreetly. We have yet to discover who in the department leaked the information. Also, I have agreed to speak to my lawyers. Your portion upon marriage or your twenty-fifth birthday, will be forty thousand pounds. Your mother's dowry.'

Nancy gasped. In two years, she would be a wealthy and independent woman. Something that she'd never dreamed possible before. Even if she didn't marry, she would be safe. She would never know hunger or homelessness again. Never be forced with the choice of selling her body for sustenance. Nor dependent on such a fickle thing as love or her feelings for Matthew.

Her aunt had done this for her. No doubt that money would have gone to Aunt Marianne's own sons. Twenty thousand pounds was not an amount to sneeze at. If she ever doubted that her aunt cared for her before, she knew now that she did. Matthew had been right. Aunt Marianne was worthy of her trust and her confidences. She had helped clear up things with Alastair and ensured Nancy's future no matter what the outcome of her *ton* season.

Her grandfather stood and pulled out a stack of books on the shelf behind him revealing a safe. He opened it with a key from his desk—very easy for her to obtain—and brought out a jewellery box. Lifting the lid of the box, he handed Nancy a multistrand string of pearls.

'This necklace is for you. They were your mother's.'

For once, Nancy was more interested in their sentimental value than their worth. She held them reverently. The only token she had from her mother was her grandmother's memorial medallion. Next, her grandfather handed her the box and in it was a magnificent sapphire set with a necklace, bracelet, and pair of earbobs. Her old instincts kicked in and she evaluated their worth to be close to five thousand pounds on the black market. She let out a low whistle.

'These are the Brampton sapphires. They were made for my mother and have been worn by your grandmother and mother. They are a part of the estate, but you may wear them until you marry.'

Nancy fingered the jewels and thought that she had never seen anything more lovely, certainly, she'd never worn anything so expensive before. She would be displaying a fortune around her neck. In the slums, such gems would get her throat slit.

'The jewellery is kept in this safe, but your aunt wished for you to wear the pearls with your day gowns and the Brampton sapphires at your coming-out ball tonight to symbolise your acceptance into the family.' He paused for over a minute. 'Your mother wore them for her coming-out party, as well.'

Unexpectedly, a tear slid down her cheek. Nancy wished, as she had so many times before, that she had a real memory of her mother. Not just her father or Aunt Marianne's stories.

Her grandfather stood up and moved to sit by her. 'You never stop missing them.'

Nancy nodded; Matthew had said something similar earlier that day. 'I used to pray to her as a small child and tell her about my day. My father thought it was sweet, but my Scottish granny was shocked and forbade me to do it any more. She even took me to confess to a priest. I couldn't have been more than seven.'

'What did he tell you about her?'

She didn't need to ask her grandfather whom he meant by 'he'. 'Oh, Father loved to talk about Lady Susan. We never called her my mother. He said that she was the only person he loved more than me. He would tell me stories about her quiet wit. He loved her voice. He said that she sang to me from the day that I was made until I was born. But his favourite thing about her was how she danced. He swore that her feet never touched the floor.'

'Then you don't believe that he married my daughter for her money.'

'Oh, no. He did,' Nancy admitted. 'That's one lie my father never told me. He wanted to marry an heiress and he found a willing one. But what you don't understand, perhaps something someone like you could never understand, was that he felt honoured that such a fine and aristocratic lady loved him. How could he not worship her? Who knows if she had outlived childbirth, if they would have continued to be happy, but for the nine months they were together, living on her pawned jewels, they were. Poverty had not marked her yet.'

Her grandfather looked at her closely. 'Has poverty marked you?'

'Yes.' She didn't even attempt to lie. 'The scars are not only on my skin, they are on my soul. I cannot go into a room without judging how much each item inside of it would fetch. Nor meet a person, without knowing how many coins are in their pocket or coin purse. On average, you carry the enormous sum of twelve gold sovereigns in your right upper pocket... Lord Matthew carries ten guineas. Mostly, I've stolen money for food and blankets, but when my father and I started working with a London criminal lord, we stole anything and everything we were told to, in exchange for his protection. Including government secrets to a French agent.'

'Then your father had no morals.'

Nancy scoffed, shaking her head. 'Poor people cannot afford morals, my lord. Not if they want to eat and have a roof over their family's heads. Nor to be kept safe from rival slum bosses and criminal gangs. But you'll be happy to know that my father taught me one moral: *never steal from friends.*'

Even though apparently her father did not keep that rule either.

The older man swallowed heavily. 'And are we friends?'

'Well, you just gave me pearls and promised me a fortune on my twenty-fifth birthday,' Nancy said with a wry smile. 'I am definitely willing to try.'

Her grandfather awkwardly patted her on the hand.

'You'd best go get ready for tonight. I'll put back the pearls.'

Nancy turned over her hand and showed him the key to the safe in her palm. 'You'll be needing this.'

Grandfather laughed. A dry, raspy sound. 'I thought we were friends now.'

She placed the small key in his hand. 'We are. That is why I am giving it back to you.'

Nancy went to her bedchamber where her abigail was waiting. For the next two hours, Miss Arnold helped her dress for the ball. Nancy glanced down at her deceptively plain white gown with small tulip sleeves. It was low-cut, with lace and embroidered beads across her waistline. The same lace and beading on the flounces of her gown and train. Every curl was perfectly placed and the sapphire jewellery set brought attention to her eyes. She thanked her maid and turned to leave the room.

'Wait, miss,' Arnold said. 'You received two bouquets. You need to pick one to carry. Her Ladyship was quite insistent about that.'

For the first time, Nancy noticed the flowers on the table next to the door. One bouquet was of exquisite white lilies. Nancy sliced open the card with a flick of her knife and saw that it was from her cousin, Viscount Delfarthing, not Matthew. The note was only signed, no message. His mother might have welcomed her into the bosom of the family, but her cousin was still only doing his duty by her. She couldn't help but wish that it had been from Matthew.

Perhaps the next one would be. The second bouquet

was composed of white roses and blue forget-me-nots. Nancy opened the card and read.

> *Blue Eyes, please accept my humble offering in remembrance of our long friendship and continued acquaintance. Between us there can be no half-measures.*
>   *Sincerely, Sir Alastair Lymington*

She dropped it on the floor as if it were on fire. *Half-measures.* Did Alastair know that she'd only given him half of the documents? Nancy stooped down to pick the note up and read it again. Blue Eyes was an endearment that he'd given her when she was fourteen and joined his crew. She'd liked it then. She'd been going under the name Nancy Brown at the time and enjoyed a nickname that was all her own. One that was not a lie, like so much of her life was. She wished now that she had never bumped into him on Bond Street, or been tailed by Mick. If only he had never learned her true name!

Sighing, she picked up the white lilies and smelled them. If Alastair hadn't met her there, he would have at Frederica's ball. And he might even be invited tonight. Aunt Marianne had sent hundreds of invitations before Nancy had confided the truth of her acquaintance with the bad baronet.

'Thank you, Arnold. I will carry this one,' she said. 'Please put the other bouquet in a vase with some water.'

Nancy left the room, walking down to the entryway where her grandfather and aunt stood waiting. He handed her a narrow box with a silk ribbon bow on top of it.

'What is this?'

Grandfather raised his dark eyebrows and sighed. 'It was brought over by the Stringhams' footman an hour ago.'

Accepting it with trembling hands, Nancy's heart soared as she opened the lid and pulled out the most exquisite dagger she'd ever seen. It was encased in a leather pouch. There were rubies in the hilt and scroll-work on the blade. There was also a small note.

Happy coming-out ball. Matthew

Nancy's heart fluttered in her chest. Instead of giving her what society thought was appropriate, he'd bought a present that he'd thought she'd like and want. Her fingers gently closed over the hilt of the blade. 'It's beautiful.'

'But not appropriate for a party,' Aunt Marianne said, taking the box and dagger from her hands. 'Take this up to Miss Black's room and not a word of it to the other servants.'

Arnold bobbed a curtsy and took the box, before heading back up the stair to Nancy's bedchamber.

Grandfather gave her a rare smile of approval. 'Nancy, you look beautiful. I am proud that you are my granddaughter.'

'She does us both credit,' Aunt Marianne said stiffly, but the warmth in her eyes belied her formal words.

They all stood near the main door in the entry and greeted each guest as they arrived for the ball. Lord after lady entered the house and Nancy could read-ily believe why they called London parties 'notorious squeezes' for people seemed to be everywhere. Her aunt's tight smile seemed to widen as time went on. Her party was a success.

Nancy caught sight of a tall young man with blond hair—Matthew. He arrived with two of his sisters on his arms, Lady Glastonbury and Lady Frederica. They made polite small talk with her grandfather and aunt, before standing in front of her.

Lady Glastonbury pointed to Nancy's bouquet of white flowers. 'I told you, Matthew, that you should have sent her flowers.'

Frederica laughed, nudging her brother with her elbow. 'He got Nancy something better.'

Matthew cleared his throat and gave his sister a stern glare. 'Don't mention the weapon in front of others, Frederica. Show some discretion.'

'Like you did in the conservatory?'

Frederica giggled and so did Mantheria.

Matthew took both of his misbehaving sisters by their elbows and dragged them out of the entryway.

One of the last guests to arrive was Sir Alastair Lymington. Her aunt stiffened and gave him a griffin-like stare. Her grandfather, unaware of his criminal connection with her, greeted him warmly. Alastair had more fine lines around his eyes and mouth, but his smile was as beguiling as ever. He wore a fashionable suit of dark blue with high collar points and an exquisitely tied cravat in the mathematical style. In his left hand, he carried an ornate cane with a silver sphere on the end: his sword-stick. As always, Alastair was deadly.

He bowed over her gloved hand. 'Miss Black, how

enchanting you are this evening. Might I steal a waltz with you?'

Relieved, she pulled back her hand. 'I am afraid that they are all taken.'

'A country dance then.'

She lowered her head. 'I should be honoured.'

And then he moved on, this time leaning on his cane as he walked. Nancy knew that he didn't need support from the cane. She wondered if he was reminding her of how dangerous he was. He needn't have bothered. Her hands were clammy and her mouth dry. She knew just how vile he could be.

The very last guest to arrive was none other than Beau Brummell. Aunt Marianne hissed his name to her in an undertone. It was no surprise to Nancy that the man was an arbiter of fashion. His brown hair was swept in perfect disorder, the elegance of his suit unmatched, and his cravat was tied intricately to perfection. Unlike her dandified cousin, his dark suit was understated simplicity. He bowed to Nancy and her breath caught. He was not precisely a handsome man, but certainly an unforgettable one. Lifting his quizzing glass, he examined her with it.

The action caught her sense of humour and she gave him a dazzling smile. 'Do I meet your approval or shall you wink and ruin me?'

Beau Brummell dropped his quizzing glass and laughed. 'I do not wink, Miss Black. I merely raise one eyebrow.'

'Which one?'

'Which eyebrow?'

'Yes.'

'The left one.' He laughed again and then offered his arm, 'May I escort you into the ballroom? No doubt there are plenty of young bucks that will ask you to dance.'

She could hardly believe it. With one action, he was signalling not only his approval of her, but establishing her as a member of the *ton*. Something that not even her aunt's position as a viscountess was able to do.

Nancy took his arm. 'I believe that you don't intend to dance with me.'

'No indeed,' Brummell said, without apology. 'My escort is gift enough.'

'True,' Nancy agreed, finding herself smiling again. 'One should never be greedy. Especially when it comes to eyebrows.'

Brummell laughed in surprise and the many guests of the ball saw the pair at their finest. Nancy—unfortunately—opened the ball with her cousin, Viscount Delfarthing. And for a half an hour he did not say a syllable, nor was he an accomplished dancer. Her next three partners were much more agreeable and chattier. Nancy smiled when Cousin Basil came to claim his dance. Her triumph was his triumph, because he had selected the cut and cloth for her gown. He did not stop talking the entire set about how thrilled he was to have his idol, Beau Brummell, in attendance.

'And your Lord Matthew is a very good sort, coz,' he said, leading her off the dance floor after the music ended. 'He sent me two bottles of cologne.'

Nancy smiled bemusedly. She was glad that Matthew had not forgotten his promise to her cousin.

'Shall we dance another?' Basil asked. 'I didn't have

time to tell you all about my new snuff box with its very own little shovel. How whimsical.'

She pulled her hand from his. Basil was best enjoyed in brief conversations. 'I am afraid that—'

Alastair took her shaking hand before it could fall to her side. 'Miss Black has already given that dance to me.'

She hadn't, but Nancy didn't dare make a scene. Alastair knew too much. She allowed him to lead her back to the dance floor. This was not their first pairing. They'd danced together at much less elegant parties and buildings. On a couple of jobs, she'd even pretended to be his wife. Including the one time she'd met his cousin, the baronet who died.

Alastair stood on one side of the line and she on the other. The musicians struck up a song and the couples began to weave through the figures.

Taking Alastair's hand, she lied, 'I cannot thank you enough for your timely arrival. Cousin Basil is a bit tedious.'

'And there is certainly plenty of him.'

Feeling a need to defend her foppish and pure-hearted cousin, Nancy said, 'Beauty comes in all shapes and sizes.'

She was grateful that this particular country dance allowed her to spend almost half of her time away from her partner.

When their hands met, he said, 'You didn't wear my flowers, Blue Eyes.'

'I no longer answer to that name.'

'And I take it you are no longer Nancy Green or Nancy Brown or Nancy White?'

He knew all her aliases and so many of her past indiscretions. Just one of them would ruin her reputation in society. She had to handle him more carefully than a hot poker. 'My cousin, Viscount Delfarthing, sent these and I accepted, since I have ceased to play the role of your new bride.'

Alastair threw his head back and chuckled. 'I'd forgotten that. We made a rather splendid pair.'

They promenaded forward and then released hands. Alastair circled back and grasped Nancy's hand again in a bruising grip.

'We are no pair,' she gritted out.

He smirked. 'But think how useful you could be to me now. You live with the secretary of war. Political and military secrets are probably lying about in your home.'

Nancy's stays seemed to restrict her breathing, even though they were not tight. She never wished to work for Alastair again. She no longer needed his protection, nor his money. They clasped hands with the couple next to them and danced forward.

'And are you enjoying *your* new home, Sir Alastair?'

He inclined his head. 'Very much.'

'I daresay your cousin did too, until his untimely death,' she whispered so that only he could hear. 'You could ruin me. But I could also do the same to you.'

The musicians played their last note. Nancy and Alastair bowed to each other like worthy foes.

Alastair took her gloved hand. 'You forget, Blue Eyes. You helped me then and you will help me now. I want the other half of the government documents with the locations and supply lines. My French contact is growing impatient.'

Swallowing, Nancy tried not to allow her fear to show on her face. 'I don't have them in my possession any more.'

'Then get them back.'

He escorted her to the side of the room, where Matthew stood waiting beside Aunt Marianne for their waltz. She watched her old boss and her new admirer size each other up like roosters before a cockfight. They both had their chests out and stood at their very tallest. Matthew was several inches taller than Alastair, but the crime lord was broader. They were both extremely handsome men, but Matthew had a freshness to his looks and Alastair wore the weary mantle of experience. She thought that Alastair would have the better of Matthew in a street brawl.

Aunt Marianne bowed to Sir Alastair.

Nancy tugged her hand away from his and set it on Matthew's arm. 'It is our waltz, I believe. And I don't want to miss even one moment of it. Goodbye, Sir Alastair.'

Matthew gave her old friend one last glare, before escorting Nancy onto the dance floor and gathering her into his arms. The one place she truly felt safe.

Chapter Sixteen

Matthew couldn't stop himself from asking, 'Are those his flowers?'

Nancy glanced down at the bouquet attached to her hand. 'No. These are from my cousin, Viscount Delfarthing. We were unfortunately paired for the first two dances and he said not one full sentence.'

The burning sensation in his chest, lessened. 'Did he speak in fragmented sentences with dangling participles?'

She laughed, a light, pretty sound. 'I forgot. You are a wordsmith. Let's just say that he spoke in one-syllable words.'

Matthew opened his mouth to proclaim that he wasn't jealous of the viscount or the dance she'd shared with the rogue Lymington. But he closed it again, knowing that it was a downright lie. He'd never felt this way about a young woman before, nor had he ever known the pangs of jealousy. They made him feel possessive. He pulled her closer to him, keeping Nancy only for himself. He was also thinking in one syllable words: *Mine. Mine. Mine.*

'And Sir Alastair?'

The man who had once employed both herself and her father, who still seemed to have a hold over her.

Nancy flushed, a pretty pink in her once pale neck and cheeks. 'He only spoke in threats.'

His hand tightened on hers. 'How dare he threaten you in your grandfather's house? I should put him in his place.'

The pink on her neck turned to a blotchy red. 'There isn't anything Alastair wouldn't dare do. At any time. At any place... Please do not entangle yourself with him. Let us not waste our dance speaking of unpleasant things. You smell absolutely delicious. I've never encountered this particular scent before.'

His own temperature rose. She was changing the subject and he allowed her to. He needed to be patient. Let her know that she could trust him and come to him for help, instead of demanding her confidences. 'My mother made this cologne specifically for me.'

'So, no one else in the world smells exactly like you.'

Smiling, he said, 'I hope not.'

Nancy fluttered her long, dark eyelashes. It was easy to forget the danger she was in when he lost himself in the depths of her bright blue eyes. 'And no one has ever given me a dagger before either.'

'Flowers are entirely too cliché.'

She gurgled with laughter. 'I wish I could have worn a scabbard around my waist to display my new dagger like my flowers.'

Matthew's hand tightened on her waist, protectively. 'Stay away from Sir Alastair and you shouldn't need any weapon in your grandfather's house.'

She briefly leaned her head against his chest. 'I feel safe when I am with you.'

It wasn't the usual compliment for a suitor, but he knew that from Nancy it was the highest praise.

'Have I rendered you speechless?'

Matthew twirled her around. 'Utterly.'

'Where does a couple go at a party like this, if they wish to be private?'

He lowered his voice. 'They slip outside to the garden behind the house for a few minutes. Perhaps behind an obliging shrub or tree.'

Nancy stroked his back lightly with her hand. 'I've always been fond of obliging shrubs.'

Matthew needed no further encouragement to waltz her towards the back of the ballroom and surreptitiously to the back door. Pulling her against him, they hid briefly in the servant's stairwell to avoid another couple, before leaving the house. *Foolish amateurs,* he thought, echoing his sister Frederica's words.

Holding Nancy's hand, he did not take her behind the first shrub, nor even the second. He wanted to make certain that they would find no previous occupants. He led her to the edge of the property and a stone wall, with a lavender bush that conveniently blocked it from the view of the back door. It was impossible to see the little flowers in the dim light, but he'd grown up with a perfumer and he could recognise the scent of almost any flower or root.

Nancy's smile slowly built on her face in the shadowed moonlight. She was a beautiful mix of brightness and darkness. Matthew felt the hair rise on his arms and nape. He was suddenly light-headed as her arms stole around his neck and she pressed her body against his. Then after a moment of breathless anticipation, he slanted his mouth towards her luscious lips. With their first kiss, she'd been passive in the embrace. Unsure of what to do. But no longer. Nancy brushed her lips against his mouth in teasing little motions, driving him wild. When he didn't think his heart or his body could endure any more, she licked his lips with her honeyed tongue.

And for the first time in his life, Matthew felt speechless. Sentences could not possibly describe the sensations his body and heart were feeling. Metaphors would have been poor comparisons. Similes fell short. Perhaps only one small, four-letter word could begin to describe it: *love.* Still as a noun or as a verb, it was not nearly strong enough.

Matthew's hands encircled the narrowest part of her waist and he slightly parted his legs. He could not get close enough. Nancy's lips continued their attack and surrender upon his own. Her tongue darting into his mouth and tangling with his, in a pleasureful joust he'd never experienced before. His entire body shivered in response to her caresses. Her fingers moved over to his heart, feeling the pounding of it against his chest. Her touch aflamed him. He burned a trail of kisses from her mouth, down her throat, and to the edge of her gown. Gently, he tugged down the sleeve, exposing her shoulder, where it would not be seen. He sucked on her skin as she moaned. The sound drove him wild.

She leaned her head back slightly, still enclosed in his embrace. 'If this is a battle, I think I won.'

Matthew kissed her neck. 'Then let me surrender more fully.'

Nancy giggled softly. 'Next time.'

She straightened her sleeve and her hair. Matthew offered her his arm and they re-entered the house. She looked radiant and happy. As she deserved to be.

Chapter Seventeen

Nancy looked stunning in a yellow organdie dress at Almack's Assembly. Matthew would have to ask his grandfather's clothier factories to produce more organdie. The material seemed to float on her lovely frame. When she walked, he could see the small outline of her dagger on her thigh. He wondered how she had attached it there, but realised focusing on her leg was unwise at a public party. Nancy's eyes lit up when they met his and Matthew's heart did a little flip-flop. But before he could ask her to dance, she was awkwardly whisked away by her cousin, Viscount Delfarthing. Then for a second set by the dandy, Lord Norwich. Matthew could have growled at the earl like one of his father's lions.

He felt a sharp elbow to his stomach.

'Dance with someone for goodness' sake and stop watching Nancy like she's your prey,' Frederica said.

Reluctantly, he moved his gaze. 'Why aren't you dancing?'

Frederica tilted her head to the side in satisfaction. 'I've sent Lord Edgewell to fetch me some lemonade.'

Matthew huffed, folding his arms across his chest. 'Earls make decent footman, almost as good as a duke's son. And a lemonade is pretty much all the refreshment you can expect at an Almack's Assembly. That, weak tea, and thinly sliced day-old bread.'

His sister, like himself, had a healthy appetite. She wrinkled her nose at his accurate and unflattering description of the food.

Frederica rolled her eyes. 'Oh, dear. Edgewell has found me again.'

'Didn't you send him for a drink?'

'I was hoping that he would take a hint and be on his way.'

He watched his sister smile and thank the young man for the punch. The Earl of Edgewell's ears stuck out and his face was covered in red spots. He owned a draughty abbey in Warwickshire and was up to his protruding ears in debt. It was well-known among the *ton* that he needed to marry an heiress to save his estates. Still the fool had refused to sell a parcel of his land for Matthew's railroad.

'Lord Edgewell,' Frederica began, 'May I introduce you to my brother, Lord Matthew Stringham?'

Matthew gave him a curt nod. The young man appeared to be not much younger than himself, but the multitude of red spots on his face gave him a more youthful appearance. Unfortunately, in an unflattering way. 'We have met before. On a business matter.'

Edgewell bowed with a flourish of his arms, one hand hitting Nancy in the stomach. The poor man's face flushed with red and Matthew could see that Nancy was trying hard to hold in her laugh. The effort was causing her own face to colour.

'Do forgive me, Miss Black, I believe?'

'I believe I am Miss Black,' Nancy said with a friendly smile. 'And you are?'

He bowed again, but this time with less of an arm flourish. 'Lord Arthur Whitely, the Earl of Edgewell. I have heard much of your great beauty and none of it has been exaggerated.'

Frederica leaned closer and whispered in Matthew's ear. 'I think my fortune-hunter believes he has found an easier target.'

Matthew snorted. 'I wouldn't have thought her twenty-thousand-pound dowry sufficient to meet his debtors.'

Nancy's upper lip curled and she began to speak in French. '*Est-ce que tu profites du ballon?*'

Edgewell bowed to her, speaking in flawless French. '*Oui, oui, mademoiselle.*'

It took Matthew a moment longer to translate what she had said because she had spoken so quickly: she'd asked if the man was enjoying the party.

'How very accomplished you are Miss Black to speak French so well,' Lord Edgewell said. 'Almost with no accent. May I ask who taught you?'

'*Une prostituée,*' Nancy said, smiling at the other young man. '*Je jure comme un marin.*'

Lord Edgewell's face turned the same colour as his spots a second time when Nancy said that a prostitute had taught her French. She also claimed to swear like a sailor, causing Matthew's sister to break out into a peal of laughter. He couldn't help but smile at her. Frederica took a sip of her lemonade.

Edgewell gave a jerky nod. 'May I have the next dance, Miss Black?'

'How kind,' she said finally in English. 'But Lord Matthew has reserved my next two dances and it has been impressed on me by my aunt, that she will choose all my partners. She doesn't wish for me to be taken in by a fortune-hunter.'

Frederica handed the young earl her empty glass. Matthew offered his arm to Nancy and his other to his sister and they left Edgewell standing alone looking ridiculous.

'I haven't been so amused in months,' Frederica said with a laugh. 'Tell me the name of the incognita that taught you French.'

Matthew watched Nancy for her reply.

She blinked twice before answering, 'Giselle. At least that is her stage name.'

He was not in the business of purchasing a woman's favours, but he had heard of the courtesan Giselle, a flawlessly beautiful Frenchwoman. Perhaps he would pay for her company after all and see what she knew about Nancy, Alastair, and the late Mr Felix Black.

Frederica laughed merrily. 'That's famous! Where did you meet her?'

But before Nancy could speak, Mr Pratt came and asked Frederica for the next dance. She released Matthew's arm and left them both without another glance.

'I hope you don't think I am a fortune-hunter.'

'No,' she said archly. 'You're hunting after much bigger game.'

He raised his eyebrows. 'And that is?'

Nancy smiled at him. 'My heart.'

His own organ was behaving most irregularly, clenching inside his chest. 'And do I have a chance?'

She leaned closer to him. 'You'll have to wait and see. You don't know all of my secrets yet, Matthew. And once you know them, perhaps it is *you* who will change your mind. I care for you too much to trick you into a relationship that you will someday regret.'

Matthew doubted anything Nancy had done could change the way he felt about her. Like the thief she was, she had already stolen his love.

'Lord Matthew, I declare it has been an age since I last saw you,' Lady Jersey said, beaming at him. 'What new exotic creature has your father bought from Sir Frederick to rehabilitate at Hampford Castle?'

'A caracal. He believes it has a connection to the ancient lynx.'

'I want to see it. Tell your mother to send me an invitation to her next house party. I declare no one throws better parties than the Duchess of Hampford.'

Matthew politely nodded. 'Of course, Lady Jersey. Are you at all acquainted with the Earl of Brampton's granddaughter, Miss Black?'

Nancy curtsied to her.

Lady Jersey smiled, nodding her head. 'What a charming young woman you are. I knew that you had to be, for this is the first time in nearly five years that Lord Matthew has graced the rooms of Almack's Assembly. But I daresay, he doesn't care if I make your acquaintance or not, he simply wants me to give you permission to waltz. And how can I refuse such a handsome young man? Miss Black, you may waltz with whomever you choose.'

'Thank you, my lady,' Nancy said with another curtsy.

'You are most welcome, my dear girl,' Lady Jersey said, winking at her. 'I am quite jealous you know. Do save a waltz for me later, Lord Matthew.'

He bowed. 'If you'll keep your *Silence*, it would be my pleasure.'

The older lady tittered with laughter as Matthew took Nancy by the hand and led her to the dance floor. With one seamless movement, he brought her into his arms. Nancy smiled up at him. There was a tie between them. Some intangible pull that held them close.

'You should have asked me if I could waltz at Almack's,' Nancy said. 'I already have Lady Sefton's permission. And you rushed us away from Lady Jersey quickly as if there was a fire.'

He twirled her around. '*Silence* is always talking. I didn't want her to waste my entire waltz with you.'

'That would have been a great pity.'

'I might have cried.'

Nancy's lips broke into a smile and a laugh bubbled out of her. 'Me too.'

Matthew felt the familiar thrill of pulling her into his arms and holding her close to him. He only wished it could have been closer. That neither society, nor secrets stood between them.

Nancy squeezed his hand, smiling at him. 'Five years is a long time to avoid the famous Almack's Assembly. May I ask why?'

Pressing his hand into her back, he led her in a turn avoiding another couple. 'I swore off Almack's and all *ton* parties that were a part of the marriage mart after the failure of my first love. I realised it was all spectacle and no substance.'

She looked down, her dark eyelashes against her pale cheeks. He could see a few light freckles.

'Did she break your heart?'

'No, but she hurt my pride,' he admitted. 'I was all of one and twenty, and a scholar fresh from Oxford. I suppose I was easy pickings. Lady Annabelle Lindsay used me to bring the Earl of Trent up to scratch. I thought I loved her and that she loved me. I begged her to know why she had accepted the hand of a man more than twice her age. I suppose she could have lied to me, but she said that second sons were of no use to her. Particularly when they were connected with trade.'

Nancy bit her lower lip.

A surge of desire burned through his body. He wanted to take that plump lower lip between his own teeth and suck on it.

'Surely, not all young ladies of the *ton* are like Lady Trent?'

Matthew scoffed. 'No, some debutantes are willing to look over my unfortunate birth order and smell of the shop in exchange for my fortune. I am not interested in those young ladies either. I wish to be loved for myself alone.'

Nancy finally met his eyes. 'I care for you greatly. But I might be a fortune-hunter, Matthew. I want a home of my own and security more than anything else in the world. All my life, I've wished to feel safe.'

'There is safety in love,' he whispered. 'And even more in trust.'

She nodded, but her eyes fell from his. Nancy had admitted to caring for him, but she wasn't ready to trust him with all of her secrets. It smarted a little, but Matthew had grown up in a large and loving family that had several homes. He'd never once known want or fear. Nancy had enjoyed none of those privileges. It would take her longer to believe that he would not discard her or use her, like her father and Alastair had.

The waltz ended entirely too quickly, as did the country dance after that. Matthew should have brought her back to her aunt, but instead, he took Nancy to greet his mother. It was never difficult to find the Duchess of Hampford in a room. Matthew's mother was a tall woman with a queenly bearing to match her height. Besides, tonight she wore a blue turban with feathers that reached well above his own six feet.

Nancy smiled, but she didn't show her teeth. She sunk into a deep curtsy that was more fit for a queen, but his mother didn't seem to mind.

'Miss Black, my daughter said that you helped get rid of the impecunious Lord Edgewell.'

Nancy tucked her chin and laughed. 'I am glad my common French was useful.'

He was relieved that Nancy hadn't told his mother that she knew how to swear like a sailor in French. Nor that she had learned it from a famous courtesan. Neither titbits would have met with his mother's approval.

Mama's lips did not smile, but her eyes did. 'Do you speak any other languages?'

'Irish and Gaelic, Your Grace,' she said, with a bow of her head. 'My Scottish granny taught me Gaelic and Irish as a child. I thought Irish was our secret language.'

Matthew wondered why. Another one of Nancy's secrets that he longed to discover.

Mama folded her arms. The edges of her lips slightly upturned. 'Frederica tells me that you are quite handy with a knife.'

A little colour stole into Nancy's cheeks. 'Dagger-drawing is hardly a ladylike accomplishment, Your Grace, but I have found it to be a useful one.'

His mother nodded. 'I couldn't agree more. A lady should always be able to defend herself, should the need arise.'

'And a gentleman, too, no doubt?' Matthew added with a saucy wink.

Mama huffed. 'I daresay you would simply talk your way out of trouble, like you do with everything else that you don't want to do.'

Nancy let out a gurgle of laughter.

Matthew brought his hand to his chest. 'You malign me, Mama.'

Both Nancy and his mother stopped smiling and he looked over his shoulder to see Viscountess Delfarthing coming towards them. The Nose had her most prominent feature high in the air. His mother stiffened and Nancy swallowed.

Viscountess Delfarthing bowed her head a little, still keeping her hooked aristocratic nose at attention. 'I believe, Lord Matthew, that a gentleman is supposed to return a young lady to her chaperone after a dance.'

He swept the Nose an exaggerated bow. 'Forgive me, Viscountess. I wished to expand Nancy's acquaintance with my mother.'

'I am sure you mean, Miss Black,' she said haughtily.

'Such familiarity with my niece's name could result in unpleasant gossip that she can ill afford.'

Glancing at Nancy, he saw her gritting her teeth. Her position in society was precarious because of her birth and her past.

'Or in accurate truths,' he countered. 'The *ton* could safely assume that I am courting your niece and that I intend to marry her by the end of summer.'

Nancy gasped.

Neither his mother nor Viscountess Delfarthing appeared to be pleased. Matthew couldn't help but grin at the expressions on their faces.

His mother recovered first. 'Lady Delfarthing, it would appear that we will soon be connected quite closely. I suppose we ought to get to know one another a bit better. I thought I saw your son, Viscount Delfarthing, earlier this evening.'

'You did, Your Grace,' the Nose said. 'But it appears that my son has slipped away whilst I was keeping a watchful eye on my niece.'

'Children rarely do what you wish them to,' Mama said.

Viscountess Delfarthing bowed her head. 'Truer words have never been spoken. Come, Nancy. You already have a partner for the next dance. Lord Matthew, Your Grace.'

Matthew took Nancy by the elbow and whispered in her ear, 'Come to my grandfather's house tomorrow for dinner. I will send a card with the address. We'll have more time to talk there.'

Releasing her arm, he watched as the Nose dragged Nancy away and led her to dance with Lord Norwich again. The earl had a glittering sense of style; his dark green suit sparkled. Emeralds adorned the buckles of his shoes and his fingers. An ugly surge of jealously reared in Matthew's chest, until Nancy turned back and smiled at him. With his words and actions, he was slowly wearing down her defences.

Despite being out until the wee hours the night before, Matthew arrived at eight o'clock sharp to his place of business. His secretary, Mr Howitt, had still beat him there.

He opened the door to Matthew's office. Thanking him, Matthew couldn't think of a butler who had done the job with more dignity. Howitt was intelligent, efficient, and deserving of a rise in salary.

'Would Your Lordship like to go over the quarterly numbers this morning?'

Matthew took a seat behind his desk. 'Yes, I would. But first, I should like you to schedule the company of the courtesan Giselle this afternoon. Do you know who she is?'

His secretary dropped his book, the little brown one that he kept all of his notes in, his cheeks suffused with colour. 'Yes, Giselle is famous. I believe gentlemen have to book her favours several weeks, if not months, in advance.'

Matthew waved a hand. 'I don't care how much it costs, I want to speak to her tonight before dinner. She is the final piece of the puzzle.'

Mr Howitt's face was now red. 'Yes, my lord.'

'And I have an odd request that you are welcome to say no to.'

His secretary raised one perfectly trimmed eyebrow. 'My lord?'

'Would you be willing to become a butler for Sir Alastair Lymington for a week or two? I shouldn't think it would last much longer than that. I want to know everything that happens in his house on Half Moon Street and where he spends his time and with whom.'

'I should be happy to assist you in any way,' Mr Howitt said. 'Am I to get rid of his current butler?'

Matthew had quite forgotten about him. 'Please.'

'Should you like to know how, my lord?'

Matthew leaned back in his chair and placed his hands behind his head, interlocking his fingers. 'Probably best if I don't. And I will double your current salary. I see that I have quite underestimated your abilities.'

Mr Howitt pulled out the little brown book again. 'About the other matter. Your tip about the different colours for last names proved to be invaluable, my lord.'

Chapter Eighteen

'I hope you don't mind if you have a few extras for dinner this evening,' Matthew said, standing in the door frame of his grandfather's office.

Rubbing his long beard, Grandfather Stubbs barked a laugh. 'Am I to send a note to your grandmother informing her that we are hosting a party?'

'Yes.'

His grandfather picked up his cane and pointed it at Matthew. 'I suppose one of them must be the Miss Nancy Black that Frederica keeps telling us about. It would appear that your intentions are becoming quite marked.'

Matthew came into the office and sat down on the chair closest to the desk. 'For a man renowned for his bluntness, that was remarkably tactful.'

His grandfather chortled again. 'Is that the polite way of telling me to mind my own business?'

'No, sir. I hope to marry Miss Black.'

Grandfather nodded. 'I'll have your grandmother send her family a note, as well. Rumours say she's a pocket Venus, but despite her connection to Lord

Brampton, her lineage is not without surprises. Both Irish and Scottish and not the aristocratic kind. Still, they say Brampton is all but bribing a suitor for the girl by offering forty thousand pounds for her dowry... I thought you weren't interested in making a financial marriage.'

Matthew stiffened in his chair. 'You know I am not. I don't give a fig for her fortune. And it's pretty rich coming from the son of a grocer, to hold a woman's parentage against her.'

His grandfather laughed the loudest yet. 'Aye. I can tell you aren't interested in her fortune. But what is holding you back? According to my secretary, they are offering odds at both Waiter's and White's on whether or not you'll offer for her.'

'I love her, but I would not advise you to take that bet just yet...'

Grandfather gave him a piercing look. 'Are you not going to tell me why?'

Matthew shrugged his shoulders. He wasn't sure if Nancy would say yes yet. She was keeping her cards close to her chest and her secrets even closer. He thought if he rushed his fences that she would refuse him without ever trusting him enough to tell him the truth. Or let him help her with whatever Alastair had over her head. 'Can't. It would muck up my plan of attack. But I was wondering, since you're such a gossip, what do you know about Sir Alastair Lymington? I've heard that he inherited a great deal of debt from his cousin.'

'Which he settled with his private means,' his grandfather said.

'How did Sir Alastair Lymington acquire *his private means*?'

Grandfather tugged at his beard. 'A good question. Rumour is that he didn't inherit the money from his own father and he didn't earn his fortune in trade, elsewise I would have heard of him before now. How the new baronet acquired his private means was not through respectable channels. No one seems to know much about him until after his cousin died.'

'By the by, how did Sir Gervase Lymington die?'

'An unknown sickness that caused sores, hallucinations, spasms, and vomiting. The rumour spread about was that the baronet died of the French pox, but the onset and speed of the death is a bit curious to me.'

Matthew leaned forward in his chair. 'How so?'

'Sir Gervase died within two days of his first symptom. It was rumoured that his cousin and his beautiful young wife had come to visit. They were with him when he died and attended the funeral.'

Could the 'beautiful young wife' have been Nancy? Swallowing, he asked, 'How do you know so much about his death?'

'Sir Gervase owed a colleague, Mr Ackerman, a great deal of money. Ackerman told me that the new Baronet of Buckley paid the debts in full. He also shared with me his speculations on the former baronet's death. But the most interesting part is that Sir Alastair Lymington does not have a wife in town. I wonder if she also succumbed to the illness?'

Matthew shook his head. 'Or if she was really his wife at all?'

'Exactly,' Grandfather said.

* * *

Aunt Marianne was not pleased when she learned that Nancy had accepted a dinner invitation without her. 'You cannot go without me and I cannot go with you. I have plans with Lady Finch that I cannot break.'

Her grandfather walked into the room. 'I will accompany my granddaughter.'

Nancy's heartbeat raced. She hadn't eaten dinner with her grandfather since the first night that she stayed in his London home. 'I…I am sure Lord Matthew could escort me, sir. You need not put yourself out.'

'I am not put out and you need a proper chaperone,' he said. 'I also suppose that it is time to meet Mr Stubbs. I have purchased goods from him for the army. Perhaps I have been too aloof in refusing to do business with him directly. He seems to be an honourable man, for a tradesman.'

'You'll probably get a better bargain from Mr Stubbs,' Nancy said, smirking. 'His grandson charges you snobbery fees.'

Aunt Marianne choked on a laugh that turned into a snort. She brought her handkerchief up to her face to cover her glee.

Nancy covered her own mouth with her hand. She should not have betrayed Matthew's confidence.

Her grandfather cleared his throat. 'Perhaps in the near future, I will receive the family discount. I'll have the carriage pick us up at seven o'clock.'

He left the room and Aunt Marianne lost her control. She laughed and laughed until she cried. Her handkerchief proved handy in dabbing at the tears running down her face. 'I'm beginning to like Lord Matthew despite myself. He is an original.'

'I care for him too,' Nancy whispered as they both sobered. 'I have told him bits of my past, but not the worst parts. I do not think that I can accept his proposal until I tell him everything. He deserves so much more in a wife than a former criminal.'

'He's not asking for your past,' Aunt Marianne said, wiping her nose, 'He's asking for your future and I wouldn't tell him a single thing that would give him an aversion of you. What he does not know will not hurt him. Now go and get dressed. You'll need to impress Mr Stubbs. It is rumoured that the wealthy tradesman intends to leave most of his fortune and business to his grandson.'

Nodding, Nancy left the room to get ready for the evening. A process that took over an hour. Her lady's maid picked a crimson gown that flattered her darker colouring. The white pearls gleamed against her skin and the red of the dress. Arnold added a few pearl pins to her ebony curls, but left several ringlets falling down her back out of her chignon. It was a daring and very flattering hair style.

'Will you be needing anything else, Miss Black?'

Nancy shook her head. 'Thank you. That will be all.'

Sitting on her bed, she was more than half tempted to ignore Aunt Marianne's advice and tell Matthew the whole terrible truth. But if she did, she risked losing him. The one good thing in her life. A handsome man who promised her a loving and safe future. One where she didn't have to sleep with a dagger or glance over her shoulder when she walked down the street. She'd told him that she cared for him, but that was a gross understatement. He filled her thoughts. Her hopes. And Matthew had even taught her to dream. She wanted to trust him. To tell him everything.

But trusting him would make him not love her any more.

Chapter Nineteen

Matthew's carriage brought him to a building near Drury Lane. He knew that many actresses played roles both on the stage and off. He'd never been tempted before to hire a private performance. A groom opened the door to his carriage and guided him into a house. It was decorated in scarlet and opulent to the point of vulgarity. He supposed that it was fitting for a bawdy house.

A woman of uncertain years with a low-cut dress, bowed to him. 'My lord, how honoured we are for you to give us your custom.'

He pulled the coin purse from his pocket that Mr Howitt had prepared and handed it to the woman. 'I appreciate the pleasantries, but I grow impatient to see Giselle.'

The woman placed the coin purse between her ample breasts. 'If you would follow me, my lord.'

Matthew trailed her up the stairs and to a room at the back of the hall. The woman knocked three times before turning the silver handle of the door. She gestured for him to go inside. 'Giselle is waiting for you.'

Swallowing, he walked through the door frame and

had barely stepped into the room when the door behind him was closed with a thud.

'Your first time here, my lord?' a sultry voice said with a decided French accent.

His eyes swivelled to the bed; she was spread out upon it wearing a dressing gown that showed more than it hid. Her dark curly hair was spread artistically over the pillow. Her face was painted and her lips were the crimson red of fresh blood. He covered his eyes. 'Do put on a robe or banyan, please. I am not here for your favours, but for information.'

It was silent for a few moments and then he heard the sound of movement and the swish of fabric.

'I am covered now, my lord,' she said, her voice cold. 'You may ask your questions and I will choose whether or not I answer them.'

Matthew lowered his hands and saw that she was wearing a silk robe whose only virtue had to be that it wasn't see-through. 'I believe that you are acquainted with Miss Nancy Black. That you even taught her how to speak French.'

She glanced down at her painted fingernails. 'I do not know anyone by that name.'

'Perhaps you know her as Nancy Brown or Nancy Green?' he pressed.

Giselle shrugged one elegant shoulder. 'Maybe I do. Maybe I do not. Why should I tell you, my lord?'

He cleared his throat. 'I paid a great deal of money for this interview.'

The courtesan placed her hands on the knot of her robe. 'Then let us stall no longer.'

Matthew held up his arm. 'Keep your robe on. Perhaps you will be more willing to give me information when I tell you that I intend to marry Miss Nancy Black.'

Giselle's hands tightened on her sash, but still she kept her red lips closed.

Sighing, Matthew added, 'I am also aware that she was involved in criminal activities when her father, Felix, was alive. I believe that you were a part of the same criminal gang. Sir Alastair Lymington was your leader until he ascended to his baronetcy. Now he seems to be getting rid of anyone who remembers his less than stellar past. My secretary discovered that Felix, Bones, Charles, Lily, and Peter, have all disappeared. I managed to find Mick first and gave him safe passage to a new life. The only person left is you.'

'If you know so much, why are you here?'

He cleared his throat. 'There are a few missing pieces that I still need to put Alastair in prison and keep Nancy, and consequently yourself, safe.'

Giselle turned her head, wrapping her arms around herself. 'If I tell you anything, he will kill me.'

'Alastair will kill you either way,' Matthew said flatly. 'Like he killed Lily and made it look like an overdose by locking the door from the inside.'

The blood drained from her painted face, making her cosmetics look even more bright and garish. 'How do you know that?'

'Mick was tailing Alastair at the time. And like him, I can help you start again.'

'I don't want a new life,' Giselle snapped. 'I want to live this one. I have worked hard to become the most desirable courtesan in London.'

'Very well,' he said, folding his arms. 'Help me to

implicate Alastair. Who was the lord who arranged to have him steal those papers? Documents that should never have left the Horse Guards?'

She waved a hand. 'Alastair never tells me the names of the clients he brings to me.'

Matthew considered this. 'Then how did Nancy know where to steal them from?'

Giselle wrapped one slender hand around the column of her throat. 'I made the mistake of mentioning the job to Felix, assuming that he would be the one who would do the theft. He must have learned who the lord was from another member of the gang. We did not know Alastair's plans for him.'

'Then do you know who Alastair sold or intends to sell the papers too?' he asked. 'Who the French spy is?'

'*Non*,' she said, holding herself even tighter and shaking her head.

'Do you know what hold Alastair has over Nancy?'

'Alastair does not share his secrets,' she whispered. 'But once Nancy is done being useful to him, he will remove her from his way.'

Goose bumps formed on his arms; Matthew touched his hat. 'Thank you for your time, mademoiselle, and for your information.'

Her grandfather did not speak for the first few minutes of the carriage ride. He sat on the opposite seat from her and resolutely stared out the window. She couldn't help but wonder why he'd insisted on accompanying her. Nancy fiddled with her skirt, feeling the comforting outline of her dagger underneath the silk.

'How is your season going?' he asked.

Nancy gave a breathy laugh. 'Better than I expected.'

Grandfather grunted. 'It seems that your relationship with Lord Matthew is progressing.'

'Do you not approve of him as a suitor?'

'How could I not? He's the son of a duke and wealthy into the bargain. Even the highest sticklers in England could not argue with his birth and breeding.'

Swallowing, she asked, 'Then what is the problem?'

Her grandfather took a deep breath and exhaled. Nancy scooted forward in her seat, waiting for his response.

'You will be leaving. And sooner than I thought.'

Snorting, she shook her head. 'But that is what you want. You gave me a large dowry so that I could catch the attention of young eligible men—like a carrot before a donkey. So that you could be rid of me.'

You never wanted me.

'I don't wish to be rid of you.'

Nancy couldn't help but snort again. 'You have almost nothing to do with me. Weeks have passed and I've rarely had a glimpse of you. Why should you care if I go or if I stay in your home?'

He intertwined his fingers in his lap. 'I am afraid that if you leave, you will never come back.'

Unwanted tears filled her eyes and her muscles felt numb. 'Why would you care? You don't even know me.'

Her grandfather nodded wearily. 'I know that I don't, and that is my greatest regret.'

Wiping at her running nose, she said, 'Not casting off your only daughter? I should think that would rank slightly higher on your conscience.'

'You said your father never held that against me.'

'But I did,' Nancy said, stabbing her finger into her own chest like a knife. 'I was no adventurer. I am your granddaughter and I have lived in squalor for most of my life. Hoping for another meal, not knowing if there is rent for the next week... Only to learn as a young woman, that I had a wealthy grandfather who wanted nothing to do with me.'

'Your father didn't mention me before then?'

She leaned back against the seat. 'He rarely visited my grandmother's cottage and when he did, he only mentioned Lady Susan. As a child, I wanted to know all about my mother. I did not even know you existed. Then Grandmother died and my father came to fetch me to live with him in Edinburgh at his new gaming house.'

'That must have been a great change.'

'Yes,' Nancy said with a sniff. 'I was a girl. I was inconvenient, so he dressed me as a boy. We lived above the gaming house until one night he lost it in a game of cards. We fled Edinburgh under the cover of darkness. I assume my father owed more people money. We came to London with new names and moved often, depending on my father's luck at the cards or where his criminal jobs took him.'

Her grandfather was quiet again for several moments, before asking. 'Why did you become a criminal?'

'Because I thought it was a better job than being a whore.'

He cringed at the word. 'Surely there were more choices?'

Nancy laughed, but there was no mirth in it. 'For a woman of little education and no money, the prospects are very bleak. Some are able to find work at a factory, but the hours are long and the pay is little. Even if it's respectable work, the male supervisor often preys on the female employees. When my father was in Newgate Prison, a madam took me in. And in my ignorance and trust, I signed away my life.'

'Why did you not come to me then?'

She released a shuddering breath. 'My father told me to and I tried. But I was turned away at the kitchen door like a dirty rat.'

Her grandfather flinched. 'I did not know.'

'Earls know very little about how the rest of the world lives,' she said. More tears filled her eyes. 'Growing up, my father was the only person that I could wholly trust and even he lied to me.'

'Yet, you still love him.'

Tears streamed down her face. 'Yes, but I hate him too… Like I love and hate you… You both abandoned me, but then you also took care of me.'

'You love me?' he said as if that was the most surprising thing he had learned during their conversation.

Wiping her nose with her handkerchief, she smiled through her tears. 'I was born a mercenary. I would love anybody who gave me forty thousand pounds.'

He laughed, a raspy, unpractised sound.

Then they chortled together. Tears still falling down Nancy's cheeks.

Her grandfather sobered first. 'I am here tonight, because I wish to be a part of your life, Nancy. I want to know you and I long to earn your trust.'

'I would like that,' Nancy whispered, and it was true.

Chapter Twenty

'You're doing what?' Matthew asked, louder than he'd meant to.

Mantheria blushed, but not because she had invited herself to the family dinner he had also invited people to without asking his grandparents first. 'I am going with Glastonbury, Lady Dutton, and Andrew to Italy at the end of the summer. My husband had a stroke and his health is failing. His doctors have suggested that he try a warmer, drier climate.'

'Good riddance,' Frederica said, running a finger across her throat.

Matthew wholeheartedly agreed. His sister had separated from her much older husband three years before, because he was all but living with his mistress, Lady Dutton. The parting had been mostly amicable, not that Matthew hadn't used the contracts to make the aging lecher pay for cheating on his sister, *literally*. The Duke of Glastonbury now lived openly with his mistress, Lady Dutton, but he still spent a great deal of time with his only child. His son and heir, Andrew.

'Won't it be a trifle awkward, darling?' Mama asked.

Throwing up her hands, Mantheria huffed. 'Of course, it will be awkward! I will be travelling with my estranged husband, our child, and his mistress.'

'Then why are you going?' Matthew couldn't help but ask.

His sister touched her forehead, sighing. 'Because Andrew wants to go with him and he won't go without me.'

'Fine. Go as a family,' Frederica said. 'But Lady Dutton should remain in England. She has done enough damage to your family.'

'Glastonbury would not dream of leaving Lady Dutton behind. And honestly, I would prefer that she looked after him rather than me,' Mantheria said, rubbing her temples. 'I will have plenty to occupy myself with Andrew.'

'But you'll have to see *her* every day,' Mama said.

Matthew folded his arms. 'You should have let Wick shoot your husband when he offered.'

Frederica snorted and his mother tried to hold in her laugh, but she couldn't quite do it. Even Mantheria giggled.

'I don't suppose you'd like me to call him out for a duel? Frederica could be my second. She's a better shot than me.'

Mantheria shook her head. 'It would break Andrew's heart. Despite the duke's many defects, he is a doting father.'

Frederica plunked down in a chair and sprawled her long limbs out. 'I can go with you if you like. Then you'll have someone besides Lady Dutton to speak to.'

'But you're a debutante,' Mama protested. 'You can't go to Italy.'

His little sister yawned. 'I know and it's terribly dull. I should much rather travel with Mantheria. And if I get a chance, I will wheel her husband's chair into a canal. No one will be any the wiser.'

Matthew barked a laugh.

His mother shook her head, but there was a hint of a smile on her lips. 'How did I raise such a blood-thirsty lot?'

'I own, I should like your company if it is all right with Mama,' Mantheria said.

Both of his sisters gave doe-eyed looks to their mother.

'But you are already nineteen, Frederica. You really should be taking marriage more seriously.'

Waving one hand, Frederica scoffed. 'Oh, Mama. We all know that you intend for me to marry Samuel and nothing will bring him faster to England than the knowledge that *I* am on the same continent as him.'

Matthew chuckled again, but was given a quelling look by their mother.

Mama took a deep breath. 'If that is what you wish, Mantheria, then Frederica may accompany you.'

His younger sister bounded out of her chair and hugged their mother, Mantheria, and then Matthew, for good measure.

'What is the good news?' Grandfather Stubbs asked from the doorway.

Before anyone could answer, Frederica nearly flattened him with a hug. 'I'm going to Italy! Isn't that so exciting, Grandpapa?'

He released Frederica and leaned heavily on his cane before answering. 'Very exciting, my love.'

'I hope you mean to behave yourself like a proper young Englishwoman,' Grandmother Stubbs added from behind him. She was a thin, elegant woman, with dark hair streaked with grey, brown eyes, and very proper opinions and manners.

Matthew tried to turn his laugh into a cough. His sister Frederica would never be a proper young Englishwoman. He felt her sharp elbow connect with his ribs. 'Ow!'

'I think I hear a carriage,' Mama said. 'Everyone sit down, and at least appear to have good manners.'

It was moments like this that Matthew could see the influence of his grandmother on her stepdaughter, his mother. He took a seat and picked up a book on calculus.

A little light reading before dinner, he thought wryly.

A few moments later, the butler opened the door for the Earl of Brampton and Nancy. Only a month had passed, but Lord Brampton looked older than the last time Matthew had done business with him. His face was more lined. But Matthew had no pity for a man who abandoned his own blood, like he had Nancy. At first glance, he thought that she did not resemble her maternal grandfather at all. Truly the only feature they had in common was the shape, size, and colour of their eyes—a bright blue, piercing in their intensity. Both pairs of blue eyes surveyed his family.

Matthew and the rest of his family stood to welcome them. Once everyone curtsied or bowed, respectively, his grandmother asked for everyone to be seated.

'What a beautiful home, Mrs Stubbs,' Lord Brampton said in a warmer tone than he'd ever spoken to Matthew with. 'I cannot thank you enough for including myself and my granddaughter in your invitation. My daughter-in-law would have enjoyed being here as well if she didn't have a previous engagement.'

Grandmother Stubbs inclined her head. 'I have learned from my husband that as much business can be accomplished at a dinner party as in an office.'

Matthew's eyebrows went up. His grandmother was referring to the lord secretary's refusal to work with Grandfather directly because of his lack of rank. It was the only gibe he'd ever heard her utter. She was usually a pattern card of propriety, but maybe that wasn't when her husband had been snubbed.

'I look forward to doing both with your husband in the future,' he said in a quieter voice. 'I have heard that Mr Stubbs doesn't charge snobbery fees, unlike your grandson, and extra charges for being a pompous windbag.'

Frederica was the first to burst out laughing, but soon everyone in the room had a chuckle at both him and the Earl of Brampton's remark. Nancy put her hand through her grandfather's arm, but her gaze was on Matthew. He could scarce credit the lord secretary's transformation, but perhaps zebras could change their stripes after all.

At dinner, Nancy was seated on his right side. He whispered to her in an undertone, 'I am surprised to see Brampton here.'

'As am I,' she said, looking at him, her eyes wet with unshed tears. 'But I am glad that my grandfather is. He wants to be a part of my life.'

Matthew set his napkin in his lap. 'Does that mean I have to like him now, too?'

'Will it be terribly difficult?'

'Yes, it will,' he said, not attempting to lie. 'But for you, I would suffer the company of a thousand feck-*less* lord secretaries.'

She giggled. 'How grace-*less* of you to say.'

'I'm hope-*less*.'

Nancy winked at him. ''Tis better than being aim-*less*.'

'Or worse, love-*less*.'

Her cheeks turned a pretty pink, but she offered a rejoinder, 'Doubt-*less*.'

'You make me feel help-*less*.'

'And you make me feel fear-*less*.'

Matthew hoped that it was true and not merely a play on words. He knew there were horrors in her past and he wanted to make her feel safe. 'Every minute without you feels end-*less*.'

'And meaning-*less*.'

'Even words are use-*less*.'

She toyed with her fork. 'And food is taste-*less*.'

'You have left me speech-*less*.' And it was true. Matthew had always used language to get his way, but he did not know what words to say to help Nancy trust him. Love him.

After a few moments of silence, she whispered to him, 'And me defence-*less*.'

Maybe his love for her was not purpose-*less* after all.

Chapter Twenty-One

'Nancy,' Aunt Marianne said with a smile over breakfast. 'I have arranged for you and your cousins to go riding this afternoon in the park.'

She forced her lips to go up in a painful smirk. She knew her aunt meant well. The older woman wanted her only niece to form a cousinly relationship with her two sons, but Nancy doubted that would ever happen with Peregrine. He never spoke to her or anyone else. And while she adored Basil, his monologues about male fashion would bring even the most stoic person to tears of boredom.

At half past three, she was beautifully attired in a damask riding habit with a matching bonnet that her aunt had selected. Peregrine arrived with two horses. Cousin Basil rode up on a brown mare and touched his top hat, knocking it to the side.

'Give me a moment to fix it,' Basil said.

He got down from his horse and spent the next few minutes trying to get it back to the perfect jaunty angle without a mirror.

Peregrine clumsily groped her waist as he helped her onto her horse, then swung into the saddle of his own animal. Nancy had only ridden a horse a handful of times in her life, but she felt comfortable enough on the old nag she was riding. Cousin Peregrine was clearly not a good rider, for the poor animal fretted and whinnied all the way to the park.

Basil took up the rear. 'Do not fret dear cousin. I am right behind you, but I cannot increase my pace without threatening the perch of my hat.'

His elder brother sighed heavily.

'Completely understandable, Cousin Basil,' she called over her shoulder.

By the time they reached the park at a snail's pace, Basil was a furlong behind them. They waited for him in silence.

Basil finally caught up to them, happily, his hat was still at the perfect angle. 'Did I miss much?'

Nancy was about to say that he'd missed no conversation at all, but then Peregrine finally spoke.

He took off his hat. 'Basil, I mean to ask Miss Stillwater to marry me.'

'Really?' Basil said, grinning. 'Well, I say. That's marvellous. Congratulations, brother. That is to say… which one? Isn't there a dozen of them?'

'The rector only has ten daughters,' he said. 'I am courting Miss Venetia.'

Nancy's jaw dropped. Ten sisters! What a large family.

'Is she the tall, quiet one with the light brown hair?' Peregrine nodded.

'Splendid. You'll make a great pair. I've always worried that you would fancy a short girl, and how ridiculous that would be if you towered above your wife when you stood next to her. I was afraid for a moment that you liked the Miss Stillwater with the flashy red hair. She is fetching, but I fear she will freckle.'

'And we can't have that in the family,' Nancy said mock seriously.

Wide-eyed, Basil agreed. 'No, indeed. I must leave at once and schedule an appointment with my tailor. Perry, you'll see our cousin safely home, right?'

'Of course.'

Basil waved merrily and bumped his perfectly angled hat. 'Oh, bother.'

Nancy urged her horse to walk on so that her sweet and silly cousin did not hear her gurgle of laughter. She reined in when she saw Matthew heading towards her on a splendid black stallion.

He rode up beside her and tipped his tall black hat. 'Hello, Nancy…ah, I see your escort. Good day, Delfarthing.'

Peregrine's horse whinnied, but Nancy heard him mumble a 'good day'.

'Cousin Peregrine, why don't you go and speak to your mother now and tell her the good news?' Nancy suggested innocently. 'I am sure Lord Matthew would be happy to see me home.'

Matthew turned his horse until it was adjacent to hers. 'Delighted in fact.'

Poor Peregrine mumbled, 'Mama will not approve of my choice. Neither will Grandfather.'

'Remember Aunt Marianne loves you and if that doesn't do the trick,' Nancy said, 'remind her that if she were to distance herself from you and your new bride, she would be just like Grandfather, who she dislikes intensely.'

Her cousin's face slowly turned into a grin. 'You're right. Mama won't want to be anything like him. Thank you, Cousin Nancy. Lord Matthew.'

Peregrine touched his hat, which was not at a jaunty angle, and cantered away from them. His poor hack whinnying the entire time. Nancy pressed her heels into her own mount.

'I take it that congratulations are in order for Viscount Delfarthing?' Matthew said sardonically as he urged his horse forward to match her pace.

She giggled. 'It's like a novel: *Lord Peregrine's Forbidden Love Affair.*'

Matthew's lips twitched. 'I had no idea your cousin could be so interesting. I thought him a dull dog at school.'

'Well, the young lady in question is the daughter of a rector and not a milkman, so it is not truly scandalous.'

He tapped the side of his nose. 'I am sure that the Nose will find it so. I'm surprised that your cousin didn't insist that you accompany him for protection.'

Nancy touched the dagger at her thigh and felt its reassuring shape and sharpness. 'I am afraid that Cousin Basil couldn't protect him either. The news of the wedding excited him so much that he literally galloped to his tailors to make an appointment... May I ask what a Cumberland Corset is?'

Matthew's shoulders shook as he laughed. 'Oh, dear. It shouldn't surprise me that your cousin wants a corset, but it does. The Prince Regent wears one too. A

Cumberland Corset helps gentlemen of larger stature to mould their forms into a more flattering silhouette. They also creak like a door in need of oiling.'

'How ridiculous!'

Smiling, Nancy waved to Frederica who was in a phaeton with the fashionable Lord Norwich. Frederica blew her a kiss back.

'I wish my father would go to the tailors,' he said in a low voice. 'He doesn't see why the old suit of clothes he wears is not perfectly adequate. Although they are at least five years old… My mother threatened to destroy his shabby clothing and so Papa said he'd wear nothing at all to Frederica's coming-out ball.'

Nancy let out another gurgle of laughter. 'I recall him being clothed, so he must have changed his mind about appearing in the au naturel.'

Matthew lifted one hand up and glanced briefly at the clouds. 'My humble prayers were answered…but don't be offended if he shows up at our wedding in his buckskins.'

At the word *wedding* she felt her face turn as red as poor cousin Peregrine's.

'I am hoping to get *your* permission to pay my addresses to you,' he continued.

Recovering her composure slightly, Nancy managed to ask, 'Then you are not asking me to marry you, you are asking for permission to ask me?'

'You hit the nail on the head.'

'Isn't that the same thing?'

Frowning, he looked down at his hands. 'Not at all. A proposal should be done by candlelight with roses and chocolates. At least, according to my younger sisters. But a chap can't plan all that unless he knows that his feelings are reciprocated.'

With all her heart and her soul, Nancy longed to say the small three-letter word *yes*. But Matthew didn't know that she was a murderess and that her life was currently in danger. She couldn't accept him until she told him the truth and if she told him the truth, he wouldn't accept her. The love she saw in his eyes would dissolve into disgust. He was so kind and witty. He deserved a wife that was worthy of him. Not one with a tainted past, which would bring shame upon him.

She swallowed. Her throat felt dry and gummy. 'I cannot give you leave yet to pay your addresses to me.'

Matthew made a guttural sound. 'Are you in danger, Nancy? From Sir Alastair Lymington?'

Nancy blinked, gaping. 'What makes you say that?'

He held up a hand. 'Your reactions to him at both your ball and my sister's. I wish to know everything that involves you. And I will help you in any way that I can. But I don't want to force your confidences.'

Her eyes fell to her hands, holding the reins. 'I have had few people in my life that I could wholly trust. I used to believe in my father, but I don't think he was ever the man I thought he was. One thing that I do know, is that I trust you with my life.'

'And your heart?' he asked in a low undertone.

Nancy took a deep breath. She didn't. She couldn't. But neither did she have enough resolution to push him away entirely. 'Lemongrass. The heart note in the perfume you gave me is lemongrass.'

Matthew beamed at her as if she hadn't just refused

his offer to ask her to marry him. Nancy couldn't help but smile back.

'What are your plans for this evening?' he said, deftly changing the subject.

Sighing, she rolled her eyes. 'More family time. My cousins are escorting my aunt and myself to Drury Lane Theatre.'

'You will get to see the honourable Basil in all of his sartorial splendour.'

'And hear about it too.'

Matthew talked commonplaces until they arrived at her grandfather's house. He lifted her down with two sure hands. She was glad that he hadn't pressed for her confidences or courtship. He was too dear for her to lose quite yet.

Chapter Twenty-Two

Viscount Delfarthing and Basil arrived at Brampton House to escort their mother and her to a play. Nancy thought her cousin looked like a man who had just received a guilty sentencing in court.

'You didn't speak to your mother yet, did you?'

He looked down at his hands. 'The words got stuck in my throat and I couldn't get a syllable out.'

'Do you want me to tell her?'

Peregrine violently shook his head. 'No. No. It must come from me. Venetia would want it that way.'

'I look forward to meeting her.'

Her cousin's face paled at these words.

Basil, resplendent in pink, beamed at them. 'Shall I order champagne and we can do it now?'

Peregrine managed to shake his head and Aunt Marianne came into the room.

Cousin Peregrine refused to look his mother in the eye and he jerked convulsively whenever she addressed him. Not that Aunt Marianne got more than a sentence or two in before Basil began to tell her the long and very detailed story of finding the perfect shade of pink stones for his shoe buckles. He'd gone all the way to Dover. Nancy was relieved when they reached the theatre. As much as she had grown to like her cousins, their conversation was best in small doses.

The outside of the edifice was certainly dreary, but inside the building was quite sumptuous. The carpets were crimson and newly laid, golden chandeliers hung from the ceiling in the foyer, and the woodwork on the walls depicted fruit and flowers.

Her cousins escorted them to their box on the lower level of the stage right with its own chandelier. Nancy felt like she was on her own little stage. The box was a half-circle with curtains on each side that could be pulled close. The theatre had six boxes on each side with three on top and three below. People from the pit stared into the boxes. She'd sat in the pit many times before and gazed upon her betters. Uncomfortably, she wondered if she would ever feel like she belonged in a box.

Basil lent her a pair of golden opera glasses. She peered through them and in the box above and across from her sat Alastair, a dark, older gentleman, and two ladies. One was Giselle, whom she no longer blamed for her father's death. Giselle's raven-coloured hair shone in the candlelight, brought out by her shocking crimson dress that showed a great deal of her upper chest. She was a courtesan and had the sort of beauty that poets wrote sonnets about. However, her former friend's beauty appeared almost brittle this evening. She was thinner. Her jaw was clenched and her eyes darted around the theatre as if she was afraid of something. Which was odd, because as a part of Alastair's criminal gang she should have had his protection. She caught Giselle's eye and smiled a little. Her former friend did not return the gesture, nor glance at her again. Alastair, however, brazenly returned her gaze. Nancy coloured and continued to look at the other boxes, hoping to see Matthew or Frederica. With no luck, she focused on the stage, where the players had begun their parts. Scooting to the edge of her seat, she leaned against the railing.

'If music be the food of love, play on,' one player said.

During the intermission, Peregrine excused himself on the pretence he wished to speak to an acquaintance. And Basil was determined to ask the young man in a bright green coat in the middle tier box who his tailor was. Nancy would have enjoyed a small stroll herself, but her Aunt Marianne seemed content to sit. Nancy sighed with boredom when the door to their box opened. Alastair and Giselle entered. Her mouth fell open and she touched her lips with her trembling fingers. Gentlemen did not bring courtesans to meet viscountesses.

'I spied you over here, Miss Black,' he said with a sinister smile. 'I could not let *half* of the evening go— without speaking to you.'

Nancy stood, attempting to hide her fear. He was referring again to the other half of the stolen documents that her aunt had already given to her grandfather. She had no way to return them to him. 'Better a glass *half* full than one *half* empty, I always say. But I'm glad you came to visit.'

'Lady Delfarthing, allow me to introduce my friend, Miss Overy,' Alastair said. 'She and her particular friend, Mrs Sweetapple, have an intimate acquaintance with your niece.'

Her mouth was dry and her stomach fluttered most uncomfortably. She reached down to touch the dagger sheathed against her thigh. Its familiar weight, warmth, and sharpness helped settle her nerves. She was not powerless against her former boss.

She heard Aunt Marianne ask Alastair about his family and Giselle leaned towards Nancy and whispered, 'I thought you disappeared after your father was killed.'

'And I thought you were a part of the heist. I didn't know that my father was betraying both you and Alastair.'

Giselle moved so that she was standing next to her. There were dark shadows underneath her eyes that not even her powder could hide. 'I am sorry that I told Felix about the job. I did not realise how desperate he was for money, or that his life was in danger.'

Nancy could only nod, her mouth too dry to swallow. The water in her eyes threatening to fall down her cheeks.

Her former friend grabbed her wrist in a tight hold and whispered in her ear. 'You must give Alastair back the rest of the documents. Your life is in danger.'

She forced herself to laugh, even though she would have much preferred to cry. Lifting her hand to hide her face from her aunt and Alastair, she asked, 'How do you know that?'

'Originally, I thought that Lily overdosed, but now I know that she was poisoned by Alastair. I'm the one that found her body sprawled out on the floor with a vial of laudanum in her hand.'

Bile rose in Nancy's throat, but she managed to keep it down. She hadn't known Lily as well as she had Giselle, even though they were both expensive courtesans underneath Alastair's protection. Lily had been all sweetness. It was easy to understand why men loved her even besides her golden beauty. But she'd also been addicted to laudanum drops. Could it have been an accident?

'Are you sure that she was poisoned?' Nancy whispered. 'You always warned her that one day she would take too much.'

Giselle's grasp on her wrist tightened like a vice. 'Mick said that it was meant to seem like an accident. The door was locked from the inside, but we both know whose signature parlour trick that is.'

'Alastair's,' she whispered. He made all their robberies look like inside jobs. 'What about you? Are you safe?'

Giselle gave a jerky nod, her body rigid with fear. 'He's keeping me close to him. He's never been my client before.'

Nancy shook her head, unsure if Giselle was still working for Alastair. 'I would give him the other half of the documents if I could. But they are not in my possession any more.'

Her former friend let go of her wrist and moved her hand to the pearls around Nancy's throat. 'Then if you know what's good for you, you'll pawn this necklace and run.'

Nancy had been running her entire life and looking over her shoulder. And she didn't want to live that way any more. She didn't wish to leave the family she'd only recently found.

Aunt Marianne made a strange noise and Nancy's eyes turned to her. 'And where is your estate, Sir Alastair?'

'Buckinghamshire, my lady.'

Giselle put on a flirtatious smile and took Alastair's arm, leaning on him. 'Oh, yes. He's got a large, draughty old hall up there.'

Nancy tried to play along. She clasped her hands together. 'I hope that there is at least one ghost.'

'Do not be ridiculous, Nancy,' Aunt Marianne said.

Giselle winked at her and held up three fingers. Nancy bit her lower lip to check a laugh. She'd missed the cheekiness of her old friend.

'Alas, there is only one ghost,' Alastair said in a tone that sent shivers of fear down her back. 'A poor young man, cut down in his prime. He was poisoned by belladonna berries. Such a tragic death and the culprit responsible was never found. They believe it was in his teacup.'

Nancy couldn't stop herself from taking a rasping breath. Black dots impaired her vision. She could barely see Giselle take Alastair's arm. 'We should go and visit our other friends.'

The only sign that she could see that Alastair was annoyed was that his jaw muscle twitched. He bowed. 'Very well, my love. Good evening, Viscountess Delfarthing, Miss Black. But know that there is no place that you can go, that I won't find you.'

His words sounded flirtatious, but she only felt the threat. It wasn't until he and Giselle had left the box that she was able to breathe normally again. And a few minutes later before her eyesight had completely cleared.

'I didn't invite him, Aunt Marianne,' she said in a low voice. 'I swear it.'

Her aunt harrumphed, patting Nancy's arm. 'Of course, you did not. The villain is merely trying to use your new position to his advantage. But you are no longer friendless and homeless. If Sir Alastair thinks he can threaten my niece, he will soon discover that I have more connections than a grove of trees and I know more devastating secrets than he could ever imagine.'

'Thank you,' Nancy said, and she meant it with all her heart. She'd never in her life before had such a stout defender. Someone who would be there for her when things went wrong. But whereas her aunt might be powerful socially, she wasn't physically. And if Alastair tried to permanently silence her, there wasn't much her aunt could do to stop him.

She waited a full five minutes before asking her aunt to excuse her for one moment to stretch her legs.

Nancy heard her aunt hiss, 'Not without an escort!'

But she ignored her. Nancy slipped along the wall, trying not to draw any attention to herself from the other guests. She wanted to listen outside of Alastair's box and hear him speak more to Giselle. What were his intentions towards the courtesan? Herself? Did he intend to murder them both?

Sliding around the final corner, she bumped into a man. 'Oh, I do beg your pardon, sir—my lord… Matthew.'

He took her hand and kissed it. 'No pardon needed. I was hoping to talk to you.'

'I did not know you were here,' she said stupidly.

'I came here to see you,' he said and gave her another

perfect smile. Since she was shorter than him, when she looked directly ahead it was at his cravat. She noticed at once that his chest and arms were muscular; heat stirred deep in her belly. Her eyes darted back up to his face. Despite a threat upon her life, the heat churning inside of her did not abate.

She managed a small smile. 'Are you enjoying the play?'

'It is one of my favourites of Shakespeare's plays.'

'Have you read them all?' Nancy asked.

He looked a little sheepish. 'Yes. One of my professors at Oxford said that Shakespeare made up over twenty thousand words. I tried to find them all.'

'And did you?'

Matthew shook his head. 'Just over nineteen thousand. But I've made up a few hundred words of my own.'

Nancy couldn't help but laugh. 'Do you like words or steam locomotives better?'

He shrugged his broad shoulders and she longed to place her hands again on his chest. Over his beating heart. 'Why can't I love both? Don't you have more than one passion?'

It was her turn to blush at *his* word choice. She touched her hot cheeks. Yes. She did. Nancy moved her hand from her cheek to his, cupping his face. 'Perhaps?'

'May I demonstrate mine?' he asked, pulling her behind a curtain and pressing his lips to hers. Nancy felt the caress all the way to her toes.

Inching herself closer, Nancy opened her mouth to him and deepened the kiss. Kissing him made her feel weightless—as if she were falling from the sky. Catching his lower lip with her teeth, she gently tugged on it. Matthew eased her to the wall and pressed her against it with his body. She melded to his form. Lost in the beauty of their embrace. The passion of the moment. For these stolen moments of bliss would be all they ever had. He would find a more suitable wife. One that his family approved of. And she would have her grandfather's money to keep her safe.

The sound of footsteps caused him to break the kiss and step back from her. She instantly felt a chill. With a shiver, she realised that Matthew had been right. Coins were cold comfort in the place of love.

'The play has resumed and Mama's wondering where you are,' Frederica said from behind them, one hand holding the curtain open. 'Papa is only a step away from talking to another naturalist about different types of dung. I should think you would not wish for him to see you.'

Matthew bowed his head to Nancy. 'We were only two friends talking.'

Frederica grinned at them. 'Do you take me for a flat? I know exactly how you were *talking*, but we'd best go back to our box, Matthew, before our mother sends out a search party.'

'First, let me escort Nancy back to her aunt,' Matthew said.

His sister winked at them. 'Just don't take too long *escorting* her. I'll tell Papa that I found you. I'll get to hear about more bat droppings. Goody!'

Nancy smiled at her friend's sarcasm.

Matthew offered her his arm. 'Shall we?'

She took it and watched Frederica walk the other

direction, pulling her father by his arm away from an older man with spectacles still speaking. The only word she deciphered was 'smut'.

Matthew covered her fingers on his arm with his opposite hand. 'That reminds me. My mother was wondering if you would look over some of her Irish contracts. She doesn't speak or read it fluently and wants to make sure that her perfume company is not entering a bad bargain. You would be paid for your time of course.'

Nancy couldn't resist a little extra pocket money and the temptation to spend more time with the Stringhams. 'I should like that very much.'

'With your permission, I will come and fetch you tomorrow and escort you to my parents' home. If your aunt does not deem my protection adequate, we can always have Thomas trail behind us.' He picked up her hand a second time and lightly kissed it. '*Au revoir.*'

She walked into her box alone and wished that Matthew could sit by her for the rest of the play. Aunt Marianne demanded where she went. Nancy humbly replied that she had gone to look for her Cousin Peregrine and explained woefully that she had been unable to locate him. Her aunt snorted in disbelief, but said no more of it.

Not that she could have got a word in edgewise—Basil spoke the entire second half about a French tailor by the name of Émile Blanchet.

Chapter Twenty-Three

Matthew arrived at Nancy's house too early to be fashionable and was not surprised to be told by the butler that Viscountess Delfarthing was not yet awake. He was ushered into the Earl of Brampton's library. Lord Brampton was not who he had hoped to see either.

'Sit down, Lord Matthew.'

He took a seat on the chair nearest to the door, placing his hands in his lap.

'To what do we owe the honour of such an early call?'

Matthew tried his best smile that worked brilliantly on middle-aged matrons, but less well on old earls. 'My mother has hired Nancy to proofread some foreign contracts for her. I was hoping to escort her to my parents' house this morning.'

The thin older man scowled at him. 'My granddaughter does not need your money.'

'It isn't my money. Nor did your granddaughter refuse it.'

The lord secretary's nostrils flared. 'Am I to understand that you are only interested in my granddaughter's translating skills?'

Matthew took off his hat, crossed his legs, and rested it on the top knee. 'No, my lord. I am courting her with great patience and I hope to marry her before the end of summer.'

The older man sat silently for a few moments, watching him. 'Are you going to ask my permission?'

'No. Don't think I will.'

'Why not?' he asked, his voice raspy. 'You won't see a shilling of her dowry if you displease me.'

'I don't want her dowry, so that won't be a problem. When I ask her to marry me, it will be for herself only. You forfeited that right long ago, when you left her to fend for herself in the slums of Edinburgh.'

The Earl of Brampton brought a shaking fist to his mouth. 'She had her father.'

Matthew gave another fake smile. 'Who by all accounts was a very charming gambler and a minor criminal, but completely incapable of providing for his daughter.'

'And does her birth not bother you?'

He shrugged his shoulders. 'That her father was part Irish and part Scottish? Not at all. Why should it? My grandfather Stubbs is a tradesman and I will take over his businesses when he retires, if he ever does. He'll probably be investing in a new company when he cocks up his toes.'

'Then Nancy's birth and fortune mean nothing to you?'

'Nothing at all,' Matthew said cheerfully. 'I have plenty of my own brass and I believe most of the *ton* is inbred… However, Nancy will probably want your money. She blackmailed you for it. She will see it as the security she's always longed for and I wouldn't dream of taking that from her. Happily, there are legal tricks and a whole lot of paperwork that allow a bride to keep her inheritance.'

Lord Brampton should never play cards for money, for Matthew could read the surprise and truth in the wrinkles of his face. His guess was correct. He knew it. The same way that he knew that steam locomotives and their railways were going to be the investment of the century.

The earl barked a dry laugh. 'I suppose you don't mind the blackmailing either.'

''Tis none of my business,' he said. 'If it were, I'd have got her at least double the amount of money. Alas, a lost opportunity.'

The older man was silent again and Matthew could swear he heard a step in the hall behind the door. He tapped his knee—of course! Nancy was eavesdropping on them. As she had been last night on whomever was in the box behind them at the theatre. Between him and Frederica, they'd effectively ruined it for her. Matthew stood up and opened the door. Unsurprisingly, Nancy stood outside of it.

'Do come in, Nancy,' he said loudly. 'You'll hear our conversation better from inside the library.'

A bubble of laughter floated out of her. Nancy had never been caught eavesdropping. Matthew knew her better than anyone had before.

'Your grandfather and I are having a stimulating

discussion about his money,' Matthew said, his eyebrows raised. 'I told him that I wasn't interested in it, but that you were.'

Her face felt like it was on fire, but she entered the room and gave her grandfather a sideways glance before taking a seat next to Matthew. She longed to touch him, but knew that she didn't have the right to.

'I suppose you want an explanation?' Nancy began.

Matthew looked at her grandfather and then at her. 'Oh, no! Not unless you'd like to tell me and then I'd be happy to assist you in any way that I can. Frederica will too. She can't keep her fingers out of other people's pies and she's a natural born eavesdropper. That's how I knew someone was outside the door.'

She nodded, considering what to tell him, wondering what he knew. 'How much do you already know?'

'More than you realise,' he said, a faint tinge of colour in his cheeks. 'You gave me the means to learn everything about your father and yourself when you told me that you had gone by different colour surnames.'

Gasping in surprise, Nancy touched the back of her neck. She hadn't comprehended that such a small detail could give away so much. But she should have. Matthew thrived on words. He would have known just what to do with that information.

'I would be happy to share what my diligent secretary found out about you,' he said. 'But I will not do so in front of your grandfather without your consent.'

Her grandfather growled. 'My granddaughter is under my protection.'

Matthew raised his eyebrows and opened his mouth, only to shut it again. Nancy realised that he was keeping her secrets. He was showing her again that he could be trusted.

'You can tell him everything, Matthew.'

His dark blue eyes focused on her face and not her grandfather on the other side of the room. 'I will start at the beginning. Perhaps unknown to yourself, Nancy, your grandfather did keep an eye on your welfare at first. When you stayed with your maternal grandmother, Mrs Catherine Black, at Heather Cottage in Roslin near Edinburgh. His solicitor sent her a yearly sum for your care.'

Nancy inhaled quickly and held the breath. She'd thought her grandfather had abandoned her from her birth. She would never have guessed that he had given money for her care. Or that he had watched over her in any way. His interest in her life wasn't only recent. Her father had misled her and she'd misjudged her grandfather.

'Then your grandmother died and your father, Mr Felix Black, came to claim you. It was a clever move on his part. He bled the late Viscount Delfarthing for five thousand pounds on your birth and an additional two thousand pounds after your grandmother's death for your maintenance. In reality, it was used to buy a gaming house in Edinburgh. But realising how valuable you were to him financially, he took you with him to the city, where he changed his name to Mr Felix White. Your grandfather's solicitors made an effort to find you, but had no success. They were not looking under a different surname or knew that you were dressed as a boy, Neill White. No one in Edinburgh knew a little girl named Nancy Black.'

She clenched her hands into fists. Her fingernails carving little half crescents into her palms. Aunt Marianne's husband had given her father a small fortune. Her uncle and aunt had loved her from her birth and her father had used that to extort money from them. And it made sense that her grandfather had thought she died. He'd lost all trace of her.

Matthew paused and glanced at her. Nancy nodded. She wanted to know the truth of her past.

He cleared his throat. 'Felix White was a compulsive gambler and fittingly lost the gaming house in a game of cards. He fled Edinburgh owing several thousand pounds in gaming debts and tradesman's bills. He returned to London, but under a different name: Reverend Felix Brown. He was easy to track from there… It was really very thoughtful of him to always keep his given name. It saved my secretary countless hours of searching court documents. He found one nine years ago, where Reverend Felix Brown was sent to Newgate Prison for his role in a robbery that resulted in the death of a dowager. His daughter, with no place to go, was taken by Madame Sweetapple. Another breadcrumb clue that you dropped for me, Nancy, for which I was most grateful. Madame Sweetapple, Your Lordship, is a madam whose whorehouse specialises in prostitutes that have the manners and accents of a lady. The clever crone had Nancy Brown sign a contract that said in exchange for her lessons and the roof over her head, she owed the madam ten years of her life.'

Nancy squeezed her eyes shut tightly. Wishing to forget this terrible episode of her life.

Matthew's hand covered her fist lightly. 'What

Nancy was not aware of, is that minors cannot sign legal contracts, especially under false names. It would never have been considered valid in any court.'

Her eyes popped open. All these years she'd feared Madame Sweetapple taking her back and making her a courtesan. Unclenching her fist, she turned over her hand and interlaced her fingers with Matthew's.

He gave her a small smile before continuing. 'At fourteen, still a child, Nancy didn't realise this. However, one of Madame Sweetapple's best customers did, Mr Alastair Lymington. He managed to get Reverend Felix Brown out of Newgate Prison for a transfer to an ecclesial judge, because of his imaginary role in the clergy. Reverend Brown never made it to the Church of England court. Nor Nancy to the auction for her virginity. The starting bid was to be three hundred pounds.'

She heard her grandfather growl again. His face was red and he looked livid.

'Both Mr Felix Green and his daughter, Miss Nancy Green, felt indebted to their saviour, Mr Alastair Lymington. Noble by birth but in no other way. Still, he was wise enough not to be the front of his own criminal business. He used a slum boss called Bones to oversee and protect his turf. Mr Green's Irish charm and his daughter's fresh beauty and innocence were used for many jobs over the next nine years. The fact that Nancy could swear like a cockney fishwife one day and charm as a duchess the next was highly valuable to him. But recently inheriting his cousin's baronetcy, the new Sir Alastair realised that his double life was going to come back and haunt his new prospects. Unsurprisingly, Mr Green was deeply indebted and had disappeared from his usual haunts. Alastair gave the address of his secret lodgings to the money lender, Harry Heap...'

Nancy's hand tightened on Matthew's.

'I assume Alastair believed that the money lender would kill both Mr Green and his daughter. One of his past messes would be not only cleaned up, but silenced without him having anything to do with it. Heap's men shot Mr Green, but his daughter was nowhere to be seen. Assuming she was no threat to his safety, Sir Alastair began to systematically remove anyone who knew about his past. As a new friend of Prinny's, a spot he was able to assume after Beau Brummell's and the Prince Regent's parting, it was extremely dangerous for anyone to know the truth. Hence Bones was murdered by a rival slum landlord. A prostitute named Lily with a laudanum addiction was found dead in her own rooms, the door locked from the inside. One of her favourites, a man named Charles, had a dagger in his belly. Peter's body was food for the fish in the Thames and a lad named Mick disappeared.'

A tear slipped down her cheek. He was only a boy. Another unwanted child that took to the streets of London to survive and was lost.

Matthew covered her hands with his free one. 'However, you needn't worry about Mick. He was more than happy to take up a new position in exchange for information. My secretary sent him to Leeds to work in one of my factories there. He is lodging with my superintendent's family.'

Relief flooding her soul, Nancy leaned forward and kissed Matthew's cheek.

'Is that the end of your tale?' her grandfather asked gruffly.

Matthew paused and Nancy hoped it was. She didn't want him to know about her part in Sir Gervase Lymington's death.

He smirked at her grandfather. 'Surely, you don't want me to end my tale before we reach your role in it, my lord?'

The older man sat back in his chair, his lips pursed into a thin line. 'Very well, Lord Matthew, please continue.'

'This is also where I enter the story, as well. A beautiful young woman slipped past the guards of the front gate of the Horse Guards and asked for directions to the Earl of Brampton's office. I chivalrously offered to take her there, where I left her in his care… Having successfully negotiated a contract with the government, I went to visit my family, thinking little of the incident, until I bumped into a very pale Miss Black, whose bullet wound had started to bleed again.'

She watched the colour drain from her grandfather's face as his jaw hung open. She had not told him of her injury.

'I brought her into my family's front parlour and told my sister to fetch cleaning supplies, whilst I went for food.' He paused. 'I believe in those short moments alone, Nancy hid the government documents she must have been blackmailing you with in our pianoforte. A clever move. She had no way of keeping them safe from you in your own home and she'd fled the last lodgings she had shared with her father. Wisely worried for her life.'

It was Nancy's jaw that dropped this time. 'How do you know all of this?'

'My sister Frederica said that the pianoforte sounded funny and I came across the packet of the documents. After perusing them, I didn't have much difficulty discovering the hold you had over your grandfather. But the story gets more interesting here. Lady Delfarthing, who has always loathed my mother, pays her a call. After, the documents are gone from the pianoforte. By chance, I saw Thomas walking in front of my house. I offered to take the parcel for him. He agreed. Do not be too hard on the lad, he had no idea the value of what he was carrying. I took the parcel to a dark pub and discovered that only half of the stolen government documents were there and that they were to be delivered to Sir Alastair Lymington in Half Moon Street.'

Nancy's knees knocked together and she was glad that she had been sitting down. She had no idea with the few pieces of her past how much Matthew could learn in such a short period. He knew everything—except that she was a murderess. Which made her unworthy of him.

'Knowing Lymington's role helped me piece everything else together into a mostly coherent narrative,' Matthew continued. 'Yet, why if Lymington is now an intimate of the Prince Regent would he still continue with his criminal affairs? Especially, after he had killed most of his crew. That was an interesting conundrum.'

'And?' her grandfather demanded.

Matthew bounced one knee. 'This is where my own grandfather became particularly helpful. He used his connections with the banks to learn that Sir Alastair's financial affairs were near bankruptcy. His cousin, who he most likely murdered, had been a gambler like himself and had lost the family fortune. To continue to be a Top of the Trees Corinthian and a Goer among the Goes, Lymington needed a steady income. Being a friend of Prinny's is never cheap. Alastair had already decided to dismantle his criminal kingdom, and must have chosen to source his new lifestyle by becoming a French informer. A lucrative profession. However, he is missing the most important half of the documents that he promised the French. The locations. Which is why he is still threatening Nancy and I am here to help.'

Closing her eyes, she took slow, steadying breaths, trying to calm her racing heart.

'You are perceptive, Lord Matthew,' her grandfather said, with more approval than she'd ever heard him speak with to his own grandsons.

'It's my business to be so. I have to read people as well as I read financial statements.'

She bit her lower lip. 'You offered to help me, but how?'

'Despite Lord Brampton doubting my patriotic sympathies,' Matthew said, 'I don't think it wise to allow that information to make it to France and Napoleon. My company feeds those supply lines and I don't want my employees to be put into danger. We need to not only stop the sale of the documents, but catch Sir Alastair in the act. If we're lucky, we'll be able to send him, his contact in the Horse Guards, and the French spy to a dark cell in Newgate Prison.'

'How?' Grandfather repeated.

She shifted her gaze to Matthew.

He lifted his shoulders up and then dropped them.

'I don't have a plan as yet. My secretary, Mr Howitt, is currently working as Alastair's butler. His previous servant left under mysterious circumstances.'

Nancy found herself smiling in spite of the terrible situation. She was pretty certain that Matthew knew the precise circumstances of the butler's departure. 'Your secretary's keeping watch for you.'

'Yes. But forgive me this indelicate question—do you know who Alastair's French contact is? That is one last piece of the puzzle that I could not find.'

Sighing, Nancy slumped a little in her seat. 'No. But I think my father did.' Papa must have, if he'd intended to sell the documents directly to the French spy instead of Alastair. There were so many things that he hadn't told her. So many opportunities for a safe home that he had denied her. Nancy wasn't naive enough to believe that her father wasn't selfish. He'd used her and she had trusted him more than anyone else in the world. And he had been lying to her the entire time.

Grandfather leaned forward in his chair, resting his elbows on his desk. 'And what is our next move, Lord Matthew?'

He picked up the king chess piece from the table beside him and rolled it between his fingers. 'According to my grandfather, Alastair's finances are in a bad way. He will have to act soon. We learn *his* next move and then we set our trap.'

Nancy nodded, but her stomach clenched. She feared Alastair's downfall would bring on her own.

Chapter Twenty-Four

After escorting Nancy to his mother's house, he left to work for a few hours. He was not a man of leisure and he needed to finish the contracts and check the accounts. Especially since Mr Howitt was butlering and unable to take care of his correspondence and arrange his schedule.

Matthew's hand was cramping after the fourth letter, but he continued to write terse, but accurate replies. He went through the contracts that Mr Howitt had edited and initialled the corrections that he approved of. Ringing a bell, he handed the stack to a clerk to write out on a fresh piece of paper in law-hand. He left the most unpleasant job for last: the accounts. Mathematics were a language that he usually respected. He loved that numbers could communicate so much. But today, he wanted nothing more than to go back to his parents' house and be near Nancy. He feared that she would finish her translation before he was able to return.

He was staring at a long column of numbers when a clerk brought a letter to his desk. Breaking the seal, he immediately recognised Mr Howitt's penmanship. He unfolded the letter and saw that it was mercifully brief and to the point.

> *SAL will be at Vauxhall tonight. He is taking his valise with documents. H*

His secretary was clearly made for spy work. Matthew particularly appreciated Mr Howitt's use of initials. He folded the paper back up and tore it into tiny pieces.

'That will be all, Philbin,' he said to the clerk.

The man bowed to him. He had a long thin neck. 'One last thing, Your Lordship. There is a man here who wanted to speak to Mr Howitt. Should I send him away, or would you like to meet with him?'

His first response was to consign this unknown person to perdition, but then he recalled that the man must have been hired by Mr Howitt to assist in the search of Nancy's past. He might have the final puzzle piece Matthew needed.

'Thank you, Philbin. Do send him in.'

Mr Philbin gave another long-necked bow before leaving the room. He arrived a short time later to announce, 'Mr Redwine.'

Matthew got to his feet and held out his hand to the man. He was probably between forty to forty-five years old and as tall as Matthew. Mr Redwine was a great deal broader and his crooked nose looked as if it had been broken at least twice. He had a swarthy complexion and thinning hair on top. His clothes were clean, but not fashionable. He was clearly a member of the lower classes, but he did not seem cowed by Matthew's position or ancestry. Matthew assumed that meant Mr Redwine had dealt directly with aristocrats before.

'A former Bow Street Runner, perhaps?'

Mr Redwine smiled and his front two teeth were grey. 'I heard you were a sharp one, my lord, but now I know it.'

Matthew gestured to a chair. 'Do please sit down.'

The former Bow Street Runner perched on the edge of his seat as if he was ready to fight at a moment's notice. He bounced his legs as if he was unused to staying still for long. 'I travelled up to Addingrove Park, Buckinghamshire on the mail coach. Neither the town nor the servants seemed to mourn the late Sir Gervase Lymington. His cousin, Sir Alastair, paid all of his cousin's outstanding tradesmen's bills.'

He whistled. 'Clever move. He earned their loyalty and buried all their suspicions.'

'Aye, my lord,' Mr Redwine said. ''Cept the rector was none too keen on him. It appears that Sir Alastair has yet to attend one of his fine sermons.'

'An oversight.'

'For a guilty man, certainly,' Mr Redwine said, placing his hands on his bouncing knees. 'Reverend Bailey thought it was mighty odd that Alastair Lymington visited for the first time since his grandfather died fifteen years before. It would appear that there was no love lost between the cousins. Then out of the blue, Alastair showed up with his pretty young wife and two days later, Sir Gervase is dead.'

Matthew nodded, slowly. 'The timing is certainly

suspicious. Did the reverend not believe Sir Gervase died of the French pox?'

The man shifted in his seat. 'He made a point of saying that the sores on the body didn't match previous victims of the pox that he'd buried.'

'Did no one else share his suspicions?'

'No, my lord,' Mr Redwine said. 'Everyone is happy that the late baronet cocked up his toes. However, I was able to get a description of Lymington's bride from the housekeeper. The lady never went into town, unlike Alastair. She was only seen by Sir Gervase's servants and at the time, he only had five. He'd not paid them wages in nearly a year.'

'How did the housekeeper describe Lymington's wife?'

'She said that Mrs Lymington was a proper young lass with black hair and appeared foreign in her features.'

Giselle, perhaps? She was French after all. He would have guessed her age closer to thirty, but *young* was a relative term.

'Anything else? Her age? The colour of her eyes? How she spoke? What she wore?'

'Mrs Finch said that her clothes were plain but respectable. She'd only packed an extra dress, as if they were not planning to stay long. She said that Mrs Lymington spoke like a lady, but there was something a little different in her accent. She assumed it was her foreign background, my lord. She said nowt about the wife's age, 'cept that she were young. But she did say that the lass had the brightest blue eyes that she'd ever seen.'

Giselle had brown eyes. It had to be Nancy.

She'd been a party to Sir Gervase's murder. This was the incriminating secret she was keeping from him.

'Thank you very much, Mr Redwine,' Matthew said, getting to his feet. 'Let me settle our bill and we will consider our business here complete.'

The former Bow Street Runner sprang to his feet as if ready to attack. 'You don't want me to keep searching for more clues, my lord? Sir Gervase's death is mighty suspicious.'

Matthew took out his coin purse. 'If the good people of Buckinghamshire are content, then so am I.'

He counted the coins into Mr Redwine's rough, scarred hands. As much as he would like to know precisely how Alastair orchestrated his cousin's death, he didn't want anyone tying Nancy to the murder.

Nancy discovered that she didn't know all the business words in Irish, but the Duchess of Hampford had provided her with an English translation book for each language which proved very helpful. Still, the entire process took her several hours. Setting down her quill, she had made forty-three word choice changes and felt as if she had more than earned her fee.

Matthew burst into the room where she sat alone. 'Lymington's going to Vauxhall tonight. My secretary sent a messenger.'

'I've never been there before.'

'It's a blasted garden maze, but it has several great places for one to watch people and listen to their conversations.'

Nancy set down her pen. 'But what if Alastair sees me?'

Matthew sat down on the chair beside her and took

her hand into his larger, warm one. 'That is the only positive about Vauxhall, we can go masked. Many people do. Even members of the *ton* to conceal their identity. It will not be considered uncommon.'

Nodding, she recalled that Basil had purchased her a mask in case of an invitation to a masquerade. 'I will pretend that I have a headache and stay home tonight. I can slip out of the servant's entrance at nine o'clock.'

He squeezed her hand. 'I will be there waiting for you with a carriage. I'm not much of a fighter, but I will keep you safe.'

Nancy's heart warmed, as did the rest of her body, underneath his heated gaze. She believed Matthew would protect her as no one in her past had done before. She wondered if this was what love was supposed to be like. Gentle, caring, and without demanding anything in return.

Chapter Twenty-Five

Lymington couldn't have picked a harder place than Vauxhall Gardens, Matthew thought. The garden had acres of paths lit by hundreds of lanterns, but there were plenty of dark places. The paths interweaved through shrubbery and trees. He could hear an orchestra playing and saw several supper boxes full of people. Mr Philbin had secured them a coveted supper box near the Chinese pavilion. Matthew helped Nancy into her seat. The hairs on the back of his neck stood up, but she assured him that she'd gone to much worse locations. He knew Nancy was no gentle flower, although he wished to treat her like one.

They enjoyed a tolerably good dinner, but it wasn't as succulent as his grandfather's French chef's cuisine.

Matthew picked up his wine glass. 'Any sign of our quarry?'

Nancy glanced around at the other supper boxes that were easily seen. 'No. But we are in the respectable part of the gardens. I daresay if we want to find a rogue, we'll have to go deeper in.'

'I absolutely hate the idea of you being in danger,' Matthew said, 'but I agree with you.'

Lifting up her fork, Nancy laughed. 'We'll set off after the dessert course. It would be truly a crime to leave such a divine sponge, berries, and Chantilly cream uneaten.'

He'd noticed before how much Nancy focused on her food and savoured each bite as if it might be her last. She must have known great hunger and want in her past. That thought pierced him like a knife.

They polished off their dessert plates and then left the supper box. The first path they chose was well-lit and wide, allowing both of them to walk across it at the same time. It forked into two smaller paths.

'Should we split up?' Nancy suggested.

'Not on your life,' Matthew said. 'It's not safe. Pickpockets and scoundrels abound at Vauxhall.'

Nancy's hand moved to her neck, where a beautiful multistring pearl necklace was. 'The only pickpocket I see is the one you brought with you. Besides, I have my dagger.'

He prayed that she wouldn't have need of it. 'But then who will protect me?'

Her nose scrunched up and she giggled. 'Very well. Stay close to me.'

He didn't have to be told twice. Matthew took Nancy's hand and they wound through the paths and found more than one couple enjoying a little privacy, but no Lymington. Turning back towards the main area, they took a new path and Matthew saw Lymington shadowed by a lantern. A servant, clad only in black, handed him a billet; he slipped the letter into his coat and struck down another path.

'Quietly,' Matthew whispered as he and Nancy tried to catch up. Matthew saw that Lymington was seated at a secluded supper box with another gentleman and two ladies who looked like prostitutes. Their faces were heavily painted and their gowns revealing. The brunette was sitting on the lap of the other man, obscuring his face.

'I thought you would never get here,' the other man said.

Nancy covered her mouth with her hand. 'I've heard that voice before. But where? If only the woman would not hang upon him so. I cannot see his face.'

'Nor I,' he whispered. Matthew barely heard Lymington's reply. 'Detained on a matter of business.'

'Come over 'ere by me, luv,' the buxom blonde begged.

Lymington obeyed and the blonde coaxed, 'Are you going to take me to the opera tomorrow?'

'Sorry, Bessy, but I have already promised to accompany this fellow to a masquerade ball to deliver some papers, which I have had to pay for twice, dipping into my profits,' he said. 'I'll take you to the opera the night after next.'

This answer undoubtedly pleased the blonde who kissed him loudly.

'Oi! Where's my kiss, Edgy?' the brunette said.

Edgy.

The other man was Lord Edgewell!

Matthew turned to Nancy and she nodded back. She'd recognised his spotted face too. He wanted to run, but slowly, they turned around and crept away from the secluded supper box. His heart beat so loudly, he was sure that Lymington or Edgewell could hear it through the trees.

Nancy tugged him forward down the path. Neither of them spoke for nearly five minutes, until they reached the dimly lit area outside of the tavern of Vauxhall Gardens.

Matthew raked his fingers through his hair. 'Edgewell. I would never have guessed a gazetted fortune-hunter was his front for being a French spy.'

Nancy exhaled slowly. 'I knew that I didn't like him.'

It took them several minutes to locate Matthew's carriage and climb inside. It wasn't until his back was against the upholstery that he felt as if he could breathe easily. Nancy sat next to him, her shoulder brushing his. Propriety dictated that he sit on the opposite seat with his back to the driver, but he was glad that Nancy wasn't very well acquainted with propriety.

Covering her hand with his own, Matthew said, 'You were incredible back there, Nancy. Not only did we learn that Edgewell is a French agent, we discovered that both he and Lymington will be at the masquerade ball tomorrow.'

'Where we will set our trap,' Nancy said.

'Together,' Matthew said, intertwining their fingers like the tooth and rack of a steam locomotive.

Chapter Twenty-Six

Nancy tapped her foot against the wooden floor. Matthew had promised to take her driving so that they could formulate their plan for the masquerade tonight. An open carriage was the only place a couple could be private, yet still be on display for all the proprieties. Glancing down at her pelisse of red shot silk, Nancy decided that she liked aristocratic clothes, adored the food, and delighted in having a home, but she was less fond of all the rules that came with being a lady.

Peeking out the window, she saw Matthew get into the phaeton in front of his parents' house and begin to come her way. She pushed past the butler, through the door, and down the steps. She could not wait another moment to speak to him. Pulling up on his reins, Matthew gave her a smile that warmed her all the way down to her toes.

He reached out a hand to her. 'Allow me to help you inside.'

Nancy could have climbed into the carriage without any assistance, but it was nice that he offered and so she accepted his hand. With a gentle tug, she was up in the carriage and seated next to him.

Sliding her hand through his arm, she said, 'To the park?'

Matthew cleared his throat. 'We can go there eventually, but I have been up for most of the night thinking about what we should do and I believe that we need to start at the beginning.'

Nancy blinked, her hand tightening over his coat. 'What do you mean, the beginning?'

'When you were shot. Or rather, where you were shot,' he explained. 'If you can show me the house, I can discover who owns it. In fact, I might already know them. The traitor must be someone with a high position at the Horse Guards which would give them access to government documents with the official seal imprinted upon them. Like the ones you stole. He must have brought them home and gave Alastair the tip to steal them.'

'That all fits together, but how is Alastair acquiring a second set of the official documents?'

'The traitor must hold a position of trust, if he is able to acquire an additional copy with an official seal to give to Alastair at the masquerade ball.'

Her mind whirled and her arm ached with a phantom pain. The last time she went to that house, she'd been shot. Then she'd found her father dead. It was the worst night of her life and the last thing that she wished to do was relive it. She glanced up at his beautiful blue eyes and saw both concern and tenderness. No one had ever looked at her that way before. Perhaps no one would ever again. And somewhere in her tattered heart she knew that he only asked this of her to help her. Matthew wanted to protect her from Alastair's minions and his mouth. A few words could destroy her small foothold into society and her newly found family.

'Number seventeen New Burlington Place. Do you need directions?'

'No.'

Lifting his whip, Matthew snapped it over the horses' heads and the phaeton lurched forward. Nancy held on to his arm and tried to calm the frantic beating of her heart. She was in a fancy carriage with a gentleman. No one would harm her or even speak to her. She did not need to worry about slum bosses or Harry Heap and his men. Besides, they would not recognise her now, clean and dressed like a lady. She barely recognised her outer self. But her inner self still wore the scars of a lifetime on the streets and the filth of murder. No amount of soap would ever wash that away. And no fancy gown could change what she had done.

After a few minutes of weaving through the busy London roads, Matthew said in a low voice, 'I hope you know that I would never wish to cause you any pain. I would not have insisted upon this little trip if I did not think it essential to our success tonight. Who knows if we will ever get another chance to catch Alastair holding stolen government papers.'

She gulped, her hands shaking. 'I know. It must be done. I will do it.'

He put both reins in one hand and then covered her gloved hand with his. 'And remember, that you do not have to do it alone. I am here.'

'My knight in shining armour,' Nancy quipped.

He glanced down at his apparel. 'What about a lord in a grey double-breasted riding coat?'

Somehow a laugh broke from her lips. Matthew always managed to make her smile and he did look very dashing in his riding coat. 'But how will you defend me? With your lapels or your tails?'

Matthew chuckled. 'Clearly, sweetheart, you have never worn armour before. Trust me when I tell you that I will be of much better use to you without fifty pounds of metal that makes it impossible to walk.'

Her pulse jumped when he called her 'sweetheart'. Instead of melting into his arms, Nancy quirked up one eyebrow. 'You've worn armour before?'

'Not since I was a lad of fifteen,' he admitted. 'There are many historic suits of armour at our castle and one day, my brother dared me to try one on. I couldn't see a lick out that helmet. The breastplate nearly crushed my chest and I creaked as I shuffled, attempting to walk. I couldn't even lift my own sword.'

'How lowering.'

'I can assure you that it was,' he said, pulling on the reins to lead his pair of chestnuts around a turn.

Nancy's breath caught. She'd only been on this street at night when it was dark and full of shadows made by the gas lamps. Several statues adorned the stone buildings in little alcoves. The marble men looked down at her in contempt as if they knew she did not belong here. That she was a fraud.

Matthew slowed down the horses as they passed number seventeen. A maid walked up the kitchen stairs in front of the house. Instinctively, Nancy turned her head, even though she had not run into a servant but the butler.

'Hello there,' Matthew called down to the maid.

She glanced up at him from underneath her white mob cap. A shock of red curls surrounded her round face and her nose turned up at the end. 'Can I help you, sir?'

He took a coin out of his double-breasted riding coat and held it up. 'A crown if you tell me who your master is.'

The maid rubbed her upturned nose. 'Lord Wigglesworth, sir. But I don't want no trouble.'

Matthew tossed her the coin and the maid deftly caught it. 'I promise you there will not be. Thank you, miss.'

Nancy buried her head, bonnet and all, into his shoulder as Matthew urged the team of horses forward. He did not say another word until they reached Rotten Row at Hyde Park. She watched him smile and tip his hat to several of his acquaintances as if their drive was simply another jaunt in the park. And not her entire life on the line.

'Pray, do you know who Lord Wigglesworth is?'

Matthew touched the brim of his hat and nodded at a stranger as they passed in another carriage. 'A baron and pretty high up in the Horse Guards. I've worked with him several times to ensure that army supplies reach the right locations in a timely manner. He knows all the details of General Lord Wellington's campaign in the Peninsula War. His information would be invaluable to the French forces.'

'Do you think my grandfather knows him?'

'Certainly. The Baron probably reports to him,' Matthew said, huffing. 'They are quite the triumvirate of traitors. Wigglesworth is the government informer. Alastair is the broker. Edgewell is the French spy. And all three players will be on the board at the masquerade tonight. Wigglesworth probably could not stage two burglaries without his staff becoming alarmed and drawing too much attention to him.'

Nancy bit her lower lip as she clenched her hands into tight fists. 'He will pass the second set of official documents tonight to Alastair. We will have to keep an eye all three men.'

'Luckily, Wigglesworth has a rather distinct figure. He's a large man. And Edgewell's face is spotted.'

'Won't the mask cover his entire face?'

'Only his eyes and part of his nose. A domino mask does not cover the mouth,' he said. 'But our entire plan hinges on your grandfather's government authority and bringing military guards with him to arrest them. You will need to speak to the lord secretary as soon as you arrive home.'

'I will.'

Matthew pulled the horses to a halt. 'And once this is all over, with your permission, I wish to speak to your grandfather about a most important matter. Since you told me that I have to like him now.'

Nancy did not think her body could withstand any more shocks that day. Dropping his arm, she brought her hand to cover the scar of the bullet hole. She was too damaged to deserve Matthew's love. Her past too tainted for him to marry. She'd half-heartedly tried to

warn him and push him away, but she had not been res-
olute enough to end it.

What was left of her tattered heart broke into pieces
as she said, 'Please do not speak to my grandfather. I
have no intention of marrying any time soon. I wish to
get to know my family better.'

'We could have a lengthy engagement.'

Gritting her teeth, Nancy shook her head. 'I cannot.
I thought I could marry a gentleman and no one would
be the wiser. But there will always be Alastairs. People
from my past who know who I truly am and what I have
done. I cannot spend the rest of my life pretending to
be someone I am not. Nor glancing over my shoulder.'

'They are lovely shoulders and perhaps you carry
more burdens than you need to,' he said in a soft voice
that nearly undid her. 'I am not afraid of your past. I
want your future. And if you are weighed down by it,
allow me the privilege as your husband of carrying your
burdens with you.'

Fear gripped her throat. She could not utter even a
syllable. Despair tore apart her heart and tainted soul.
She shook her head resolutely. She loved Matthew and
she would not ruin his life by marrying him. She would
not bring shame to his name or to his family.

'Please Matthew, say no more,' she whispered. 'I
cannot and will not marry you.'

Her hands flew to her mouth. No sooner had she
spoken, then she wished to take those words back. To
use different ones that would hurt him less. But the
truth was painful and she could no longer hide from it.

Without replying, he flicked the reins and the phaeton
careened along the path. Several people hailed Matthew,

but he ignored them. Ignored her as if she was not sitting next to him on the narrow seat. But what did she expect? She'd refused his offer of marriage. He was no longer courting her and had no reason to help her any more.

The lump in her throat grew and she could barely get out the words when they arrived in front of her grandfather's house. 'I suppose that you do not wish to help me now.'

'Of course, I still want to help you tonight,' Matthew said in a gentle voice, touching her chin so that she looked into his blue eyes. 'I love you. I will not withhold my support because you are unable to accept my offer of marriage. That is not what love is. With love there are no rules or requirements. Love is trust. Trust is love. And you can trust in me.'

She shook her head again. Tears fell from her eyes and he handed her down out of the carriage.

'I'll see you tonight,' he said, then drove away.

The butler opened the door and Nancy's legs were shaking as she walked up the stairs to her bedchamber. She barely made it to her four-poster bed before she fell flat on her face and sobbed. She loved Matthew so much that it hurt more than being shot or stabbed. Her entire body ached from her head to her toes. But she could not love selfishly, like her father had. She would be selfless and put Matthew's needs first. He deserved a life in the sunlight and she was only made for the shadows.

More sobs racked her body and Nancy reminded herself that a complete break was the best for both of them. She was a thief and their romance was but a stolen moment in time. He would marry a blue-blooded debutante who didn't twirl daggers and know all the vilest curse words. Nancy would live with her grandfather and have the security and family that she'd always wanted. Matthew would never grow to resent her, or worse, be shunned by society for her disgraceful past.

They would live happy separate lives.

She covered her eyes with her hands. But without Matthew she felt joy-*less*, cheer-*less*, and peer-*less*.

Chapter Twenty-Seven

Nancy wore a pale pink domino over her white gown, and a matching mask for the masquerade. Where Basil acquired the extra pink domino, Nancy didn't ask. She wondered if it might be one of his own. Her cousin took being a 'pink of the *ton*' very seriously. At least the pink part. Touching her leg, she felt the reassuring shape of her dagger. Aunt Marianne had a deep purple domino and did not bother to put on a mask, not that her figure and nose weren't very recognisable. Cousin Peregrine wore a black domino and a mask that covered the top half of his face. On the bottom half, he wore the grimace of a long-suffering son who only came to support his mother.

Grandfather planned to arrive separately with several armed guards.

Their party arrived fashionably late to the masquerade and were welcomed by all four hosts: Brummell, Mildmay, Alvanley, and Pierrepoint. None of whom wore masks as of yet. Beau Brummell was adorned in a silver domino that contoured perfectly to his figure. She didn't blame Basil for sighing longingly.

Brummell watched Nancy through his quizzing glass. 'I was not wrong to bring you into fashion, Miss Black.'

She couldn't help but smile at his audacity and curtsy to him. 'Thank you, sir. But the credit belongs to my cousin, Basil. He selected most of my wardrobe.'

Brummell's quizzing glass swivelled towards Basil's champagne-coloured domino and gold-plated mask. Nancy held her breath until he said, 'You look exquisite, sir.'

Her cousin merely grinned in reply. For once, speechless.

Then Lord Alvanley greeted Aunt Marianne and Peregrine by name. Mr Pierrepoint merely nodded in their direction and Mr Mildmay kissed Nancy's hand. Behind her, she heard a scurry of footsteps and saw the arrival of the Prince Regent, his crimson domino emphasised his full figure. Nancy could hear a creaking sound when he walked and assumed that it was his Cumberland Corset. The Prince Regent carried his mask in his hand.

'Alvanley and Pierrepoint, how do you do?' he said jovially and shook hands with both gentlemen. He next stared at both Brummell and Mildmay for over a minute without speaking one word, giving them a cut direct. He then walked towards Nancy and her aunt.

'Lady Delfarthing. Miss Black.'

Brummell's eyes narrowed on the Prince Regent's retreating figure and said quite loudly, 'Alvanley, who is your fat friend?'

The Prince Regent turned back, his cheeks coloured as red as his crimson domino. He gave the leader of fashion a blistering glare before offering Aunt Marianne his arm. She took it and Nancy followed behind them into the ballroom. She would need to slip away to find Matthew.

'Nancy, you must stay near me at all times. A gentleman need only put on a mask to become a mannerless fiend,' Aunt Marianne said in a low undertone after detaching herself from the prince.

Glancing over her shoulder, she saw her grandfather's spare form in a long grey domino entering the party. Behind him trailed six military guards. He signalled for them to go to the side of the room, before walking up to an unknown gentleman and touching the shoulder of his red domino. Grandfather's eyes met hers and she realised he was pointing out Lord Wigglesworth to her. The man who had shot her, because she had stolen the documents a day too early. A shiver of fear ran down the back of her neck and the old wound ached in memory.

Trying to forget, Nancy said, 'The Prince Regent seemed captivated with you.'

Aunt Marianne harrumphed. 'The Prince has the attention span of a butterfly and enjoys women with generous curves.'

A few minutes later, she saw the Prince Regent's very recognisable figure dancing rather closely to Lady Hertford, whose shape was similar to Aunt Marianne's. Nancy couldn't help but smile a little for the woman was rumoured to be his favourite mistress.

A short gentleman arrayed in a blue domino asked her to waltz. Her aunt gave a brief nod. Nancy needed to act normally. She couldn't afford to tip off Alastair, Edgewell, or Wigglesworth that they were being watched.

Nancy did not recognise her partner by his hair or

his voice. Whirling in a circle, she saw Basil speaking animatedly to a thin man in a dark purple domino whom she assumed was Lord Edgewell. She might have told her cousin that the earl was a connoisseur of tassels. A conversation with Basil would definitely keep him busy. The man was the right height and hair colour, and the half of his face that could be seen was covered in spots. Her lips curled as she realised he was getting to hear the story of her cousin's new snuffbox shovel. 'A gentleman need never get his fingers dirty again for a pinch.'

Edgewell was well in hand, but where the deuce was Alastair? The unknown gentleman returned her to Aunt Marianne's side, where her hand was claimed by a tall gentleman in a white domino. There was something familiar about him, but she couldn't decide what. But the dance was a vigorous country set and they barely exchanged more than a few words. The man used a falsetto voice to disguise his identity. After the dance, he offered to procure her a glass of lemonade, which she gladly accepted.

'Miss Pink Domino,' the gentleman in the white domino said, handing her a glass. 'It seems you always have a colour in your name.'

This time the man had spoken with his real voice.

'Alastair.'

She lowered the drink from her lips. Nancy knew better than to accept a drink from his hands.

'It's not poisoned with belladonna berries, Blue Eyes,' he said with a sneer. 'But I think it is time that you and the Nose went home with a headache.'

'You're not my boss any more.'

He brought his hand to her face and lightly caressed

her mask with one finger. 'And you should remember that you are no longer under my protection, Unsoiled Dove. That was your stage name, wasn't it?'

Recoiling, Nancy felt as small and as scared as she had at fourteen, when her virginity had been up for sale. She had thought Alastair was her knight in shining armour. Her saviour. She would have done anything that he asked her to do. But instead of taking advantage of her innocence, he had taught her how to protect herself. How to fight. To steal. To survive on the London streets.

She looked down at the drink in her hands. 'Very well.'

Leaving him where he stood, she rushed back to her aunt's side. Nancy touched her pounding head. She didn't need to feign a headache. She had one.

'You're paler than a ghost,' Aunt Marianne said. 'Come with me to the retiring room.'

Her aunt held Nancy's arm like she was an invalid as they walked slowly to the ladies' retiring room. Once the door closed behind them, Nancy felt like she could breathe again. She glanced down at the beautiful pink silk domino. It had been the only domino that shade and sheen in the entire room. She would be too easy for Alastair to spot.

Someone bumped into her shoulder and Nancy saw a young woman with dark hair swaying on her feet.

She grabbed the lady's arms to steady her, pushing back her bright yellow domino. 'Are you quite all right?'

The young woman's head lolled to one side. 'I d-d-drank too much from Barnabas's flask,' she said in a slurring voice.

An idea popped into Nancy's head. 'Let me help

you to a seat and why don't we take off your mask and domino? I am sure you would breathe better that way. Aunt, will you help us?'

Aunt Marianne raised an eyebrow, but didn't say a thing as Nancy took off the unknown young woman's yellow domino and mask. Her dress underneath was very fine and Nancy only felt a small tinge of guilt for stealing her clothing. Together, they lowered her into a chair. Her head lolled to one side and then she passed out. Nancy carefully arranged the young woman in the seat so that she wouldn't fall off.

She took off Basil's beloved pink domino and handed it to her aunt. 'Can you keep this safe? I should hate for anything to happen to it. Basil would never forgive me.'

'What are you doing?'

Nancy picked up the yellow domino and put it on. 'Matthew, Grandfather, and I have a plan to get rid of Sir Alastair permanently. But it will only work if he doesn't recognise me. Alastair is expecting me to be in pink. He'll assume that I have already left the masquerade.'

Nodding, Aunt Marianne picked up the unknown young woman's mask and helped Nancy put it on. 'Then your hair needs to change too.'

She held still as her aunt pulled out several pins, leaving only a small bun at the top. The rest of her black curls cascaded down her back.

Nancy glanced into the mirror. 'You're brilliant, Aunt Marianne.'

One side of her aunt's mouth went up into a half smile. 'I think the brilliance is all you, my dear. I believe that I had better stay and keep an eye on this unfortunately intoxicated young woman. If I were to come out with you, I would give us both away. Keep your dagger handy at all times.'

She touched her leg and felt the familiar outline of her weapon. 'You knew?'

Aunt Marianne tapped the side of her nose. 'My dear, they don't call me the Nose for nothing. Now go on. Get rid of that horrid little baronet.'

Instinctively, Nancy leaned forward and kissed her aunt's cheek. 'I love you, Aunt Marianne.'

A full smile formed on the older woman's face. 'And I love you, Nancy.'

She gave her aunt a hug before leaving the retiring room alone. Skirting the edge of the dance floor, she saw Alastair in his white domino walking with a rotund gentleman in scarlet. The man her grandfather had pointed out as Lord Wigglesworth.

Touching her mask to make sure it covered her face, Nancy moved as quickly as she dared to get closer to Alastair. There was no time to find Matthew or her grandfather, for Alastair was leading Wigglesworth out the door, closing it behind him.

She had to follow them. Stooping down, she pulled her jewelled dagger out of its leather holder on her thigh. Nancy was not foolish enough to follow her old criminal boss without a weapon in her hand. She popped back up and gently turned the doorknob. She didn't want Alastair to realise that she was on his tail. Nancy left the door open behind her, hoping that Matthew or her grandfather would realise what was happening and follow.

Nancy was grateful for her dancing slippers which

allowed her to silently steal across the hallway and around the corridor. Alastair opened the last door and held it for the lord, before trailing him inside.

Once she heard the door close, Nancy sprinted down the dimly lit corridor and put her hand on the doorknob. This time it didn't budge. It was locked. Oh, how she wished that she had been on a job. She would have had her lock-picking kit on her. Now all she had was a stolen domino, a dagger that was too large for the hole, and a mask. She dropped her head into her hands in frustration and one of her fingers felt the sharp prick of a hairpin. Kneeling down before the door, she set down her dagger and yanked out one of the hairpins. She shoved it into the keyhole and began working the lock. With a turn, she heard the click and opened the door with only her dagger in her hands. Both Edgewell and Wigglesworth were on the floor. She hoped that they weren't already dead. They were witnesses to Alastair's villainy.

'Blue Eyes,' Alastair said in a winded voice. 'I should have known you would pick that lock. I taught you well.'

She nodded, her hands still shaking.

Alastair nudged Edgewell's boot with his swordstick, but the young earl only moaned in response. His eyes were closed, but he wasn't dead. 'Do you really intend to fight me with that ornamental dagger?'

Matthew had given it to her for her debut. Nancy swished the dagger around in a fancy pattern before bringing it back to a ready position. 'Charles taught me how to use it, before you put a knife in his belly.'

He raised his own sword-stick to attack position. 'So you figured that out, Nancy. How clever of you. I never once regretted saving you from the stews.'

'And I regret every moment spent in your company.'

'Ah, Blue Eyes, I will miss you,' he said slowly, his sword-stick poised to strike. 'You're not leaving this room alive. You see, I worked too hard and waited too long to become a baronet and take my place in the society I was born to.'

He took another step towards her. His sword tip nearly touching her blade. 'Why are you protecting the man who shot you?'

'Not another step closer,' she warned, parrying his sword away from her with the dagger. 'I'm not protecting him. I'm arresting him. And you. You're the one who told Harry Heap where my father was hiding.'

Alastair sneered at her. 'I warned your father time and time again to stop playing when he ran out of brass. The fool put my name on the gaming vowel for security. For once in your life, see Felix for who he truly was. You were never more than a tool for him to use.'

Her heart sank, but she held her dagger higher. As much as she wanted to blame Alastair for her father's death, it wasn't his fault. Papa's gambling addiction brought his own demise, after keeping her in poverty for most of her youth. Coins were like water in his hands. Her father could not keep a hold on them. Had he loved her? Nancy didn't know. If he'd truly cared for her, wouldn't he have given his infant daughter to Aunt Marianne and Uncle George? Wouldn't he have used the money, the seven thousand pounds, for Nancy's maintenance and education, instead of for gambling? When had he ever put her first? Instead, he allowed her to be a pawn of a criminal lord and lied to her more times than she could count.

'You're right,' she said, choking on the words. 'You are right. My father only loved himself, but I believed in you. I trusted you and you used me to poison your cousin.'

'You knew there was something in that tea,' he said, now circling her.

Nancy stepped back and lifted her dagger in a defensive position. 'You told me the plan was to drug him and then steal your family's heirlooms. You said nothing about murder.'

Alastair echoed her movements. 'But I didn't murder him, my sweet. You did. The moment you poured that belladonna tea into his cup.'

He sneered before he swung his sword down at her. She parried the blow and turned on her heel, back to a defensive position. He swung high and inside, but she blocked the blow with the dagger.

'You'll never beat me like this, Blue Eyes,' he said tauntingly. 'Charles trained you well in defensive moves, but I am taller and stronger. It is only a matter of time before I find your weakness.'

For too long, Alastair had been her weakness. Her belief in his kindness and goodness had deceived her to his true nature. She attacked low and inside, slicing his upper thigh. Red blood stained his white domino. 'But you're bleeding, and I am smaller and quicker.'

His gasp of pain turned into a laugh. 'I almost wish I had taken you as my own.'

'You lied to me. You told me that I had to stay under your protection or that Madame Sweetapple could take me back. You knew her contract had no legal hold on me.'

Alastair grimaced. 'Legal has little to do with brothels, Blue Eyes. Pimps don't need papers to take you back.'

She blocked his next strike, but he pricked her left arm. Blood seeped slowly out of it. She had to win quickly, before she began to lose her strength. 'We both know that there was nothing gentle about my upbringing.'

She stumbled back towards the desk and the inanimate bodies of Wigglesworth and Edgewell. Was arresting these traitors worth dying over? Never seeing Matthew again? Or her newly found family?

'Having second thoughts, my sweet?'

Chapter Twenty-Eight

Matthew stood in the shadows at the masquerade looking for Lymington. Mr Howitt had sent him a note saying that the baronet was wearing a white domino. Alas, there had to be at least twenty men in white dominoes. Some were easy to tell that they weren't Lymington. The person in question was either too short or too wide. Viscount Delfarthing was near one of the white dominoes, but Matthew didn't think the chin looked like Lymington's.

Stealing into a corner, Matthew watched Nancy in a pale pink domino dance with a stranger dressed in blue. She looked delicious enough to eat, but he was here to keep an eye on Lymington until the documents were handed over. And he had to find him first. Matthew saw Basil speaking animatedly to Edgewell. The French spy was well in hand, but where was his accomplice? He watched a man in a white domino ask Nancy to waltz. It had to be the real Lymington. His stomach hardened as his eyes followed them around the dance floor and to the refreshments table.

Moments later she was leaning on Viscountess Delfarthing's arm and being led from the room. What had Alastair said to her? Done to her?

Matthew watched Nancy so long that he nearly lost Lymington in the crowd. He moved a few feet and found him talking to a portly man in a red domino. Matthew wasn't close enough to hear what they were saying, but both gentlemen must have found the discussion very amusing for they were laughing. Nancy did not come out of the retiring room, but he saw a tipsy young woman wearing yellow go in.

The door of the ladies' retiring room opened and the yellow domino lady came back out. Where the devil was Nancy? And Viscountess Delfarthing?

After a few minutes, Lymington and the unknown man left the room through a side door. Should he follow them? Or stay with the other quarry? Basil was holding Edgewell's arm in a death grip. He felt a small tinge of pity for the spy.

The young woman in yellow edged along the side of the room and then followed Lymington and his companion out the same side door. Was there another French agent? A woman?

He made his way to the same side door through the throngs of people. Stopping at Basil's elbow.

Matthew bowed his head. '*Comment ça va,* Edgewell?'

The spotted young man whose arm Basil was holding smiled. 'Come what?'

Edgewell could speak French fluidly. Yet the masked person before him had not recognised a common greeting. 'You're not Edgewell.'

'Course, I am,' he said, in a deeper voice that was not at all like the young lord.

Matthew pulled off the man's mask to reveal a young fellow with a great deal of red spots on his face, but who was decidedly not Lord Edgewell. 'Blast! Why were you pretending to be him?'

'Dash it! This is a masquerade. One is supposed to pretend. Besides, Edgewell and I had a bet. He said he'd give me one hundred pounds if I convinced people that I was him.' He pointed to Basil. 'I've had him believing for over an hour.'

Matthew had let Lymington go and he'd never had Edgewell. He pushed the young man out of his way and made a path to the side door. The girl in the yellow domino had left it open. Taking a breath, he stepped into the dimly lit hallway.

He tried to turn the knob of the closest door. It was locked. He would open every blasted door until he found them.

Matthew peered into a dark room, but closed the door, satisfied that no one was in there. He flung the doors open willy-nilly. But all he found were empty rooms or amorous couples that had successfully escaped their chaperones.

Turning the corner, he found a corridor that smelled like a candle burning. This had to be where they were.

When Matthew reached the door of the library, it was slightly ajar. He threw it open. Nancy was wearing the yellow domino and it was stained with blood. She held a small dagger in her hand. The one he gave her. Matthew turned to see Lymington without a mask, rushing towards her with his sword upraised. Without a weapon or a plan, he stepped between them. He had to protect her. Matthew closed his eyelids as Lymington's sword came down towards his head.

The sound of a gunshot made his eyes pop open.

Lymington dropped his sword and stumbled back a few steps, clutching his leg. Blood pooled over his hands and down to his boots. He fell to the floor with a thud and then fainted. Matthew swivelled to see Lord Brampton holding a smoking pistol in his hands. Behind him were six guards.

'Staunch their wounds and arrest all three of them,' he barked to the guards. 'But give me the documents Lymington is carrying first.'

Matthew pivoted to catch the woman he loved as she swooned. Her face was devoid of all colour and he could see blood dripping out of a wound on her arm.

He carefully set her on the floor, kneeling beside her. 'Nancy, I need to tear off the bottom of your petticoat to wrap around your arm to stop the bleeding.'

Her bloody hand covered his. 'Why did you step in front of me? You could have been killed.'

'Because I love you and I had to protect you.'

She gasped, shaking her head. 'I am not worth your life.'

Glancing down at her tenderly, he whispered, 'You are to me.'

'I love you too,' she whispered, and he would have happily stepped in front of another sword.

She grimaced in pain as he tore the bottom of her petticoat into long strips. Matthew gently took off her domino and tugged down her sleeve to reveal the wound.

Glancing up, he asked, 'Brampton, you don't happen to have any alcohol on you?'

The lord secretary pulled out an elaborately decorated silver flask from inside of his coat. 'I daresay you need a little pick me up.'

Matthew took the bottle and instead of taking a swig of it, he poured its entire contents on Nancy's wound and she swore like a fishwife. In English, possibly Gaelic, and then in French. Then he wrapped the bandage around her shoulder. Once he'd used all the strips of linen, he placed both hands on her wound and pressed down.

'Cor and bollocks!' Nancy gasped.

'Sorry,' he said, continuing to apply pressure. 'I've got to stop it from bleeding.'

'That hurts worse than being cut,' she said, gritting her teeth.

Matthew saw the guards half drag and half carry the three conspirators out of the room. The lord secretary held the government documents in his hands, there were splatters of blood on them. He hoped it wasn't Nancy's.

Once the bleeding stopped, Nancy pushed away his hand and managed to sit up. 'Do those documents contain the same information as the ones I stole?'

Brampton nodded gravely. 'Yes. I believe we have caught all three of the French conspirators.'

Matthew released a breath that he didn't realise he was holding. Nancy's grandfather did not know all the details. Including her part in the late Sir Gervase Lymington's death. The criminal baronet could still damage her reputation if he spoke out against her. 'Will there be a public trial?'

Lord Brampton cleared his throat. 'I believe that I will be able to persuade the Prince Regent to handle their trials privately. Since Sir Alastair was seen in his company, it would reflect poorly on the prince.'

And Nancy.

'What about Lord Edgewell and Lord Wigglesworth?' Matthew asked, getting to his feet and then helping Nancy to hers. She was still holding the dagger he gave her. Matthew kept an arm securely around her waist. She was still very pale and he didn't wish for her to swoon again.

'They will be taken care of discreetly,' Lord Brampton said. 'Both will be held securely in prison until their own trial for selling government secrets.'

Nancy leaned more heavily against him and Matthew tightened his hold on her. 'Good.'

He held up his free hand. 'Lord Secretary, your granddaughter, my soon to be betrothed, foiled a French plot. I do believe that she deserves to be awarded with a title for her diligence and great sacrifice.'

Lord Brampton's lips twitched. 'I can see your mother in you. What do you want?'

Matthew quirked up one eyebrow. 'It would seem that there is now an opening in the house of lords after the Earl of Edgewell's arrest.'

'You want an earldom?'

Matthew's eyes found Nancy's and she smiled, nodding. 'If you insist, Lord Secretary. We should be most grateful to accept an earldom in recompense for service to our country.'

Matthew saw the older man's face crack into a smile

for the first time. 'How is that my granddaughter did all the work and you are the one to get the title?'

'That's something that you and I will have to change in Parliament, now that I will have a seat in the House of Lords,' Matthew said, lifting his arm so Nancy could hold on to his side. 'And if you need any assistance in creating the earldom, I am always happy to help you with any contract writing. And do be sure to make the earldom inheritable to male or female heirs, since a lady was the reason it was created.'

'I don't want your help writing it. You would pen away the crown jewels and then tax me for them,' Brampton scoffed. 'You'll get your earldom and Edgewell's land for your steam locomotives, but no additional funds from the crown. You have plenty of money to maintain the title without it.'

Matthew couldn't help but grin. 'We begin to understand each other.'

The older man looked at his granddaughter. 'But perhaps we are now on the same side?'

Nancy smiled at both Matthew and then her grandfather.

'I'll drop the snobbery charges, but I refuse to give you the family rate on supplies for the army.'

'I wouldn't expect any more from you, Lord Matthew,' he said and then wrinkled his nose in apparent disgust. 'Find a room that is less gory before you drop to one knee. And don't be too wordy in your proposal to my granddaughter. She needs to go home and lie down. She has lost a great deal of blood.'

Holding Nancy tightly, he followed the older man out

of the library, through the corridor, and to the dimly lit hall. He opened the door to the empty room he had found before whilst looking for Nancy. He helped her limp inside.

The old earl gave Matthew a hard look and held up both hands. 'Ten minutes.'

He closed the door behind him leaving Matthew and Nancy blessedly alone.

Nancy leaned her head forward and Matthew's lips found hers in the middle. They kissed as if they would never get another opportunity. She licked the seam of his lips and he gladly opened them for her plundering. One of her hands curved around his neck and pulled him down to her. Placing both hands on her waist, he pressed her more tightly against him and she gasped in pain. She'd been stabbed less than a quarter of an hour ago.

He gently released her. 'I am sorry, my love. I should have been more careful.'

A little pink stole into her pale cheeks. 'I should like nothing more than to use all of the ten minutes kissing, but there are some things that must be said.'

Offering his hand, Matthew led her to a window seat and lifted her onto his lap. He was a businessman after all. Not a monk. Placing an arm carefully around her waist, he thought about how close he'd been to losing her this very evening. Nancy fit perfectly on his lap and pressed several kisses to his neck and chin until he wasn't sure that he could remember his own name. Nor could he form a coherent sentence. There was no previous experience to compare it to. The bliss. The ecstasy. The sheer joy of holding the woman he loved.

* * *

Nancy laid her head on his shoulder and Matthew stroked her curls. 'I shouldn't have kissed you until I told you the truth. You cannot marry me. I am a murderess.'

He didn't stop caressing her or even pause his movements. 'There, there, love. I am sure Alastair will recover from the stabbing wound.'

She shook her head against his shoulder, nuzzling her nose against his neck. 'Worse.'

'Are you talking about your part in Sir Gervase Lymington's death?'

Nancy's head popped up and she pulled away from him enough to see his face. There was no surprise in it. And no judgement either. 'You already know about it.'

His hand rested on her hip and his thumb caressed her in reassuring circles. 'I don't know everything, sweetheart, but I believe you played the role of Alastair's young bride? His supposed reason for visiting his cousin, who conveniently died two days later.'

Swallowing, Nancy nodded. 'I poured the tea with the belladonna berries in it.'

'How awful for you,' he said sympathetically, as if what she'd done wasn't enough to give him a disgust of her. Enough to have her hung.

She sniffed. 'You don't mind that I am a murderess?'

A wry smile formed on his beautiful lips. 'I'll certainly be careful to watch you prepare the tea in future, but I won't blame you for anything you did in your past to survive. Life dealt you a rotten hand of cards and I trust whatever you did was the best thing you could do in the situation you were given.'

A hysterical laugh formed in her throat. Only Matthew would jest about poisonous tea. Nancy shook her head back and forth. 'I didn't…I didn't know the tea was poisonous. I mean I didn't know it was deadly. I thought it was merely a sleeping drug and that Alastair planned to steal family heirlooms that he'd said his grandfather meant for him to have. I had…I had no idea it would kill him.'

Matthew brushed his lips against her temple. 'Your grandfather is the lord secretary and you just single-handedly stopped a French plot. You can start afresh… unless there is anything else you'd like to tell me before I can formally propose? I promise you, it won't change my mind or my heart. I love you just as you are.'

A deep feeling of love surged through her very soul. This handsome and perfectly wonderful man not only loved her, but trusted her implicitly. Her secrets were safe with him and so were her fears.

Although he didn't say the words, Nancy knew that he had been willing to die for her. Matthew's love was unselfish. He would never put his needs or wants before her, like her father had. Like Alastair.

She placed her other hand on the opposite side of his head, framing his face in her hands. 'No one has ever loved me like you. No one has ever been willing to sacrifice themselves for me.'

Nancy pressed her lips to his and he responded with delicious pressure. Her hands moved from his face to behind his neck.

Matthew broke the kiss and then made a trail of kisses from her mouth to her ear. 'You are more loved than you know, Nancy. And not just by me. But by your grumpy grandfather, your dragon aunt, your quiet cousin, and your dandified one. They would have all come to your aid. You are infinitely loveable.'

Words were his sword, but today, they were her salvation. Nancy felt their truth and the security of knowing that her family loved her and would never abandon her. Because of Matthew's researching of her past, she knew that they never had forgotten her. They'd helped in every way they could.

'You are pretty loveable yourself, my lord. And your fortune is the least wonderful thing about you. Nor did you need a peer's title. Although I think you will do a world of good in Parliament and I should very much like to be a countess.'

He gently tugged on the sleeve of her uninjured arm and placed his lips on the hidden skin there. She moaned as he gave her a love bite. His mouth moved down and he gave her another one where no one could see it. Heat pooled in her belly as he tugged up her sleeve, hiding his marks.

'I am glad I have a fortune,' Matthew admitted, 'if only to give you the safety and security you have always longed for. Shall we buy a house in London and let Basil decorate it for us? I daresay it would be *all the crack*.'

A laugh gurgled in her throat. 'My cousin would love that…and we should buy a house in the country too.'

'I already have one of those.'

Nancy leaned her forehead against his. 'Really?'

'A lovely place called Greystone Hall,' he said, his breath warm against her lips. 'Bought it in a foreclosure a few years ago. My sister-in-law, Louisa, grew up there. I can't wait for you to meet her and my nephews.

Especially the one named after me. He's a particularly handsome babe.'

She kissed his eyelids, his nose, and then his cheeks. 'Then he is already my favourite. But before you buy a London house, shouldn't you propose first? You can't back out now. You've already declared your intentions in front of my grandfather who is a government cabinet member.'

His lips brushed hers. 'Shall I get upon one knee? I planned to, but your current location on my lap is so agreeable that I am reluctant to move.'

Nancy grinned. Matthew was clever and kind and so witty with words that he would keep her laughing for the rest of her life. 'You can stay where you are.'

Matthew's hands moved to her back and he rubbed up and down in a slow burn. She found herself purring like a cat. 'Dearest Nancy, Countess of Whatsit or wherever your grandfather decides, I love you with all that is in me. Please say that you will be my wife. My partner. My equal. My soulmate. My everything.'

She touched his lips with one finger. 'You have a way with words.'

'I'd rather have my way with you,' he responded immediately, capturing her hand and kissing each fingertip.

Nancy grinned. 'I am a proper lady now. So you'll have to wait until after the wedding to have your way with me—but the answer is yes.'

A slow smile built on Matthew's face. 'Such a little word for the gift of a lifetime.'

Epilogue

Nancy couldn't believe that she was staying in a castle. A real English castle! Along with her grandfather, Aunt Marianne, Peregrine and his wife, Venetia, and the very fashionable Basil. Her cousin was currently trying to convince the Duchess of Hampford to redecorate one of her many parlours in sea green, but not making much headway. Happily, she and Matthew had given him free rein to design every room at their new home in St James's Place, London.

Her husband came towards her carrying a glass of wine in each hand. He gave one to her.

'A toast to the bride and groom,' Wick said, holding up his own glass. Wick was Matthew's elder brother. He was dark-haired and shorter than him by several inches. 'To the Earl and Countess of Trentham, may your marriage be long and fruitful.'

'And financially sound,' Mr Stubbs added, lifting his glass.

Matthew smiled down at her and everyone else in the room blurred to nothing as he pressed a gentle kiss to her lips, before they linked arms and drank out of each other's wine glasses.

Everyone else in the room echoed, 'To Matthew and Nancy!'

He looked impossibly handsome in his wedding suit and Nancy felt beautiful in a celestial blue gown—her favourite colour—and wearing the Brampton sapphires. Matthew released her to hug his grandparents, his brother, and his sister-in-law, Louisa, who was holding little Matthew. He then made his way down the line of his younger sisters: Mantheria, Frederica, Helen, and Becca. Hugging his nephews Andrew and Grey last, before his parents.

The Duke of Hampford had a small monkey sitting on his shoulder and his clothes were rather threadbare. He hugged Matthew enthusiastically. 'I have bought you a large wedding gift.'

Matthew's eyes widened and his mouth opened. 'Oh, no, Father. Please. We'd rather not…there is nothing that we need.'

'Everyone needs an ostrich,' Lord Hampford said, causing the room to erupt in laughter, including his wife.

Nancy's husband groaned—*she loved thinking of him as that!*—and appeared rather chagrined at the prospect.

The Duchess of Hampford grasped Matthew twice in a tight embrace and made him promise to write faithfully during their wedding trip. Then she pulled Nancy into a hug. 'My dear, I must hear from you too! For you are my daughter now.'

She'd never been someone's daughter before and the words warmed her soul. 'I will.'

The duchess handed her an exquisite glass bottle that looked like a flower. There were large white and red lily-like petals above a green base. 'Your very own scent, Nancy. I added a little heather from Scotland, distilled Irish eyebright, and a low note of sweet vetiver from England. You represent the best of all three nations.'

Nancy opened the bottle and smelled the scent—it was light and beautiful, and a little woodsy.

Her grandfather stood beside the duchess and hesitated before holding his arms out to his granddaughter. They'd never embraced before, but it was never too late to start again. Nancy walked into his arms and squeezed him tightly.

'If you're happy, I'm happy,' he whispered in her ear.

Nancy stepped back, beaming at him. 'Then you must be very happy.'

'Of course, he is,' Aunt Marianne said, surprising Nancy again by hugging her. 'You have done very well for yourself, Nancy. We love you dearly and you are a credit to all of us.'

Nancy shook hands with Peregrine, before nearly being crushed to death by Basil. On impulse she hugged Venetia, who was nearly as tall and as quiet as Peregrine. They would deal extremely well together. Far better than any society debutante her aunt had tried to foist upon him.

The Stringham sisters surrounded her and all managed to hug Nancy at the same moment. For the first time in her life, she felt safe and whole. A part of not only one family, but two.

'Where are you taking Nancy on the wedding trip?' Frederica asked.

'To Paris?' Helen offered, her eyes bright.

'We're at war with France,' Becca reminded her.

Folding her arms across her chest, Helen scowled. 'You're not going to spend your wedding trip in Rome with Mantheria and Glastonbury, are you? It will be dreadful.'

Frederica elbowed her sister. 'I'll be there too!'

Matthew shook his head, putting an arm around Nancy's shoulders. 'We are going on a rather peculiar wedding trip. First, to the village of Roslin, then to Edinburgh, Leeds, and finally Greystone Hall, which will have a new mistress.'

He wanted her to show him everywhere that she had lived. Her husband wished to meet her friends and the people she had grown up around. Despite them being from a different social class than himself.

Helen wrinkled her nose. 'Why Leeds?'

Nancy put her arm around Matthew's waist, leaning against him. 'We're going to ride on the steam locomotive, *The Salamanca*. The future of exports and travel.'

Matthew's sisters shook their heads in dismay and Nancy smiled as he kissed her in front of them.

She heard Helen say, 'Ugh, gross!'

'I think it's lovely,' Becca said. 'I want someone to kiss me like that.'

'Still such amateurs,' Frederica added.

Matthew slanted his head, deepening his kiss and Nancy was unable to listen or think any words.

* * * * *

If you enjoyed this story, make sure to pick up
Samantha Hastings' brilliant debut,

The Marquess and the Runaway Lady.

Get 3 FREE REWARDS!

We'll send you 2 FREE Books plus a FREE Mystery Gift.

FREE Value Over **$20**

Both the **Harlequin® Historical** and **Harlequin® Romance** series feature compelling novels filled with emotion and simmering romance.

YES! Please send me 2 FREE novels from the Harlequin Historical or Harlequin Romance series and my FREE Mystery Gift (gift is worth about $10 retail). After receiving them, if I don't wish to receive any more books, I can return the shipping statement marked "cancel." If I don't cancel, I will receive 6 brand-new Harlequin Historical books every month and be billed just $6.19 each in the U.S. or $6.74 each in Canada, a savings of at least 11% off the cover price, or 4 brand-new Harlequin Romance Larger-Print books every month and be billed just $6.09 each in the U.S. or $6.24 each in Canada, a savings of at least 13% off the cover price. It's quite a bargain! Shipping and handling is just 50¢ per book in the U.S. and $1.25 per book in Canada.* I understand that accepting the 2 free books and gift places me under no obligation to buy anything. I can always return a shipment and cancel at any time by calling the number below. The free books and gift are mine to keep no matter what I decide.

Choose one: ☐ **Harlequin Historical**
(246/349 BPA GRNX)

☐ **Harlequin Romance Larger-Print**
(119/319 BPA GRNX)

☐ **Or Try Both!**
(246/349 & 119/319 BPA GRRD)

Name (please print)

Address _____ Apt. #

City _____ State/Province _____ Zip/Postal Code

Email: Please check this box ☐ if you would like to receive newsletters and promotional emails from Harlequin Enterprises ULC and its affiliates. You can unsubscribe anytime.

Mail to the Harlequin Reader Service:
IN U.S.A.: P.O. Box 1341, Buffalo, NY 14240-8531
IN CANADA: P.O. Box 603, Fort Erie, Ontario L2A 5X3

Want to try 2 free books from another series? Call 1-800-873-8635 or visit www.ReaderService.com.

Get 3 FREE REWARDS!

We'll send you 2 FREE Books plus a FREE Mystery Gift.

FREE Value Over **$20**

Both the **Harlequin® Desire** and **Harlequin Presents®** series feature compelling novels filled with passion, sensuality and intriguing scandals.

HARLEQUIN
PLUS

Try the best multimedia subscription service for romance readers like you!

Read, Watch and Play.

Experience the easiest way to get the romance content you crave.

Start your **FREE TRIAL** at
<u>www.harlequinplus.com/freetrial</u>.